I0891235

everything we never said

everything we never said

SLOAN HARLOW

putnam

G. P. Putnam's Sons

G. P. Putnam's Sons
An imprint of Penguin Random House LLC, New York

Produced by Alloy Entertainment
First published in the United States of America by G. P. Putnam's Sons,
an imprint of Penguin Random House LLC, 2024

Visit us online at PenguinRandomHouse.com.

Library of Congress Cataloging-in-Publication Data is available.

ISBN 9780593855720

6th Printing

Printed in the United States of America

LSCC

Design by Cindy De la Cruz
Text set in Adobe Garamond Pro and Proxima Nova

To all the Hayleys and Ellas in the world
and anyone else who's ever felt lost and alone

chapter 1
ella

Thick waves of rain assault my bedroom window, the lightning and thunder of a Georgia storm cracking this Monday morning wide open. I've been awake for hours, listening to the wind howl, fantasizing that a swirling gale will rip through my wall and sweep me away.

The floor creaks just outside my room. I can see Mom's shadow shift beneath the door. The wood groans beneath her feet. The sound of indecision. To knock on her daughter's door or not?

Mom leaves, her footfalls retreating back to her bedroom.

Not, apparently.

A year ago, she would have burst in, and I would have gotten an earful for still being under the covers. A year ago, her silence would have been inconceivable. But a year ago, everything was different. I've earned this silence, heavy as a stone around my neck. And with this penance, I throw back the covers and do the impossible:

I get ready for my first day of senior year at North Davis High.

Even though it feels like a different lifetime, I still remember how stressed I was on the first day of eleventh grade. No amount of argan oil could sleek away the Georgia humidity from my frizzy black hair. The cat-eye makeup that had looked so femme fatale the night before now made me look like I wanted to hold Gotham City for ransom with laughing gas.

Panicked, I had texted a selfie to my favorite person in the world with the caption Help.

Hayley's response had been immediate. Are you kidding? You look hot AF. Just come over real quick, I can help your hair. Georgia summers got nothing on my straightener.

But today?

Today, I put on the first thing my toes touch on the bedroom floor: the same jeans I wore yesterday (and the day before that, and the day before that) and a gray sweatshirt stained with last week's salsa. I can't remember the last time I looked in a mirror.

Grief has opened a canyon between me and that stupid girl from a year ago, whose greatest disasters were bad eyeliner and flyaways. How I hate her.

How I long for her.

Walking back into the halls of North Davis High, I feel like I'm not returning as Ella, but as Shadow Ella, the living ghost girl. The thought feels like a paper cut on my heart. I wish I *were* a ghost. Maybe then I could stretch across the realms and actually still talk to Hayley. Tell her the important things.

Like the fact that Albert Wonsky now has her locker. She'd groan and say something like *Please, please rescue my pictures of Pedro Pascal before my husband is drowned in anime porn*, and I would laugh and tell her, *Sorry, too late.*

I'd tell her the dent is still there. The one from when I kicked a locker after getting a B in Latin. And so is the dent she kicked right next to it. "For plausible deniability," she had said. "Not what that means," I'd said back.

I'd tell her there's still pink birthday candle wax smeared in the alcove by the music room. The one where Sawyer Hawkins and I had crouched, grinning madly as we jumped out with balloons and a lit cupcake to scream, "Happy birthday!"

Sawyer.

His name feels like a fist twisting my stomach. I can't think about him today. It's already too much. If I do, my rib cage will crack all over again.

Which is why this is the exact moment Sawyer walks into view. There he is, at the end of the hall, towering above Mike Lim as they discuss something that has Sawyer's handsome face breaking out into a crooked grin.

It hits me so hard, I have to stop walking. I lean against a wall and clutch my books so tightly that the words CALCULUS I will probably be embossed into my sternum for days.

As if he can sense my presence, Sawyer suddenly glances in my direction. I stop breathing. For the first time since the funeral, I'm seeing Sawyer's soft brown eyes.

Except there's nothing soft about the look he's giving me.

Sawyer, the only boy I've ever known to celebrate month anniversaries with tiny, perfect gifts, who happily supplied us with popcorn and Sprite throughout an entire *Twilight* marathon when Hayley felt sick, who loved my best friend as much as I did . . .

That Sawyer is currently shooting me a look of such fury that I instantly feel like puking.

I knew it. *He blames me.*

I should hold his gaze. I should let his judgment sear me. It's what I deserve, for what I stole from him. From her.

But instead, I whirl around, swallowing a sob, ready to sprint down the hall, out of school, maybe forever. But I end up slamming directly into Mr. Wilkens.

"*Oof!* Easy, there, tiger!" The school psychologist stumbles back, his hands shooting out to grasp my shoulders and keep me from falling.

"God, I'm *so* sorry," I choke out, mortified.

"No, no, Ella, you're fine. I'm fine." He ducks his chin, trying to catch my eye. "Hey. *Hey.* I'm glad we bumped into each other. How are you?"

I shrug, not trusting my voice.

"That well, huh?" Mr. Wilkens is usually clean shaven, but he has some scruff along his jaw. His typically bright blue eyes look smudged today, the color of bruises. Maybe he's one of those counselors who actually cares about his students. Maybe he's sad this morning too.

It's a nice thought.

"Ella," he says, "I know today is hard. And I hope you know I'm here for you." He looks like he wants to say more, but the bell rings, interrupting his thought. "Ah, saved by the bell." He laughs. "Don't be late to class. We'll talk soon, okay?"

He watches me walk away, concern furrowing his brow. It's so kind, how he's worried. How he wants to help. *Don't bother, Mr. Wilkens,* I should tell him. *Save your effort and time for students who aren't lost causes. Students who deserve it.*

Students who didn't kill their best friends.

FOR THE ENTIRE day, I try to be invisible. I try to ignore the accusing glares and the soft stares of sympathy, eyes full of pity. But it's impossible. When I walk by a crowd of girls at the water fountain, a hush falls over them. In English, Seema Patel, a girl I haven't spoken to since elementary school, leans over and offers me a bag of Sour Patch Kids. "Figured you could use it."

And when I'm standing at my locker before lunch, I'm swarmed by people I'd hoped to avoid all day: the old crew. Well, what's left of them, anyway. Nia Wiley, Beth Harris, Rachael Evans, and even Scott Logan appear at my shoulder. Sawyer's absence is notable. But there's no hole that can compare to the most obvious one, the size of a crater.

These are Hayley's friends, really. Nia and Beth ran track with her, Beth and Rachael have been dating since freshman year, and Scott is like a barnacle that you can't scrape off, no matter how hard you try—half comic relief, half arrogant teenage boy. Hayley brought me into the group, and without her here, the center won't hold. Another week or so of me avoiding their calls and I'll be flung off into my own orbit, which will make everyone more comfortable.

For now, though, Beth throws her arms around my neck.

"Ella, where have you been? I was so worried when I didn't hear from you! I called you, like, every day this summer!"

Nia reaches over to gently pry Beth off me. "And, like *I* said, I probably wouldn't have picked up either if you were binge calling me every day."

Beth pouts, leaning back against Rachael, and Nia shakes her head, shooting me an apologetic look. "We just wanted to see how you were doing, Ella. I mean, other than the obvious."

"Yeah, we miss you." Rachael gives me a small smile; Beth nods in agreement. Nia elbows Scott, who's standing behind them, frowning down at his phone.

"Yes, Ella, ditto, we're totally here for you." Scott only looks up from his phone for half a second.

Nia glares at him, then turns to me, her eyes softening. "Girl. How are you?"

Beth and Rachael look nervous. Scott's not paying attention. I'd take all of that over Nia's compassionate, too-knowing gaze.

"It's been tough, but I'm fine. I promise." I do my best to smile as I close my locker. "You guys don't have to worry about me. I appreciate it, I do. But I'm good."

Beth and Rachael look relieved. Nia frowns.

"Ella, you know you can—"

"You heard her," Scott cuts in as the bell rings. "She's fine. Her chakras are unblocked, her aura's good, her Mercury's in retrograde or whatever. I'm gonna be late to Spanish."

Nia glares at his retreating form but doesn't push it. For once, I'm grateful that Scott's sort of a dick.

It doesn't end with my old friends. Every teacher wants to check in with me too.

Just like Mr. Wilkens, they take me gently by the elbow, their voices low, and ask me how I'm doing. What do they expect me to tell them? What are *any of them* expecting me to tell them during the three minutes between classes? All the things that I haven't been able to tell my parents or the parade of mental health professionals in the four months Hayley has been gone? I give them the only answer I can, the only answer they want to hear: "Fine. I'm doing fine."

By some miracle, time keeps moving, bringing me closer and closer to the end of the day. Even so, it feels like I'm in a rowboat, the wooden sides filled with leaking holes, each one a memory—the now-empty desk in third period, the lunch table we'd sat at for three years taken over by freshmen. The ocean is churning, and I'm fighting to plug up each leak, to keep the rushing waters at bay. The waves crash and I nearly capsize, but I manage to stay afloat.

At 3:15 p.m., the bell rings.

Finally.

I'm sprinting toward the front doors when a voice stops me.

"Ms. Graham! I've been looking for you." Ms. Langley, the pottery teacher, is beckoning to me from the doorway of the art room. I glance longingly at the double doors at the end of the hall, at the flickering EXIT sign, then walk over to her.

"Hi, Ms. Langley," I say, readjusting the bag of books at my shoulder, every one of my polite Southern instincts at war with my desperation to leave.

"I just wanted to give you something real quick." She holds up a finger, and then reappears a moment later with a small cardboard box in her hands. On the side, handwritten in Sharpie, are the words ELLA AND HAYLEY. Inside are two handmade ceramic mugs.

And just like that, the tiny rowboat that I'd managed to keep upright all day starts to go under.

"I thought you might want these," Ms. Langley whispers, sounding nearly as sad as I feel. "They didn't get fired in the kiln until after . . . Well, I've been holding on to them for you."

"Um," I say, blinking down into the box.

It had been Hayley's idea to make mugs for each other. Coffee cups for when we roomed together at the University of Georgia. Hayley had been so proud when she'd shown me her design, a mug with an ornate *D* stamped into the side. *D* as in . . . *denture*. When I'd protested that I was *not* going to be drinking out of a *denture mug*, she'd held up a hand.

"Wait, listen. This is a mug you'll use for life. I'm just preparing for the best phase of our friendship: when we're old and senile. Think of how fun that'll be." Hayley's eyes had flashed their green mischief. "Every time we see each other, we'll be new best friends all over again." She'd shrugged. "And you'll have a place to keep your dentures."

Both mugs had turned out beautifully.

I barely register saying goodbye to Ms. Langley. I exit the school in a daze, unable to stop looking down at the mugs, clinking against each other in the cardboard box. I'd like to look away. I want to, I do. I want to chuck them into a ravine, but I know it would be like pulling out an organ and stomping on it. I somehow need these mugs to keep going.

I run my hand over the one Hayley made. There's an indent on the bottom, one she forgot to smooth. I peer closer and see little swirling lines, a pattern.

Hayley's fingerprint.

Distantly, I register that there is a world around me. Maybe some grass, a sky. Raised voices from far away.

But right now, all I can focus on is pressing my finger into that little indent.

It all happens so fast.

One moment, there are headlights in front of me, a bus barreling at my face. There are screams, the bellowing of a horn like a great dragon. My heart is in my throat, my last thought, *Protect the mugs,* and then I'm flying backward.

I don't die.

I slam back into something solid. My brain thinks, ridiculously, of a brick wall, but this wall is warm and has a heartbeat. Someone pulled me out of the way. Someone saved me.

I tilt my chin up to find myself looking into the wide, panicked eyes of Sawyer Hawkins.

"Sawyer!" I gasp, stumbling out of his arms to face him. My book bag has spilled onto the school lawn, but I'm still clutching the cardboard box, mugs miraculously unbroken.

"Ella." Sawyer's panting, his face slack with shock, one hand on his chest, the other pulling at the roots of his thick hair. He takes a few steadying breaths, closes his eyes. When he opens them once more, they're blazing with anger.

"Ella," he growls, "what the *hell* were you thinking? You could have *died*. Like, literally *died*. If I hadn't been here, if I hadn't been watching? *Christ.*"

"Why were you?" It takes me a minute to realize I've said this out loud.

"What?" He stops short, confused.

"Watching me? In fact"—I swallow—"why even save me?" Horribly, my eyes spill over. I can't pretend I'm fine anymore.

Color drains from Sawyer's face. The anger in his features evaporates, and if it's at all possible, he seems more stricken by my words than by my near miss. He licks his lips, mouth dropping open, but nothing comes out.

I want to hear his answer. A microscopic diamond of hope embedded in my stomach is begging me to stay, to listen to what he has to say.

But I don't. I can't.

I know the answer. And anything kind out of his mouth would be pity, or a mercy I don't deserve. I whirl around and walk away.

He doesn't call after me. That tiny prick of hope wants me to look over my shoulder, just once. But I don't.

And I vow to never speak to Sawyer again.

chapter 2
ella

On the bus ride home, I press my forehead against the dirty window, replaying on repeat the moment I thought I would die. The rush of headlights, the smell of burning rubber and diesel. No time to scream, to think of anything but the mugs currently clinking in the box on my lap.

Hayley, did you have time to think?

Knowing Hayley, she probably would have cracked her knuckles and said, *All right, let's see what you got.*

I still don't understand how she can be gone, while I'm still here.

And, it seems, neither can Sawyer.

What would he have said if I'd waited for his answer? Would he have told me how he *really* felt?

I know Sawyer. He's no monster. Of *course* he was going to say, *Why, yes, Ella, I am quite glad you did not become a meat smear on the pavement before my very eyes.* Even if deep down, he thinks it should have been me.

The truth is, it was so close to being me. Or at least, that's what they told me in the hospital, where I had awoken with cracked ribs, a concussion, and no memory of the previous twenty-four hours.

"A trauma response," the doctors said. "It's normal." As if there's anything normal about any of this. They said I might get my memories back, but so far . . . nothing. And based on what the cops told me, I don't know if I do want them back.

It had happened after a party at Scott's house last spring, just weeks before the end of junior year. Witnesses said they'd seen me drinking a beer, then ushering a drunk, upset Hayley to my car before I got behind the wheel. We'd been driving home when I crashed my car through the guardrail just before the Silver River Bridge. They found me in the driver's seat, crumpled against a boulder on the sloped embankment above the churning water of the river.

And they hadn't found Hayley at all.

All that remained was a shattered hole in the windshield where she'd been flung from the car, her blood on the jagged glass. She hadn't been wearing her seat belt, and they told me if the impact hadn't killed her, the river surely would have. Infamous for its strong current, jagged rocks, and sudden drops—there's not one soul in Cedarbrook who doesn't know how treacherous those waters are.

So treacherous, in fact, that they couldn't even retrieve her body. They tried, of course, but with the sweep of the current, there was no telling where she'd ended up, and even their best divers were hesitant to enter the river. After a fruitless week and a close call for one of the rescuers, they called it off.

Hayley was gone, and it was all my fault. It was me who'd had the beer. Me who had driven. Me who had killed her.

The bus makes a groaning stop, and we are finally at my neighborhood.

By the time I'm stepping onto my driveway, the afternoon sun is golden and casting long shadows on the lawn. Even with the waning light, the humidity is stifling.

The house is quiet when I step inside. A year ago, Mom would have swarmed me at the door. *Let's go over your syllabi, have you gotten the swim meet schedule yet, did Mrs. Prescott get my email?* My younger sister, Jess, would have given me a sympathetic eye roll, and not too long after, Dad would have gotten home from work, rescuing me with a quick joke that would have Mom smacking his arm, laughing despite herself.

Half the time, Hayley was with me, in which case Mom would have fussed over her instead, overbearing as a mother hen with her chick, paying no mind that she was of a different brood. Hayley had loved it. Even when Mom had been scolding her for getting Cs.

I hear a mewl at my feet, where a little gray cat is rubbing against my leg. She blinks her green eyes up at me and meows again.

"Where's your collar, Midna? You're naked again." I balance the box of mugs on one hip and lean down to scoop her up in one arm. She purrs when I press my face into her fur as I carry her up to my room. I shoulder my door open, Midna hopping from my arm to curl up on my desk, the mugs tinkling at the movement. With a pinch of my heart, I set the box down, slide it under my bed.

That's when I notice what Midna's pawing at on my desk. I pick up the dog-eared copy of *The Coven's Secrets,* the second book in the Realms of Wonder series. A favorite of mine.

"You haven't read it yet, right?" Jess is leaning against my door frame, her green eye shadow and dark lip gloss making her striking features pop, no doubt courtesy of her best friend, Kelly, who's already a beauty guru at age fourteen. I tamp down the spike of envy at the image of Kelly giggling as she swipes a brush across my sister's eyelids.

I clear my throat.

"I didn't even know it was out yet," I whisper. With everything that's happened, I'd forgotten about it completely. Something I'd marked on my calendar a year ago, eagerly awaited. I can't remember the last time I'd even thought to pick up a book.

"No spoilers, but it's good." Jess shrugs a shoulder. "Thought it'd be a nice distraction."

"Thanks," I say, genuinely touched. The one word is all I can manage right now, but I hope she knows how much I mean it.

Jess nods. "Also." She raises her hand, a worn purple collar dangling from her finger, bell tinkling. "It was in Mom's monstera pot. The leaves are all squished again. She won't be happy."

"Girls?" My mom's voice follows the sounds of the back door opening and shutting as Jess and I fasten the collar back on a squirming Midna. Midna has trotted off (probably to go sleep in Mom's plants again) by the time Mom appears in the doorway. She's been gardening. Her forehead is glistening with sweat, and she smells like the sun. But her peach blouse is still immaculate, her fingernails clean.

My perfect mother. Standing here, I feel it acutely: the gap between who I am today and who I once was—her perfect daughter.

And with the way her dark eyes are holding my gaze, it looks like she feels it too. But that sorrow? That disappointment? Yeah, I deserve it.

After a second of uncomfortable silence, Jess clears her throat.

That seems to snap Mom out of it. "Can you both come downstairs and help me with dinner? Your dad will be home soon."

In the kitchen, my mom pulls potatoes out of the pantry and hands them to Jess while I go to the sink to wash dishes.

"So," Mom says, looking at me. "How did today go?"

The question I'd been dreading. And have no idea how to answer. Thankfully, I don't have to.

"Fine," Jess cuts in. "Everyone said sophomore year is way harder, but I think it was just a scare tactic. And Kelly's in two of my classes. In fact . . ."

I send a silent prayer of thanks to Jess as she chatters while slicing through potatoes. I pick up a sponge and start scrubbing. But Jess is done too soon, and Mom's eyes turn to me. The front door opens, and I'm saved again.

"Hey, I'm home," Dad calls.

He strides into the kitchen, arms open, his dark beard stretched into a smile. "There are my beautiful women!" He hugs Jess, kisses Mom on the head, and turns to me, his hazel eyes softening. "How you doing, kiddo?"

"Um," I say, biting my lip, and I nearly tear up at the gentle tone of his voice.

"Did you get to talk to Coach Carter today?" Mom joins me at the sink to rinse the pot of rice for dinner.

I close my eyes. Coach Carter, the swim coach. I had hoped to avoid this conversation for at least another week. I toy with the idea of lying, but honestly? I don't have the energy for it.

"No."

Jess ceases her chopping, and Dad shifts uncomfortably at my side.

"Was she out sick?" My mom's hand swirls in the pot of rice, turning the water milky white.

"Mom," I say, avoiding her gaze, "I didn't talk to Coach Carter because I'm not rejoining swim team."

Her hand stills. Her shoulders tense. She stiffly carries the heavy pot to the rice cooker, all three pairs of our eyes following her. All three of us waiting for her fierce reprisal.

But to my shock, all she says is "But you love swimming." She keeps her back to us, her tone uncharacteristically measured. "Since you were little. You broke a school record last year." When she turns to face me, I'm startled at the pain in her face, the fear. "What about your future, Ella? Coach Carter said last year that scouts from all the top schools were already emailing her. Think about that, Ella. Think about—"

Dad puts a hand on Mom's shoulder. "It's only the first day back, Michelle," he murmurs.

For an instant, something familiar and razor-sharp flashes in my mom's dark brown eyes. We all feel it, Jess and Dad going stiff. But in a moment, it's gone. Deflated, Mom gives a single nod before turning back to the rice cooker in silence.

Jess resumes chopping potatoes with pursed lips, and Dad kisses my head. "Be right back. Gotta get out of these stuffy clothes." He yanks on his tie with a half-hearted goofy face, trying to lighten the mood. It only works a little. He shoots me a sad smile and makes his way upstairs.

I blink at my mom's back in disbelief.

Mom comes from a line of fierce, machete-wielding warrior women. She used to tell the story of how her lola (Tagalog for "grandmother," so my mom's grandmother) dragged *my* lola and her siblings into sugarcane fields to hide from enemy troops in the Philippines during World War II. My lola still has some bullet shrapnel in her left foot.

I'm glad Mom never had to test her guerrilla chops, but without a doubt, this is a woman who could make a soldier cry. She's a woman who wasn't too frightened to leave all her friends and family behind to build a life from nothing in a strange land.

A woman who's currently crumpling in our kitchen, her shoulders sagging as she swallows her words.

And I did this to her. I did this to all of us. For a wild moment, I'd give anything to hear the strident cadence of a classic Mom lecture. To hear her voice raised at me for an A-minus on a World History exam. Because that would mean that, on top of everything else I've done, I hadn't broken this family.

That I hadn't broken my unbreakable mother.

Wordlessly, Jess finishes her chopping and goes upstairs to change her clothes. I continue to finish washing the dishes, the silence stretching between my mother and me, until she says this:

"Hayley's mom called earlier."

I drop the plate I'm holding into the sink, where it shatters with a loud crash. Mom frowns at the broken plate but keeps her mouth shut, no admonishment to be careful.

"What did she want?" With trembling fingers, I pluck the shards of ceramic out of the washbasin, my heartbeat fluttering in my throat.

"You need to go over there after school Friday. She wants your help." Mom sighs. "She sounded *awful.*"

Nausea rises in me, sudden and fierce. "Mom, what could I possibly . . . How can I help her?"

"She wants you to pack up Hayley's room." I don't realize I've been squeezing my fist until I feel a sharp pain. When I look down at the shards in my hand, my palm is filling with blood.

"Mom," I croak. "Please, don't make me do this. Please."

I'll rejoin the swim team, I want to tell her. *I'll go to any school you want me to, but please don't send me into the den of my dead best friend's memories.*

Mom turns from the stove to face me. I'm surprised to see the tinge of regret in her eyes. "Ella, she told me she can't even go inside Hayley's room." Her lips tighten. "She is all alone in that house now. She has no one else. And no one else knew Hayley the way you did. You'll know what she would have wanted to do with her things."

I can't breathe. I want to scream, *How the hell should I know what Hayley would have wanted? No seventeen-year-old discusses their own death and plans for it.*

"I can't do it," I say.

Mom looks sadly at me. "I know you don't want to, Ella. I'm sorry. But you have no choice." She opens the lid of the rice cooker, the smell of steamed rice, usually so lovely, making my stomach roil.

"Friday afternoon. Go there straight after school. She'll be expecting you."

chapter 3
ella

"Anyone? Anyone at all? Come on." Mr. Moss always uses his middle finger to shove his glasses up the bridge of his nose when he's frustrated. This is the third time he's done it in the last minute. "I'm sure none of y'all thought about your poor Latin teacher all summer."

Understatement of the year.

"But can none of you *really* remember the difference between the nominative case and genitive case? None of you?"

I do. I remember. Old Ella would have given the rest of the class a chance to answer, but only for a beat or two. She would have glowed under Mr. Moss's praise when she told him the correct answer.

But right now, I'm praying Mr. Moss can't see me where I'm hiding in the last desk in the back row, strategically slinking behind Thomas Jones's crown of wild red curls.

Mr. Moss sighs, presses his glasses up his nose once more, and turns to the dry-erase board, writing the answer, the only sound the disapproving squeak of the marker.

Every muscle in my body sags in relief, and I let the air out of my lungs. I scan the room. No one's looking my way. They're either scribbling in their notebooks, thumbing through the *Ecce Romani* textbook, or slyly browsing their phones beneath their desks.

Rachael's in this class with me. She'd waved for me to sit next to her, but I didn't miss the way her shoulders relaxed when I politely turned her down. I can't blame her. How is *she* supposed to know what to say to me when my own family is at a loss? When *I'm* at a loss?

I slink farther down in my seat, thinking, *Ten more minutes down.* I do some math, scribbling numbers on my blank notebook page. My heart sinks when I see the number. *Over seventy-three thousand more minutes to go in the school year.* Somehow, I need to figure out a way to stay invisible and numb for the next seventy-three thousand minutes.

The PA system crackles, making all of us jump.

"Mr. Moss, please have Ella Graham come down to the front office." The voice on the intercom sounds bored.

Mr. Moss blinks in my direction, like he'd forgotten I was there. Chairs creak as every eye turns my way. Rachael shoots me a sympathetic look.

So much for invisible.

I have no idea why an administrator would need me except for one reason: what happened with Hayley. I had wondered if there would be some consequence, some punishment for the fact that I'd been drinking. Last year, Dr. Cantrell, our school principal, had been congratulating me on breaking a state swim record. Now he would be expelling me from school.

I bite my lip to keep from crying as Mr. Moss opens the classroom door. I let my hair sweep over my face, hunch my shoulders, wishing I could just teleport out of the room to avoid this walk of shame, every eye like the flash of a paparazzi bulb.

On the long walk down the empty halls to the front office, I decide that I am okay with this. I'll get my GED. Go to college somewhere no one knows me. Go by my middle name.

I shoulder open the door to the front office, imagining answering to "Anna."

"Is Dr. Cantrell ready for me?" I ask Ms. Bertram at the front desk.

"Ella?" I turn around and see Mr. Wilkens peeking out from around a corner. "Come on back."

I hesitate, confused. "I thought that Dr. Cantrell wanted to see me, that he wanted . . ." I chew my lip, suddenly embarrassed. "To expel me?"

"Ella, I'm sorry to make you worry," Mr. Wilkens says, rubbing the back of his neck. "I called you down here, not Dr. Cantrell. Come to my office. I'll explain everything there."

"Oh," I say, feeling stupid as I follow him down the hall.

Mr. Wilkens's office isn't so much an office as a conference room, really. Bookshelves line the wall, and several armchairs and a couch form a loose circle in the center of the space.

And every seat is taken by other students.

Well, not every seat. There's a spot on the couch, presumably for me.

And it's right next to Sawyer Hawkins.

Of course.

He doesn't look up when I walk in, doesn't even seem to notice someone else has entered the room. His arms are folded tight against his chest, his leg bouncing irritably. My throat and stomach clench.

"Sorry, everyone," Mr. Wilkens says, gesturing for me to sit. "Now that Ella's here, we can begin."

At the sound of my name, Sawyer's head snaps up. I slink to the couch and slide into the empty spot between him and Mary Collins, trying desperately not to press against him.

"All right," Mr. Wilkens says gently, leaning back on his desk, one long leg crossed over the other. "Thank you all for coming. I'm sure you're all wondering why you're here." His voice goes soft. "Hayley Miller."

My body reacts to the sound of her name, guilt and sorrow spasming through me. I wonder if I imagine the same flinch in Sawyer beside me.

"This is a big loss, and grief comes in waves. Now that we're back at school, I'm sure many of you are truly feeling Hayley's absence," Mr. Wilkens says. "The administration asked me to hold group sessions with all the seniors, to give you space to heal and be heard. Does anyone want to go first and share what's on your mind? How about you, Scott?"

I'd been so preoccupied with Sawyer, I hadn't noticed Scott. His light brown hair is intentionally rumpled like usual, his clothes casual even though I know just how much his white leather shoes and watch cost—namely because he's made sure everyone knows. Scott wasn't rich until his mom remarried a man who ran a successful marketing company in Atlanta, but now he never lets anyone forget it. Hayley always rolled her eyes about it: "He's the irritating pest you put up with for jokes. He acts like an idiot, but somewhere in there, he's got a good heart. I think."

Now he is rubbing his hands eagerly, his trademark smirk in place. "Oh, goodie, Mr. W, now the healing can finally begin. Let's see . . ." He begins ticking off his fingers, his voice dripping with false sincerity. "I can't believe Hayley's gone; she was such a force of nature. Gosh, it's so unfair, I'm furious she's dead. Maybe if my mom and stepdad weren't always out of town, I wouldn't have thrown that awesome party, and she'd still be here. Wow, I can't believe how incredibly *sad* I am—"

"Scott—" Mr. Wilkens cuts in, his tone disapproving.

"Wait, I'm almost done, I just have one stage left. Even though I'll miss Hayley, I know that I will learn to love life again." Scott's handsome face twists into a mocking grin. "Boom. Done. Five stages of grief in record time."

Mr. Wilkens regards Scott with a hand on his chin. "Sometimes when our feelings are particularly painful, humor can be a way of deflecting. A way of not feeling. That's understandable, Scott."

For a moment, Scott's eyes flare, but before he can say anything, Jackie Nevins cuts in.

"Mr. Wilkens," she sobs. "It's just been so awful! I can't stop thinking about her."

I roll my eyes. Jackie had run track with Hayley for about three minutes and had shared a total of about two conversations.

"Thank you for being brave, Jackie. I know it's not easy. But please, share anything you're willing to." Mr. Wilkens clasps his hands and gives Jackie his undivided attention, which, when she bats her eyes up at him, I'm realizing was probably what she was going for in the first place.

Mr. Wilkens is admittedly hot, for a teacher. He'd grown up in Cedarbrook, and back when he went here, he'd been prom king, valedictorian, and star pitcher on the baseball team. If he wasn't so down-to-earth, he'd be impossible to stomach. But everyone knows that Mr. Wilkens is dating a stunning art teacher at our rival high school. Of *course* the man's not single.

Sorry, Jackie.

I feel a light pressure on my leg and realize with surprise that Sawyer is nudging me. He gives a tiny jerk of his head toward Jackie, who is now openly weeping. Somehow, I know exactly what he's trying to communicate. *Who the hell is she?*

Chewing the inside of my cheek, I pull out a pencil and scrap of paper, as smoothly and silently as I can manage.

Was in track with H—kicked off team after half a semester, I scribble.

Sawyer's eyes follow my fingers, and the corner of his mouth twitches when he's read the whole message. He raises an eyebrow, the one with the scar, and shakes his head at his lap, a small smile on his lips. A little candle of heat blossoms in my chest, the warmth of an inside joke.

After Jackie is done with her tale of woe, all the other students join in. There's a boy named Andrew who had asked Hayley out once during freshman year, who she had gently, but firmly, turned down. Though the way he tells it, she was the one that got away.

"If only we'd had more time." Andrew sighs.

Scott scoffs in disgust, folding his arms. I try to catch Sawyer's eye because *come on*, but he seems to have forgotten anyone else is in the room with him. He's back to frowning down at his shoes, none of the lightness that was there a moment ago. And we're back to reality, where Hayley is gone.

At this point, I just want it to be over.

When the bell rings, the relief is so palpable, I close my eyes. Everyone sits up, stretches.

"Hold on, everyone," Mr. Wilkens says. "Not everyone got a chance to share." He smiles encouragingly at me. "Ella, I can't imagine how hard this has been for you. How are you holding up?"

Oh, dear God, no.

My heart starts beating so fast, it feels like it'll rattle up my throat. Sawyer stiffens beside me, and Scott eyes me with interest. Everyone else shuffles reluctantly, settling back in their seats.

My mouth is dry. I clutch my books tight against my chest. "I appreciate that. I do, really, I do." Against my will, my voice is going quiet, swallowed by my panic. "I just don't know what I can possibly say—or, um, *how* I can possibly say . . ."

"That's okay," Mr. Wilkens says softly. "There's no wrong way to talk about—"

"You know, this is the problem with you shrinks," Sawyer cuts in, startling me. "You like the sound of your own advice so much, you don't ever *listen*. Which, correct me if I'm wrong, is your only job." He wipes a hand across his jaw, shaking his head in faux pity. "Imagine getting a master's in just 'sitting there and shutting up' and still sucking at it." Sawyer's face goes cold. Lethal. "She said she doesn't want to talk."

I stare open-mouthed at Sawyer as a chorus of gasps echo around the room. Even Scott looks half surprised, half impressed. Never in a million years could I imagine talking to a school staff member like this.

Mr. Wilkens straightens up, crosses his arms. "All right, settle down, everyone." He levels Sawyer with a thoughtful look. "You know what? He's right."

The silence is stunning. Sawyer's dark brown eyes flash, the set of his jaw defiant.

Mr. Wilkens looks around the room. "Sawyer's right. I wasn't listening." He turns to me. "Ella, I shouldn't have pushed for you to share before you were ready. I apologize." Mr. Wilkens pins Sawyer with a serious stare. "Ordinarily, I wouldn't tolerate language like that, Mr. Hawkins. But anger, in your circumstance, is absolutely normal." He tilts his head slightly. "And, often, displaced."

Scott lets out a low laugh. Sawyer's voice goes soft, acidic. "Wow," he says. It's somehow scarier than when he was yelling. "What a breakthrough."

I can feel the trembling in Sawyer's clenched fists, can sense how every muscle in his body becomes a rigid line before he explodes off the couch, the sudden movement knocking over the textbooks on my lap. He strides out of the room, slamming the door, sending Mr. Wilkens's diploma crashing to the floor.

There's a collective breath. Even Mr. Wilkens seems shaken, his movements jerky and unsure. My hands tremble, and my mind is racing.

What the hell was that?

chapter 4
sawyer

Outside, I slam my back against the side of the school and lean my head against the wall. My hair snags and scrapes on the rough brick, a soft, pleasant pain. I close my eyes.

I should not have lost my cool like that.

But . . . who the hell wouldn't have? Trapped in that freak show of a grief group like that? Listening to Scott's bullshit? Watching Wilkens zero in on Ella, forcing her to talk?

Who could have just sat quietly by while her brown eyes went all soft and scared? While she collapsed in on herself, folding like a bad poker hand? If you knew Ella like I do (which, as Hayley's best friend, is *pretty damn well*), then you'd know that Ella's always been pocket aces, but that she'd never bet on herself.

That's why I lost it. Hayley used to tell me, "There's something about Ella that makes me want to stand over her and snarl at the world like a lioness." Back then I'd tease her, asking, "Is she your best friend or your cub?"

But now . . . after barely yanking Ella out of the way of that bus, after catching the twitch of her lips as she scribbled that note to me, after watching the way she tucked her hair behind her ear as Wilkens kept *pushing* . . . after realizing that it's only me now, only me here to stand above her and snarl at the world?

Well, of course I stood up and roared.

But still.

Bad move, Sawyer.

I wipe a hand down my face. I'm barely keeping it together as it is. The last thing I need is to get expelled, show up on the principal's radar, on *anyone's* radar. I'm lucky Wilkens isn't turning me in to an administrator.

Honestly, though, I'm also lucky my outburst wasn't worse, given the toxic snarl of sludge that's been filling me from gut to throat for the past four months, threatening to spill over. I can't remember the last time I slept through the night. Can't remember the last time I woke up without the feeling of molten rocks in my gut, the taste of ash in my mouth.

Absentmindedly, I run my thumb along the scar on my left palm, a thin pink river, puffy, still tender. I forget about most of my scars, but I can't ignore this one. Seriously: Try ignoring your hands. It's impossible.

I'm feeling a little calmer now, more levelheaded. Until I see her.

Ella's walking right toward me, staring at the ground, chewing her bottom lip, holding her books tight to her chest. This is the first time I've gotten a chance to look at her. I mean really look at her. I can't imagine how hard this has all been on her. The thought fills me with molten guilt. I've been so wrapped up in my own pain, I'd forgotten I'm not the only one in this hellhole of a school year. There are shadows under her eyes. Looks like I'm not the only one struggling to sleep.

As soon as her eyes land on me, she freezes.

Once more, *I'm* the one making her scared, and it's a kick in the gut. Like accidentally stepping on a puppy's tail.

I'm still trying to figure out what to say when she hunches over, trying to shrink, and starts backing up slowly. It's exactly what I used to do when I was sneaking Oreos from the pantry, thinking I was so slick, while Mom stood over me, arms folded, watching the whole time.

I can't help it. I snort a laugh.

"Hey, Graham," I call out, "I can see you. But if you want, I can pretend we didn't make eye contact."

She stiffens, and it's clear she's embarrassed, a flush creeping up her neck. She throws a look over her shoulder, like she might flee anyway. But she seems to think better of it, straightening and facing me.

I soften my expression, hoping I look as sorry as I feel. Ella's still looking at me like I might turn into a teen werewolf any minute, her shoulders still around her ears, and it's killing me, so I find myself blurting out—

"Hey, how's your cat?" Smooth, Sawyer. Real smooth.

"My . . . cat?" Ella blinks at me.

"Yeah, uh, Edna? How is she?" I rub the back of my neck, wincing.

Ella snorts, a noise that seems to surprise her and gives me hope. She shakes her head. "You mean Midna?" Ella's mouth twitches. "She's . . . um, great. We switched her food, so she gets fewer hairballs now."

I can't believe this is the first conversation we're having since Hayley's funeral. If Ella's face is any indicator, she feels the same.

"Yeah, *Midna*, that's what I meant. And hey, congrats on . . . fewer hairballs. Always good to not have . . . as many of them." I clear my throat.

And there it is. Ella's smile. Even though it's small, it lights up her whole face, her eyes as stunning as a sunrise. That's when I notice how the wind is catching her long, dark hair, the sun turning the little strands into red-gold filaments and making her eyes look impossible, like glowing amber. How had I never noticed before?

Jesus, of course. Because it wasn't okay to notice.

Is it okay even now?

Hell, how long has it been since I've said something?

Ella clears her throat, shifting uncomfortably on her feet.

Crap. *That* long. I blink a few times, trying to clear my head.

"So, um, your books." I clear my throat and look away. "I . . . didn't ruin any of them, did I?"

"My books?" She frowns.

"When I stormed out and knocked them over." I rub the back of my neck.

"Oh, right."

"I'm sorry. I should have at least stayed behind to pick them up. I was a dick."

She tilts her head a little. "You got really mad."

I breathe out harshly through my nostrils. *Steady.* "Yeah. I mean, that chick acting like Hayley was her dead conjoined twin?"

Ella snorts. "I think she was just trying to get Mr. Wilkens to look down her shirt. Which, gross."

My thumb presses into my scar. "The whole thing was gross. Everyone there was just looking for a reason to get out of seventh period." I suddenly feel very tired. "But I shouldn't have yelled," I say quietly. I feel the urge to be honest with her. "My life's been kind of a nightmare. Some days I can keep it together. And then some days I stub my toe on a chair, and I get so furious that I wish, like, I *actually* wish, the chair were alive so I could kill it slowly."

Her eyes widen, and okay, maybe that was a little too honest. I clear my throat. "To, uh, give you an idea of, um, how very well I've been handling everything."

I expect her to be a little more closed off, but when I meet Ella's gaze, she's blinking rapidly, and her eyes are filling with tears.

"I do this thing," she says, "where when I wake up, I roll over and grab my phone to text Hayley, like always. But then I *remember*. And I just want to crawl inside my mattress." She shakes her head. "Most nights are just me staring at the water damage on my ceiling. I never knew how *quiet* three a.m. is."

"Someone told me once," I say, "that eating a banana before bed helps fight insomnia."

"And?" Ella raises a brow.

"And . . . yeah, it worked exactly none of the time."

When she laughs, I can't help but notice how her face lights up. "I'm sorry you're having trouble sleeping," I say. "It's the worst thing in the world."

Ella's smile falters, because, *no*, obviously insomnia isn't the worst thing in the world.

A large, Hayley-shaped silence settles between us. Ella's shoulders are hunching again, and I have this sudden panic, like I'm losing her, which, does that even make sense, because I don't even have her?

"Well," Ella says, and it already sounds like a goodbye, "I'll tell Midna you said hi." She turns to walk away, her hair flowing behind her, silky and black.

"Ella, wait."

I reach out and catch her wrist to stop her. Her honey eyes flick to mine, and she lets out this little gasp.

It's the gasp that gets me, the way her mouth falls open.

I drop her wrist, like her skin burned me.

There's a tight, hot feeling suddenly rising from the bottom of my gut, all from me touching this girl's arm, and of course, the problem isn't that all this is happening with a girl, but that it's happening with *this* girl.

Come on, man, it's Ella. *Ella.*

"That grief support group is bullshit." My voice is a little rough, and I have to clear my throat. "They don't know what the hell any of this feels like. But I do. If you ever need to talk . . ." I step back to give her some space. To give *me* some space. "I'm here."

Ella nods. "Thanks, that means a lot." She gives me a tight smile. "See you later, Sawyer."

I watch her walk away, rubbing the back of my neck, feeling both lighter and heavier at the same time. My stomach churns. It feels like I messed up somehow, and guilt sears my belly.

Because touching her? It felt new, but familiar.

Because the last time touching a girl felt like that?

Well, I was touching Hayley.

chapter 5
ella

On Friday after school, I find myself standing on the porch of Hayley's house. Already, I can feel her absence. Without Hayley tending the azalea bushes by the front steps, they have browned and shriveled, as has the herb garden that once overflowed with basil. Hayley had set up dozens of "hydration stations" for bees, which were just little ceramic pots filled with cobalt-blue marbles for bees to drink from without drowning. But the water in them is murky and brown, and I see at least one bee floating on the surface. I take a deep breath, close my eyes, and fight the urge to run.

Before I can do anything, though, the door swings open. The man in the doorway starts, as shocked by my presence as I am by his. He narrows his piercing green eyes.

"Well, if it isn't little miss Ella."

"Sean," I say, suddenly wary. Surprise makes me blunt. "What are you doing here?"

"Well, hello to you too," he says, pulling a pack of cigarettes from his pocket.

Sean Adams is Hayley's mom's ex. His dirty-blond hair is messy, the rough scruff along his jaw doing nothing to dampen his rugged good looks. The first time I'd ever met him, I was shocked at how much younger he was than Phoebe. That hadn't been the only thing striking about him.

"Don't you dare say it," Hayley had said, catching the look in my eye.

"I won't!" I said. "I will not mention how hot your mom's boyfriend is—"

"*Gross*, Ella!"

"Come on, you have to admit it."

Hayley refused to admit it out loud, but I knew she thought he was hot too. And so did Nia and a number of our classmates. Sean's an electrician, and the school had hired his company to rewire an old wing of the building to bring it up to code last year. Hayley seethed whenever she'd catch anyone eyeing him as we passed him in the halls; she'd stared daggers at Jackie when she'd dared to flirt with him once, Sean smirking the whole time.

Unfortunately for her, it took his company months to finish the job, and by then, the novelty of Sean's charms had long expired. He drank, lied, and had screaming fights with Phoebe. Then he started sneaking out of the house, and Phoebe found out that he'd been cheating on her with a much younger woman. I never found out who—Hayley didn't like to talk about Sean or Phoebe—but at least he had been gone from their lives.

Or so I had thought.

Now I can't stop my lip from curling in disgust. Sean eyes my face, the cigarette hovering around his mouth. "Judge me all you want, but you don't know the whole story. I loved Hayley too, you know."

He drops the cigarette butt, twists his boot heel on the filter, the many keys at his belt jangling. "That storm fried a few breakers at that school of yours, so I guess I'll be seeing you around."

He gives me one last crooked smile before getting into a gleaming black BMW parked at the curb. It must be new; back when he and Phoebe were a fixture, he'd only driven a white van with the words CEDARBROOK ELECTRICAL SERVICES emblazoned across the sides. It billowed foul smoke, and only started half the time.

"Serves him right," Hayley had said. "He totaled his car going ninety in a school zone. Dingus doesn't even deserve a clunky work loaner."

The SUV is a major upgrade. I can imagine Hayley's derisive snort. "Would've been cheaper for him to just get a shirt that said, 'I'm Compensating for Something.'"

After Sean drives off, I push open the front door and find the entire house dark, the only light filtering through the cracks in the blinds.

"Phoebe?" I call out.

"Kitchen," a rough voice calls back.

I pick my way through a series of open cardboard boxes, contents spilling over. Pictures have been taken off the walls; shelves are half-empty. I don't recognize this place, once my second home. It feels abandoned, like a house that had been ransacked, then hastily fled.

I make it to the kitchen, and it's the same thing in here: open drawers and cabinets, each half-full. There, sitting at the kitchen table, amongst boxes filled with ladles and forks, lighting a cigarette with trembling fingers, is Phoebe. She's sitting where Hayley would normally sit when she, Sawyer, and I would eat snacks in between movies during a sleepover. In front of her is a cup that has Bugs Bunny and Taz on it, and the Six Flags Over Georgia logo, from when Hayley and I went over spring break a few years ago.

Phoebe holds her cigarette in one hand and uses the other to trace a finger on the table, frowning deeply. She doesn't notice when ash falls onto the linoleum floor.

Hayley's mom has never been someone I'd call a paragon of parenthood. But she had always looked sleek and polished. The gaunt woman before me is wearing a gray T-shirt full of holes, the design so faded I barely make out the Atlanta Braves symbol on the front. Her auburn hair is limp and greasy, and her face sags with sorrow. Even her once-brilliant green eyes are now nothing but black wells of pain, like grief has changed her very DNA.

This is not the Phoebe I know. And how could it be? A tornado has ripped through her entire life, and she's standing on the rubble, staring confusedly at splinters in her hands, wondering, *Was this my daughter's bed or the living room floor?*

I feel guilty at my surprise, at the thought that rises up in me: *So she did actually care about her daughter.*

It reminds me of something my lola told me when I was little and furious at my mother.

"I hate her!" I'd wept.

"No, anak," she'd said gently. "You love your nanay." When I insisted that I couldn't love her if I hated her, Lola had wiped my tears with a knowing smile.

"Love isn't like stepping into a river, where either you're wet or you're not. Love is the river itself. Sometimes the current is tranquil and steady, like my love for you." She'd kissed me.

"And sometimes," she'd continued, "it has sharp rocks and bruising rapids. The sudden drops and turns are confusing and painful, but it's still the same river. It's still love."

Lola's words come back to me now, and I feel like I finally understand them. How easy it would be if things were so simple, if love were binary, if it either *was* or *wasn't*. But as I regard Phoebe's red-rimmed eyes, I now know the truth is far more complicated.

I clear my throat softly. "Hi, Phoebe."

"So." Her mom leans back in her chair, and when she turns her bleary eyes to me, I catch a glimpse of the old sharpness there. "You came."

I nod, looking around at all the boxes. It's almost shocking how many kitchen utensils there are in the Miller household. In all the time I had known Hayley, the only time Mrs. Miller was in the kitchen was when she was retrieving a bottle opener or a corkscrew.

"Are you . . . are you moving?" I ask. For some reason the idea feels like a dart to my chest. Even though Hayley hated living with Phoebe, so many of *my* memories live here.

"No point in staying here, just me," Phoebe says. "I've done most of the house, but I need you to do Hayley's room." Pain flickers over her face when she says her daughter's name.

It's twisted, but I wonder if it would touch Hayley to see her mother like this. So broken over her death.

I clear my throat. "So . . . do you want me to pack all of it for you to store, or . . . ?" I can't quite bring myself to say the alternative aloud: throw out what remains of her daughter's life.

She laughs mirthlessly. "I do want a few items, but I can't look at them now. Besides, I think Hayley would prefer you be the one to go through her stuff."

She's right. She would have hated the idea of her mother scrabbling through her belongings, no reverence for the correct things, Hayley's beloved gems, understanding none of it.

"I'll set aside things I think you might like and that Hayley would have liked you to have," I promise.

She leads me down the hallway and stands before Hayley's closed door. There are still pictures of Pedro Pascal and BTS that Hayley had cut out from magazines and printed illicitly on the color printer at school. At the center is a Polaroid taken at the homecoming dance last year. It's of Sawyer, Hayley, and me. Hayley's whispering something in my ear that is clearly hilarious, because my head is thrown back, mouth open, captured at the peak of my laugh. Sawyer is looking at us both, his face one of quiet amusement, his long lashes fanning delicate shadows on his cheeks.

We look so radiant. So beautiful. Impossibly eternal. I remember that night. Thinking that this would be us forever, thinking that Hayley was gorgeous, even I felt gorgeous, and that night, I allowed myself to think Sawyer was gorgeous too.

I look down at my feet and blink hard.

"I tried to do it myself," Phoebe says quietly. "But as soon as I stepped in, I didn't feel right. Like I didn't belong. And as I looked at her walls, her things, I realized it was the room of a stranger. My own daughter."

I stand there awkwardly, not sure what to do. Tentatively, I put a hand on her shoulder, but as soon as Phoebe feels my touch, she jerks back. She gives a harsh sniff and faces me with stiff shoulders.

"Phoebe, I'm so sorry. I know that you and Hayley—"

Phoebe cuts me off with a cruel bark of laughter. "Oh, don't bother, Ella. What's the point? She's gone. So gone that I don't even have a body to visit. Can't even bring her flowers like a normal mom would." I shrink back from her, from the razor edge in her voice.

"But it doesn't matter," she continues, her laughter unsteady, turning into something else entirely, "because I don't even know what her favorite flowers were. What kind of mother doesn't know that?" She meets my eyes suddenly. "I bet you know, though. Don't you?" Her voice is deadly quiet.

"Sunflowers," I whisper, wondering if she knew about the little sunflower tattooed on Hayley's left ankle. If she didn't, she never will.

"Sunflowers." Phoebe blinks, as if remembering where she is. "Sunflowers, huh," she says again, stepping back from me.

"Keep whatever you want," she says, her voice suddenly neutral. "I'll donate the rest."

And then she turns on her heel and walks back to the kitchen, leaving me alone with what remains of Hayley.

chapter 6
ella

I take a deep breath. Grief flutters in my lungs, but I have a duty to fulfill, and I need to keep my shit together. I stall by carefully removing the pictures from the front of Hayley's door, trying not to linger on that Polaroid of us.

Then I rip the Band-Aid off and turn the doorknob.

The first thing that hits me is the scent of jasmine—Hayley's perfume. And just like that, she's in the room with me. For a moment, I truly believe that she's hiding underneath her bedcovers, giggling while she scrolls through Archive of Our Own, reading smutty Pokémon fan fiction.

How am I supposed to do this when it feels like Hayley can walk back in any moment? When this room is a perfectly preserved time capsule of when she was alive?

Her fairy lights are still plugged in, LED bulbs going strong.

There's an opened can of Sprite on her dresser, mauve lipstick stains on the rim. Scrawled in her handwriting on the framed chalkboard above her bed are the words *Goal of senior year: Finally get Ella some well-deserved hot, hot man-snack.* Except she had crossed out *snack* and written *meal.*

This is such a mind warp, I actually get dizzy. I take a step back to steady myself and knock into a lamp by the door. It falls backward, against the wall, and a bulb shatters.

I startle at the sound, and suddenly, my best friend is dead again. I'm here in Hayley's room with a job to do.

"Where to start," I mutter to myself, scanning the room for something simple and not too sentimental. There's her dresser and closet, both stuffed with stories and inside jokes. Nope. There's a pile of clothes and her school backpack on the papasan that was "my spot." No way. Her desk seems the safest. Hayley was supposed to use it to do homework, but I never saw her use it for anything other than a dumping ground.

Cautiously, as if walking through a minefield, I make my way to the desk. Sure enough, it's piled high with wrinkled papers. At the top of the stack is an assortment of coupons for eyebrow threading and earwax removal from the local mall.

"Ew, Hayley." I laugh softly.

The coupons help center me, tamp down my grief, so I can get to work. The rest is mostly junk, useless things she had shoved in her backpack, only to toss them on her desk when she got home. There are several flyers for the various fundraising carnivals North Davis High organizes for the school's clubs and teams.

Hayley loved those carnivals. Especially since they're one of the main reasons she and Sawyer got together. He didn't have any classes with us, so he had just been the "Hot Lunchroom Guy" for months. Then, one day, she showed up at our table with Sawyer in tow. They'd hung out at a carnival I'd missed because I'd been sick, and in the space of a week, Hot Lunchroom Guy became a staple in our life.

Going through the pile (of, let's face it, Hay, *trash*) flies by too quickly, and finally I have no choice but to face the wall I've been ignoring, the one above her bed that's covered in a mix of photos, doodles, and notes we scrawled to each other during class.

I climb on the mattress, running my fingers along the edges of a photo of me sticking my tongue out at the camera. Underneath it is a little haiku I wrote. I was embarrassed when Hayley taped it to her wall, but she told me to shut up, because it was *art*.

> **Why did you drop chem???**
> **Now Will C sits next to me.**
> **He farts in his sleep.**

It's not art, but I find myself laughing, and I'm suddenly eternally grateful Hayley never threw anything out.

Not too far away is a photo Jess took of me and Hayley sitting at my dinner table, our mouths full of food. I never noticed my mom in the background, looking mildly horrified. Underneath that picture is another ripped piece of notebook paper, where Hayley and I passed notes back and forth.

> *E, I'm on my period and I think I will murder someone if I don't get any of your mom's lumpia tonight*
>
> 😠
>
> *did you seriously just draw an angry face at me*
>
> **yes! you know mom only makes that for birthdays and special occasions, and your period is not one, sorry**
>
> *fine what's the recipe we can make it ourselves*

we need ingredients but Manila Mart is super far away dude and Atl traffic is the devil so we won't get back till late anyway and ☹☹☹

E, my poor anxious bb bird, dont worry it gonna be ok

I smile, remembering how Hayley and I were making a shopping list at the kitchen table when Mom came up behind us, saw what we were writing, and rolled her eyes. Turned out, Mom had lumpia wraps in the freezer and, since she'd had the day off and was in a good mood, helped us make a delicious crispy pile of lumpia. Mom had enjoyed teaching us how to wrap the meat, how to make sure not to overfill the rolls.

She did *not* enjoy when Hayley bet me I couldn't fit three lumpia in my mouth at once, and I proved to her that I could, in fact, fit four.

But there's also so much I had forgotten, like a picture taken during a picnic at Centennial Park. It was our whole group. There's Nia looking gorgeous as always, holding pink cotton candy to her lips. Beth is right beside her, arms thrown around Rachael, who's smiling widely. Then, of course, there's Scott. In the picture, his arm is around my shoulder, but he's looking at Hayley, who is biting Sawyer's shoulder playfully.

There are more random snapshots: Sawyer dipping Hayley backward in the rain, their clothes soaking wet. Scott kissing Hayley's cheek while she scrunches up her face, in laughter or disgust, it's impossible to say. Another where he's flicking off the camera, a few strands of hair falling in front of his bored gaze. Hayley in motion on the track, Nia next to her, both steps away from the finish line as the rest of us cheer for them in the stands. Beth and Rachael dressed as characters from *Schitt's Creek* on Halloween.

My sadness deepens because I realize, even before Hayley died, it had been months since I could remember us all being happy together, the way we were in these pictures. Toward the end, it had mostly been Hayley, Sawyer, and me.

I had swim team and AP exams to prep for. And Hayley was captain of track, which, toward the end, *really* stressed her out. Her coach was putting a lot of pressure on her. "It's almost not fun anymore," she told me, with a defeated look in her eyes I'd never seen before.

I frown, smoothing the corner of a photo. Come to think of it, Hayley was stressed out all the time at the end, wasn't she? School, sports, the same old crap from Phoebe . . . The last month of junior year had taken its toll. I'd hoped that after summer started, she'd be able to relax and feel like her old, happy self again.

But she never got that chance.

Over the next couple hours, I quietly dismantle the life that Hayley and I built together. I carefully stack pictures into a box, setting aside any that I think Hayley would be okay with me giving to her mother.

Her clothes aren't as hard as I thought they'd be. I know her wardrobe so well, it's easy to separate what to keep and what to donate. There's a Field Day T-shirt from elementary school that Hayley used to wear as a crop top that I set aside for Phoebe, along with Hayley's jewelry. A few of the pieces are family heirlooms, passed down from Phoebe's grandmother. Hayley rarely wore any of them, preferring to keep them safe in her jewelry box.

"After all," she once told me with a wry grin, "these are the only things of Phoebe's I can inherit that don't involve trauma or alcoholism."

Now all of Phoebe's legacies end with her.

There's only one piece of jewelry I keep, one of Hayley's necklaces. It's a delicate gold chain with one charm: a tiny gold circle with the outline of the state of Georgia stamped in the center. I was surprised when she used her first paycheck to buy it.

"But you're always complaining about how much this state sucks!" I said.

"But it's where we met and fell in love," she said, pinching my nose.

I fasten the chain around my neck and press the little gold circle into the hollow of my throat. It's tiny, but I feel a warmth in my chest, knowing that this was Hayley's.

After hours of work, I have reduced the entirety of what is left of Hayley and her room into cardboard boxes. Feeling numb, I sit down on the bare mattress, staring hard at the room, looking for anything familiar. Anything that reminds me of the little corner of the world we carved out together.

Soon, another family will move in, make their own memories, never knowing a girl named Hayley and a girl named Ella once tackled life's greatest mysteries under this very roof.

It hits me then: no body, no room, no house.

It'll be like Hayley never existed.

Tears rise up in my throat, a terrible hollowing void. But then I feel something strange under my hand. I press down on the bed, and no, I didn't imagine it. There's something tucked underneath the mattress.

Frowning, I shove my hand in the tight space between the box spring and mattress. My fingers brush against something hard. I pull out a black book with no markings on the cloth cover. I open it to the first page, and see the words *This diary belongs to Hayley*—and immediately slam it shut.

Hayley's diary.

I can hear movement in the hall, footsteps. Phoebe. If Hayley ever found out that her mom had read her diary, she'd rise up from the grave just to die again of embarrassment.

Without another thought, I slip the diary into my schoolbag. Then I turn off the lights and leave Hayley's room for the last time.

chapter 7
ella

The following Thursday, the clock hits 3:15, and the bell rings. One more school day down.

I slowly pack up my items, nodding at Mr. Wilkens and Ms. Langley, who are chatting in front of her classroom, on the way out of school. I see Nia, Rachael, and Beth up ahead, hugging before they head off to their separate activities, Nia to tennis and Rachael and Beth probably off to Beth's house in her beat-up Honda.

Everyone is rushing to the next thing, except me. Mom has a long shift at the hospital, Dad's working late, and Jess is at Kelly's. As hard as it's been to be with my parents, to feel their disappointment, I also can't bear the idea of hours of silence alone in the house.

With my head down and thoughts anywhere except the present, I don't pay attention to where my feet carry me. But it makes a twisted kind of sense: the bleachers beside the football and track field.

This was where I used to wait for Hayley during her practice. I'd settle in the bleachers, do my homework, read, or listen to music, and occasionally glance up at Hayley. She was usually focused on her two-hundred-meter-sprint time, but every so often, I'd catch her eye and make goofy faces or point to a dude and mouth, *This is the jerk I was talking about.*

But today, my usual spot is taken up by a group of sophomore boys. They're splayed across the bleachers, vaping, Froot Loop–scented clouds lingering above their heads. The air smells like candy as they have a smoke-ring-blowing competition, oblivious to me.

Their stuff is spread out, their long limbs starfishing across the metal benches, so there's no way for me to walk by them without stepping into their space.

For a moment, I stand and watch.

One of the boys has just released a particularly impressive ring when he spots me.

"Oh, shit!" he yelps, nearly falling over. It'd be funnier if they weren't all looking at me (or rather, *not* looking at me) like I was a Gorgon about to turn them into stone with my eyes alone.

I clear my throat. "Mind if I squeeze by you?"

In response, all the boys spring to their feet, scooping their belongings up. I've never seen tenth-grade boys work so efficiently.

I take my customary seat on the bleachers, watching the practice below. It's fall, which means it's cross-country season, and the team is currently warming up, stretching and high-stepping to get loose.

Even through the mess of thoughts in my brain, there's been one particular thing that has been on my mind since I packed up Hayley's room last Friday. It's currently burning a hole in my backpack, calling to me.

Hayley's diary.

I shouldn't even dare to consider it. I am guarding the book of Hayley's most private thoughts like it's the One Ring of Power. To

Hayley, if that book fell into the wrong hands, it would destroy her universe.

She was an open book in so many ways. So when Sawyer once joked about "seeing if there was anything in there about me," he and I were both taken aback by the vehemence of her response.

"Absolutely not," she had snapped. "I need just one place, *one* place I can dump everything. *Everything.* Even my darkest, most vile confessions, without thinking someone might judge me."

My hand goes to the necklace at my throat, absently tracing the tiny charm's edge.

Her diary, her thoughts, her handwriting. It's as close as I'll ever get to a resurrection. Besides, there's nothing in there she wouldn't have shared with me anyway.

Right?

Fingers tingling, I unzip my bag and carefully draw out the black book. I smooth a hand over the cloth, run a finger down the spine. I'm surprised by the choice. Hayley was more of a stickers-all-over-the-front kind of gal. But, if you really need your thoughts hidden, I suppose the unassuming black journal is the way to go.

Still, it's odd, and probably another reason I should *not* read this.

And yet.

I slide my finger inside the cover, tap it so it bounces up.

Just one page, Hayley. I promise that whatever you say I'll take it to my grave. I just need you for one page.

I open the book.

The loud clang of footsteps on the bleachers startles me. Heart pounding, I shove the diary into my backpack and whirl toward the noise. Sawyer is standing there, staring at me.

"Oh, shit!" I yelp, and it does not escape me that I sound just like that dumb tenth grader from before. "Sorry. I wasn't expecting you."

"Clearly." Sawyer's mouth twitches. "You know, we should really stop meeting like this. Let's see . . ." He taps his fingers. "You nearly gave me a heart attack the first day of school. Then I freaked you out during that grief thing. And just now, you acted like I'm the slasher in a teen horror movie. I'm up one, so scare me one more time and then we'll be even."

He sits down, leaning back on the bleachers behind him, elbows propped up on the metal seats. His jeans are sitting low on his hips, and when he reclines, there's a glimpse of flat, tanned skin peeking between his belt and the hem of his shirt. I look quickly away.

"One jump scare," I say. "Got it. I can do that."

He shoots me a sideways glance. "You're kinda blowing up my spot here, Graham. I come here sometimes. Usually it's empty. I like the solitude."

I feel my cheeks grow hotter.

"Oh, I can go . . ." I lean forward to grab my bag, when his hand covers mine.

"I'm kidding."

"Oh, duh. Sorry." I breathe, feeling dumb. And what the hell am I supposed to do with my hands? Especially when his is still on top of mine?

Sawyer pulls his hand back. "You know, I used to wonder if that was your first word."

"Which word?" I ask, my head spinning. "'Duh'?"

Sawyer laughs. "'Sorry.' It's your favorite word, especially when there's nothing to be sorry about. You should say it less."

My response is automatic. "You're right. I'm sor—" I clap my hands over my mouth. His head falls forward, and he huffs a laugh.

For a moment, all we do is stare at the cross-country team as they begin running around the track, distant echoes of whistles and shouts ringing out in the humid air. Somehow, the silence with Sawyer is expansive, freeing. So unlike the claustrophobic, tense quiet at home.

Then I realize something.

"Wait a minute, shouldn't you be out there?" I ask, waving at the stadium.

"Hm?"

"Don't you run cross-country? I seem to recall Hayley bailing on me a few times so she could go to your meets."

Something flashes in his gaze. "You could've come too, you know," he says after a beat.

"Tempting. It sounds riveting, staring at an empty finish line while you run three miles," I tease.

Sawyer gives me a brief smile. "Had to quit. Not enough hours in the day. School, sports, waiting tables: I could only choose two."

I follow his gaze back to the track. "You must miss it," I say softly.

He shrugs.

"It's not a big deal. I make good tips, and the manager at La Michoacana gives me whatever hours I want. I was never gonna win any Olympic medals anyway. Besides." That small smile's back. "I get unlimited chips and salsa."

"Oh, well, you should have led with that. That explains everything."

We both laugh. I sneak a look at Sawyer, at the dark fringe of his lashes, at the silver scar slashing his eyebrow in two, a newish-looking scar on his palm, still reddish and puffy. Then his expression goes serious.

"I miss her, though," he says quietly.

My chest tightens. "So do I. So much so, sometimes I feel like I can't even breathe."

His eyes close and a shadow passes over his face. Part of me is desperate to know what he's thinking; the other part is desperate not to.

"What were your last words to her?" I ask instead.

Sawyer shifts his weight, wiping a hand down his jaw, not meeting my eyes. "You want the truth?"

"Always."

He sighs. "I couldn't tell you if my life depended on it. I hate that it was probably something mundane. But . . . well, those last couple months were . . ." He clears his throat. "Just—there was a lot going on. It's all jumbled in my head, those last few weeks. Maybe it's best I can't recall the painful parts."

"I would take it," I say, my voice breaking. "Painful, bad, whatever. I'd take it. Because, Sawyer? I don't remember my last day with Hayley. None of it. Getting ready, the party, the—the drive home . . . it's all a bright, blinding fog. I want it back so badly. I just want *her* back—"

My voice isn't working, and I realize I'm sobbing too hard to continue.

Suddenly I'm surrounded by Sawyer. He slides his arms around me, one arm wrapping around my waist, his other hand cradling the back of my skull, fingers tangled in my hair. He pulls me close, pressing me against him, tight. I can feel the thrumming of his pulse against his cheek, and I'm dizzy from the smell of his cologne.

"I know," he murmurs into my ear. "I know, Ella."

And the thing is, he does know. He might be the only one who does.

"All of this . . ." I take a shuddering breath. "It's all my fault. If I'd driven slower, if I'd been more responsible, more careful . . ."

"Hey. No." He pulls back to fix me with a fervent stare. "Listen to me." He squeezes my shoulders painfully hard. "*None* of this is your fault."

With an impossible gentleness, he brushes his thumb along my cheek, wiping away my tears. His face is grave, serious.

"None of it," he murmurs.

And maybe it's the purge of a good cry. Maybe it's the way early twilight has made me feel like we're the only two people in the world, lending a certain ceremony to his words. Or maybe it's just the way Sawyer is looking at me right now, like, for the first time, someone isn't feeling sorry *for* me, but sorry *with* me.

Whatever it is, I believe him.

"Thank you," I whisper.

The sky is a soft scarlet gold from the setting sun. With all the teams filing into the athletic building, the field is quiet again. The crickets are warming up for their night music. Frog songs carry across the field, from some damp, humid brush. As the pinks of the sky turn to purple, it feels like night is being ushered in, just for us. A breeze lifts the scent of wisteria and honeysuckle to us, gently tousling our hair. I watch Sawyer's thick, dark locks dance on the wind. I'm suddenly very aware of his thumbs grazing the corners of my lips, how very close our faces are.

Unbidden, the thought comes to me: *Golden hour looks good on Sawyer.*

I remember now how ludicrously, maniacally happy Hayley was when she started dating Sawyer. Every touch, every look, every word between them left Hayley dizzy, smiling, unfocused. I had to prod her to do homework, repeat things I said to her. I'd get annoyed, but Hayley would just grab my hands and spin me around. "You'll understand someday, E," she would say.

And now, God help me, I do.

chapter 8
sawyer

It is well and truly night when I skid to a stop at the front door to my house. I lean against the scuffed wood, take a moment before walking in. My heartbeat is a little slower by the time I'm turning the lock and stepping through the door.

"Oh my goodness! Wow, Callan, come here, you'll never believe it, the president's finally arrived!" The voice comes from somewhere underneath the kitchen table. "I mean, can you believe that we are actually *worthy* to have dinner with?"

I roll my eyes. "You're the reason Callan's such a drama queen, Mom."

Mom's head pops up from underneath the table, her hazel eyes wide in mock surprise. "*Moi?* Dramatic? Never. Now come over here—I need your help fixing this." Her head disappears again.

"Shit, I thought I fixed that," I mutter, joining her under the table.

"Language," Mom says half-heartedly as she grapples with the broken table leg. "Hold this up while I grab the wood glue."

This will be the third time we've repaired this leg. Neither of us says the obvious: We need a new table. But the rent just went up last month, and it's not like Mom could get a *fourth* job.

I keep both hands on the leg, eyeing Mom as she frowns in concentration, applying the glue. Her fine brown hair is swept back from her face, her makeup light. For years, anytime we've gone out anywhere, people assume we're brother and sister. When they hear that she's my mother, they don't believe it. "You look way too young to have a kid as old as him!"

And they're right. Mom's only thirty-three years old. I'm eighteen next May. You do the math.

She looks young because she is young. *Although*, I think, anxiously watching her grimace from effort, she's been dragging a lot recently. Three jobs, two kids, no help. It's getting to her.

"I can hear your fretting from over here." Mom grunts. "Stop that. I'm fine." She applies the last of the glue with a flourish. "Done!" Mom's nose wrinkles. She leans toward me and sniffs. "Whoa, Saw-Saw. I thought I'd forgotten my deodorant, but it's you!"

"Mom." How? How does she make me feel eight years old?

"Did you go on a run?" she asks, crawling backward from underneath the table.

I stand up, brushing off my jeans. "Something like that," I mumble.

"Hey, that's great!" Mom grabs her Waffle House apron and purse. She pauses, face falling a little. "I'm sure you've been missing cross-country."

It's almost exactly what Ella said on the bleachers. But honestly, I hadn't realized I'd been running until I was about a mile in. I hadn't meant to.

One moment, I was holding Ella's face; the next minute, I was sputtering that I was late for dinner, nearly falling down the bleachers from how fast I was trying to get away.

She's one of your closest friends, I was thinking. Calm and reasonable. *You were just being there for a friend during her time of need.* And that's when I realized the wind was stinging my eyes and my lungs were burning.

I was full-on *sprinting.*

I guess I thought that, maybe, if I ran fast enough, I'd burn up whatever the hell this feeling is, the one that's refusing to go ignored. The harder my legs pumped and lungs ached, the easier it was to focus only on the strain in my muscles.

But a three-mile sprint only left me exhausted and gasping at my front step. And as soon as I stopped, I was slammed by the memory of Ella in my arms, the warmth of her body. Her large amber eyes, swimming with tears, looking up at me like I have the answers to everything.

Shit.

No way do I have feelings for Ella. Not happening.

"Hey, Broody Brooderson, I'm talking to you. Do you like her?"

"What?" I panic and pinch the bridge of my nose. "*No.* Maybe. Yes? Ugh, but I can't . . ." I drop my hand. "No. The answer is no."

Mom blinks at me. "You . . . have some very complicated feelings about our new coffee maker." She's standing next to the sink, her hand on a coffee maker that wasn't there this morning. Mom refers to every inanimate object in the world as "she." Lamps, toothbrushes, burgers. She says it makes her feel better. Like she's getting back at the patriarchy or something.

"I'm sorry you don't like her, but Linda from work gave her to me. They just got the newest Keurig, and our old one was on the fritz." She eyes me shrewdly. "Unless you weren't talking about Mrs. Coffee here."

"Ugh, Mom." I turn away from her to hide my burning cheeks. "You know caffeine stunts growth."

"All right, Mr. President, if you're gonna be all tight-lipped." Mom blows a strand of hair out of her face. "*Callan,*" she bursts out, "if I have to come get you, I swear to *God*—"

A little blue blur slams into my gut, knocking the wind out of me.

"Finally," Mom sighs while I clutch at my chest and wheeze.

"Mr. President! Mr. President!" my little brother, Callan, dressed in Thomas the Tank Engine pajamas, chants into my shirt, jumping up and down, hands wrapped tight around my waist.

"Hey, buddy," I say, ruffling his mop of brown hair. Even when he's causing me bodily harm, no one can make me smile quite as easily as Callan.

"Callan," Mom says suspiciously, "what were you doing? Were you eating crayons again? Tell me you weren't eating crayons again."

"Nope!" Callan says, before throwing back his head and giving me the most colorful smile I've ever seen. There's black, blue, red, magenta . . . yeah, the whole rainbow. I'm amazed he can talk through the wax.

Mom sighs. "Just make sure he doesn't swallow too much of it, Saw." She checks her watch. "Shit, I'm late."

"Shit!" Callan yells jubilantly. "Shit, shit, shit!" He marches into the living room, saluting with each word. Mom shoots me a long-suffering look.

"I got it," I say.

"Thanks, Saw." She gives me a tired smile. "Dinner's in the oven. You're good to wait with Callan for the bus tomorrow?"

"Of course." A piece of paper on the side of the fridge catches my eye. I catch the words "invited" and "third round of interviews." I snatch it off the fridge and stop my mom at the door.

"Mom!" I shake the paper at her. "Mom, this is amazing. Why didn't you tell me? This is huge!"

"Oh, Sawyer, it's not a big deal. I'd be an executive assistant, not an astronaut."

"Mom, I saw the job description. I saw how many zeroes were in that salary. And the benefits—"

"Sawyer, don't get your hopes—"

"If you've already made it this far—at this point it's just a culture fit, and no one's more likable than you! Mom, if you got this job . . ."

"Don't say it." She softens, her eyes sparkling. "But thanks, Saw." She tilts her head back to call out, "Callan, Mommy's leaving, you gonna come say goodbye or what?"

There's another incoming blue blur, but I manage to grab Callan before he slams into Mom. He gives her a tight squeeze, and she kisses the top of his head at least ten times.

I would have protested, even at Callan's age, but he just squeezes her tighter.

"Ugh, I'm so late now I might as well not show up." Mom pulls back and sighs. "Kidding. Unfortunately. *Bye.*"

We wave to Mom as she pulls out of the driveway. It's starting to drizzle a little, and I can hear the screech of the windshield wipers as they drag against the glass.

Those I will *need to replace,* I think.

I know it's dangerous to get my hopes up, but I can't help but imagine what it'll be like if Mom gets that job. I wouldn't have to prioritize all the things that need to be replaced or fixed around the house. I could just go to AutoZone, get the wipers, maybe even a rain repellant for the windows. I wouldn't have to worry about Mom driving in a surprise thunderstorm anymore.

We could eat dinner at a table without fear that our spaghetti could collapse to the ground at any moment. Mom could have a day off—no, *weekends*! Two whole days! She could take Callan to the library, or the park, or even the zoo. Callan's greatest dream is to meet a silverback gorilla.

Mom's greatest dream is to get a full seven hours of sleep. This job would give them that and more.

I feel a tug on my shirt. "Saw-Saw," Callan whispers.

"Yeah, bud?"

"Do we have to keep standing at the door? I'm hungry," he continues to whisper.

"Sorry, Cal." I close and lock the front door. "We gotta clean all the crayons out of your teeth first. First step, crayons. Second step, food."

Callan whines all the way to the bathroom, chanting, "First step, food! First step, food!" Other than that, he's pretty compliant, holding his mouth open for me as I brush thick chunks of colorful wax from between his teeth. I do the best that I can, but some of it's *really* crammed in there. I stare at the rainbow-filled gaps between his teeth, wondering what to do.

"You look angry," Callan says.

I laugh. "I'm not angry, bud. This is my thinking face."

In the end, I just decide to see how it looks after dinner. Maybe some of the food will loosen the wax, and he's eaten crayons before. Though I think that was an eight-pack, and we made the mistake of buying him a sixteen-pack to replace it. Callan's been patient, but there's no way he's letting me floss him, so dinner it is.

Callan chatters to me about his school day while I pull out the casserole dish from the oven and switch it off. It fills the kitchen with the smell of beef and onion. Even Callan stops talking for a moment to appreciate how good it smells.

I can't believe with everything going on, Mom still took the time to make us dinner. She's been doing it on her own for so long, she'd probably say she's used to it. With everything she's been through, and with all she has to do to keep this family going, I can't help but think that this is not something any human being should ever have to get *used* to.

Pointing a finger to my face, Callan interrupts my thoughts. "Angry or thinking?"

Both.

"Thinking," I say. "Callan, what would you say to a dinner picnic in the living room?"

"I would say great idea!" Callan claps his hands and jumps up and down.

"Very good. I knew you were a smart man." Callan seems to take this very seriously. "Why don't you get a few pillows and put them in front of the TV. You wanna choose something on Netflix?"

I've hardly finished my sentence before he's zooming out of there. Mom hates when we eat in front of the TV, but the wood glue needs to cure overnight, and I really don't want to risk anything falling on Callan.

I serve the two of us and wrap the rest for Mom. I grab a fistful of napkins Mom brought home from Waffle House and carry the plates into the living room.

As I thought, we will be watching *Avatar: The Last Airbender* for the fortieth time. And I am not mad about it.

"Chew and swallow first, buddy," I say, sighing, when Callan tries to act out the opening credits with a mouthful of beef and noodle.

As soon as Callan settles down, his chin propped on his hands as he watches the TV, his plate empty, I realize we've reached the part of the evening I have been dreading.

The part when there's nothing distracting enough to keep me from thinking about Ella.

I'm sitting on the floor, my back leaning against our ratty old couch, and everything in the living room gets hazy as images from the bleachers float back to me.

I wanted to kiss her.

As soon as the unbidden thought appears in my head, I know it's true.

And it's not the first time.

That one makes me curl my hands into fists, because, dammit, that one is too.

But I've never—I mean, while Hayley and I were together, there was a *very clear line* in my head that I *never*—

Still, there was this one time last year. Ella was moping because some asshat turned her down when she asked him to homecoming. We were sitting in Hayley's room. I was on the floor, Ella was curled up on the bed, and Hayley was stomping back and forth, ranting that she couldn't believe anyone in the world would ever turn Ella down.

"Sawyer! I mean, Ella is gorgeous! Right? That's an objective truth! Don't you think Ella's gorgeous?" Hayley said.

Ella turned bright scarlet. "Sawyer," she pleaded, "don't answer that."

"She's like my sister, Hay," I said, my heartbeat picking up inexplicably fast. I turned to Ella. "You're like my sister. You know, it's weird if I say—"

"You're so full of *shit*, Sawyer!" Hayley yelled, marching out of the room and slamming the door shut.

Then it was just me and Ella, squirming in the most god-awful awkward silence.

I don't know *why* I couldn't even think about Hayley's question. I just couldn't. There was a block or something.

But I did blurt out, "Ella, that guy is a moron. The biggest idiot ever."

She turned onto her stomach, buried her face into a pillow. "You don't have to say things just to make me feel better. It makes me feel pathetic."

I rubbed the back of my neck. "You're not pathetic. And I'm . . . I'm not. Just saying it."

But I said the last part kinda quiet, so I don't think she heard me, and I remember thinking, *Maybe it's for the best.*

And maybe it's for the best, even now.

Because being that close to Ella, it was hard to ignore what she is.

Which is gorgeous. I couldn't say it then, but Ella is gorgeous. And she's smart, and kind, and funny, and she smells like vanilla, and she's—

Hayley's best friend.

First and foremost, Ella is Hayley's best friend.

Which is why I'm going to scoop all these thoughts I just had, put them in a box, stuff them in the back corner of my mind, and never, ever open them again.

chapter 9
ella

On Monday, I pull my gym bag out of my locker and slam the door harder than I need to.

It's been a few days, and I *still* can't stop replaying what happened on the bleachers with Sawyer. Anytime I close my eyes, I can feel his warm breath against my ear, his pulse against my skin. I can also see the terror in his eyes when he came to his senses and ripped away from me, stammering something about dinner before he ran. Like he couldn't get away fast enough.

This is a good reminder for me. That he thinks of me as a friend. Nothing but a friend. I mean, I was crying like a baby. What was he going to do? Pat my head and leave? He didn't, because he was being a good *friend*.

Then why can't I stop thinking about it? *Why?*

The more I try to stop myself from thinking about Sawyer, the more detailed my thoughts get. Like the flood of *true* understanding in his eyes as I confessed my guilt. The heat of his palms on my shoulders, the callus of his thumb as he wiped tears from my cheek, telling me, "It's not your fault . . ."

I have to stop. How the *hell* am I gonna stop?

I ask the universe to help me get my mind off Sawyer, and the universe delivers.

On the way to gym class, I feel myself get my period.

"Shit," I hiss, scurrying into the girls' locker room. "Shit, shit, shit."

Why is it three days early? The stress? I'm cursed? Either way, since it's unexpected, chances are I don't have any tampons.

Then I have another realization. I fumble through my gym bag, panicked, whispering, "Please, no, please, please," but to no avail. I did, indeed, pack white shorts for gym class this morning. What was I *thinking*? Why do white shorts even exist? Why do white chairs, white carpets, white pants, white *anything* exist?

I dig violently through both my gym bag and my backpack, shoving my fingers in every nook and cranny, but turns out, past Ella was not very nice to present-day Ella, and she did not pack a secret emergency tampon stash.

Sitting down hard on one of the cold concrete benches, I fight back tears. Six months ago, this would have hardly been a blip. Hayley was always stuffing extra tampons and pads in the side pockets of her backpack, because "You never know when Shark Week will strike, and you never know when a sister will be in need."

A sister is currently in dire, dire need.

I cast a gloomy eye around the room. Clusters of girls are scattered around the locker room, applying deodorant, adjusting their shorts, staring at me and whispering. I drop my eyes, not wanting to give anyone more to talk about, or more reasons to feel sorry for me.

I bury my head in my hands. I'll just wait until they're all out of the locker room and stuff a giant wad of paper towels in my panties and pray.

There's a tap on my shoulder.

I look up to see Seema Patel, the girl who had offered me Sour Patch Kids on the first day. "Just a guess," she says, "but is this what you need?"

She holds an array of tampons in my face, fanning them out like a deck of cards. She's got light, regular, super, and super plus.

Seema and I were friends in elementary school. She'd come over a lot for playdates, and I know somewhere in the back of my closet is a friendship bracelet she made for me at camp. But when I got close with Hayley, Seema and I lost touch, each of us drifting into our respective friendship groups. I hadn't seen her much until a few months ago, when she was also hired as a lifeguard at the Y. And now she's here, like a guardian angel.

She watches me blink at the tampons.

"You take too much longer, you're gonna be leaving a bloody butt print on that bench."

I breathe a surprised laugh, grab a regular and my gym clothes, and head to a bathroom stall.

"You sure?" she calls after me. "Don't be embarrassed to snag a super plus. Especially on my account. Shit, some days I'm just *destroying* ultras. Dude, it's so much blood, I'm like, *How am I even alive right now?*"

When I walk out of the stall, she's still there, leaning back against one of the lockers plastered in flyers for the upcoming fall festival. The fall festival had always been my favorite event of the year—corn mazes, candy apples, and bales of hay strewn around. Hayley and I usually volunteered for the s'mores booth. Last year, she'd somehow talked Scott into volunteering for the dunk tank—it'd been brilliant watching the baseball team nail the target time after time, sending Scott plunging into the water. Now I can't even imagine going.

"Thanks, Seema. You know, I'm impressed at your . . . lack of *ick*, with this subject," I say. More than impressed, it actually makes me feel downright sentimental. Because I've only ever known one other person who didn't shy away from unfairly stigmatized subjects.

"What? This is nothing." Seema waves a dismissive hand. "I worked as a vet assistant at Cedarbrook Animal Hospital the past two summers. My favorite thing was helping lance cat abscesses. Periods are boring."

That shocks a loud, good-natured laugh out of me.

Hayley would have loved this girl. Immediately, the thought has my gut twisting with guilt, sorrow . . . envy? I shake my head, trying to rattle the shitty feelings into dust.

"Well . . . I owe you big-time," I say, feeling awkward as we head to the gym doors.

"Oooh, I'll remember that," she says, her voice playful.

My hand is on the door handle when she stops me.

"Give me your phone," she says.

"What? Why?" I take a step back.

She rolls her eyes. "Sheesh. I just want to exchange numbers. We work together and we have gym and English together, and now we share tampons. I'm pretty sure that means we're friends again. Plus, I'm *not* getting stuck with Robert when we have group projects."

On the other side of the door, I can hear Coach Cud, the gym teacher, blow his whistle. If we aren't out there in five seconds, he'll mark us tardy and we'll get detention.

Seema's holding out her hand, waiting for my phone.

"Fine, here."

We exchange numbers and enter the gym. Coach Cud glares when he sees us but doesn't mark us as tardy. He was Hayley's track coach, a former North Davis High star sprinter himself. He's young enough that he remembers what it's like to be a teenager and doesn't want us to think he's a dick. Hayley half loved and half hated him. "Is he Coach Cud or Coach 'Bud'? That dude needs to pick a lane," she'd always say as we groaned. But sometimes, like today, his need to be cool works in our favor.

I groan when I see students dribbling and shooting basketballs. I hate basketball. I'm terrible at it, and I'm not in the mood to make a fool out of myself today.

"Want to partner up?" Seema asks, but I hardly hear her because on the far end of the court, wearing a dark gray shirt and gym shorts, Sawyer Hawkins is having a chin-up competition with Thomas Jones.

It's clear from the sour look on Thomas's freckled face that Sawyer is winning, and my stomach flips as I watch the muscles of his sculpted arms coil and unfurl with every chin-up he does.

On the bleachers the other day, Sawyer was so gentle.

But what if he wasn't gentle? What would that be like? What if instead of that metal bar, he was clasping my wrists? Gripping them just as tightly? What if he was pinning those wrists down?

Pinning *me* down?

Dear, sweet God in heaven, what is *wrong* with me? I touch fingers to my cheek and find my skin on fire, praying no one notices.

It's not like I'm a *nun*. I mean, Bradley Clark and I dated for most of tenth grade. We kissed, did stuff. Not *sex*—I haven't done *that* quite yet—but . . . I mean, some other stuff. Everything about Brad was simple and clean. When he moved out of state, I didn't even cry. Hayley had asked if I was okay, and I told her I was more than okay. Things with Brad had been nice, after all.

Fine.

When I told Hayley that, used the word "fine," particularly when describing my hookups with Brad, she marched me to her car and drove us to a shop that sold incense and vibrators. She was so pissed when they wouldn't let us in the door because we were under eighteen.

"Girls deserve orgasms too, asshole!" she shouted at the window before sitting next to me on the curb.

"How'd you know I didn't have one?" I asked, playing with my shoelaces. "Because, I don't know . . . it was pretty nice, so maybe I did?"

"Please." She tossed her long red hair over her shoulder. "When you know, you *know*. And you really deserve to know, dammit." Hayley threw a dirty look at the clerk through the window.

"It's okay! I don't mind. I promise." I shrugged. "I really don't care about, um, having one."

The *look* Hayley gave me. She pulled me to her chest and rocked me back and forth. "Oh, my sweet, *sweet*, tiny, organically grown strawberry."

"Why are you like this?" My voice was muffled by her shirt.

"One day. One day, you'll understand, baby bird." And she kissed my forehead.

I really hadn't thought about Hayley's words since then.

But for some reason they come back to me now, as I watch Sawyer stretch his calves.

Hayley never talked about her sex life with Sawyer. Of course, she *wanted* to. But there was something about knowing it was *Sawyer* that she'd be talking about, and I'd have to sit next to him on the couch during movie night or across from him at Starbucks. It made me all embarrassed and awkward to think that he'd be passing me the ketchup, and I'd be staring at his fingers, thinking, *He used those to do* that *to Hayley?*

But now I'm sort of wishing I knew . . .

Just then, pain explodes against the side of my head as something slams into me with such force I stumble to my knees. At first, I think it's karma, fast and swift. But then I see a basketball rolling away from me.

"What the hell is wrong with you, Scott?" Seema appears in front of me, crouching to catch my watering eyes. "You okay, Ella?"

"It was an *accident.*" Scott swims in my vision, but I can make out the cruel curl of his lip. "Ella knows what an *accident* is. Don't you, Ella? At least this is just a little one, where no one died."

"Shut up, dickweed," Seema snarls.

My throat constricts. My eyes are watering, and I must have bitten my tongue, because I'm tasting blood. The loud screech of gym shoes, the echoing yell of rowdy teenagers, the accusing glint in Scott's eyes . . . I need to get out of here.

I launch to my feet and stagger toward the door.

"Coach Cud, I need to go to the nurse's office," I say in a wobbly voice. My eyes shoot over to where Sawyer is watching Thomas struggle through a chin-up. He didn't see my embarrassing display, thank God.

"Grab the hall pass, Graham," Coach Cud calls. "And you, Logan, five laps for being an ass."

"Want me to come with you?" Seema asks over Scott's protests.

But all I want is Hayley.

She'd know what to do. She'd pick me up, brush me off, and tell me I should have taken out my tampon and thrown it in Scott's face.

Ew. I laugh and wipe the tears from my eyes. And that's when I know the only thing that will make me feel better.

"I'll be okay," I tell Seema. "But thank you, really."

Then I run to the girls' locker room, change back into my school clothes, and head in the opposite direction from the school nurse.

One of Hayley's and my favorite spots to hide out was the encyclopedia aisle of the library. I don't think anyone's checked out an encyclopedia since Google was invented, so it was the perfect place for us to curl up in the corner and eat Sour Skittles.

As I head to the library, I pass Mr. Wilkens's office, and for a second I falter, wondering if I should try talking to him about what I'm feeling. But his door is closed, a sign on the front reading, IN SESSION.

And with nothing else to stop me, I push open the double doors of the library and head to the back. I settle on the floor, tucking myself against the shelves. Then I unzip my backpack and slowly, reverently, draw out Hayley's diary. I run my fingers along the corners, cradle it like a relic. I close my eyes.

Forgive me, Hayley. For all of it. For Sawyer. For this. I'm a mess. I don't know how to get through this. In fact, I don't think I can. I'm ruined without you, and the only person who can get me through losing you . . . is you.

And with that final, desperate plea, I open Hayley's diary and begin to read.

chapter 10
hayley's diary

I used to scoff at movies or stories where a terribly ordinary girl is having her morning cereal before school, on some terribly ordinary Tuesday, and bam, *they find out they're secretly a princess. Well, I should say, I'd* publicly *scoff, because the truth is, buried deep in my little heart, it would make me ache and yearn for such a thing to happen, and it was only because I* knew *it never,* ever, *ever would.*

Until now.

*I can hardly hold my pen for how hard my hand is shaking because—because—*because *what I am is so much* better *than finding out I'm a secret princess from some invented country.*

What I am is maddeningly, gut-wrenchingly, toe-curlingly in love. *And I know it's true because it's so potent, and I don't even care that I just wrote something so saccharine. The Hayley from before could never have penned anything so cloying, but now I just want to sink into a meadow and imagine his lips and . . . But let me back up.*

It started at that fundraising carnival E and I signed up to volunteer at. I wish I could remember which one it was, but after three years, they all blend together in a single, lovely, sticky, cotton-candy-flavored blur.

Besides, that's the point, isn't it? That it was some terribly ordinary carnival in some terribly ordinary school parking lot. But fortuitous just the same. E got sick, so I had to do my volunteer shift at the ring-toss booth all alone. The evening smelled like grass and funnel cake, and I was running the ring-toss game spectacularly. *I had my hair gathered in one hand and was fanning myself with the other when S strode to the counter, eating popcorn from a paper cup.*

I was hit with the smell of cologne and warm butter, and I had to look away for a moment, he was so beautiful.

He surveyed my booth, taking in the glass bottles, the cheap plastic rings, and then, finally, me. I swore I saw his eyes linger on the bare stretch of my neck but was sure it had to be wishful thinking.

Either way, it flustered me, and I found myself blurting out: "Wanna play?"

He set down his popcorn and picked up one of the many plastic rings scattered across the wood.

"I feel like I'd be missing out if I didn't." He tossed the ring up and caught it. "Everyone's saying it's the best game at the carnival."

"Then what are you waiting for?" I dropped my hair, sweeping it over one bare shoulder. I didn't miss the way his eyes followed

the movement, and it made me drop one of the plastic rings, my fingers fumbling.

I gathered a handful of rings and dumped them in a pile before him. S managed to catch two of them before they rolled off the counter.

"It's five dollars." I held out my palm.

"You only take cash?"

"No. But if you pay with card, it's fifteen dollars," I said.

He barked out a laugh, but when I only raised my eyebrows, he stopped.

"I should have known you weren't kidding," he mumbled. He dug into his pocket, searching. I could hear the rattle of coins. "Let me guess. You recently found out that the Square processing fees are used to fund some terrible anti-fungus group, and you're a friend to all mushrooms."

It was my turn to laugh.

"I love mushrooms dearly, but that's not it. I like Square just fine. It's a handy little thing for small businesses," I said. "The truth is, I forgot to grab the Square reader from Ms. Langley, and not only would I need to track her down, but I'd have to then *track down Principal Cantrell for an adapter because my phone doesn't have the right port. But mostly?" I plucked the proffered five-dollar bill from his hand. "I forgot to download the app, and that's the biggest bother of all."*

S's mouth twitched, like he was keeping one in, and it was like all the laughter rose from his chest and gathered in his eyes, making them sparkle.

He cleared his throat. "Fair enough."

I explained the rules and stepped aside, watching as he brushed his hair out of his eyes and focused on the grid of glass bottles.

S carefully tossed ten rings and missed every single one. He was fishing in his pocket to try again when I thrust a St. Louis Cardinals basketball in his face.

"What's that?" His eyes were wary.

"Your prize."

"But I didn't land any rings."

"That's because this game is rigged." I slammed the ball on the counter. "You were never going to win." I held up the ring and showed him how it was only slightly wider than the neck of the bottle. "I'm doing my part to give power back to the people."

S smiled down at his shoes and shook his head. "It's all making sense now. You've just been giving prizes away all night."

"I'm only giving back what ring-toss games have stolen from innocents for decades."

He narrowed an eye at me, leaning on the counter. "You don't think Principal Cantrell's gonna get mad?"

"Why?" I asked. "You gonna snitch on me?"

"Of course not. Besides"—something hot and dark flashed through his gaze—"I like having a secret with you."

I don't faint. I'm not a fainter. But the way he said it, the way his voice got low, made me a little light-headed. As I watched him walk away, I had to shake my head, clear it, because had I imagined it or had S been flirting with me? *Because, yes, I know, it's unlike me, but the truth is, I'd figured I was not S's type.*

Was he mine?

That's the magic of S: He's everybody's *type.*

Even when you don't think he could be.

Which is why, after that night at the carnival, I couldn't stop thinking about him. I was beginning to lose hope when I didn't see him at school for the whole next week. I began to imagine that, perhaps, it had *been all in my head.*

But then, one day after school, after grabbing my iced coffee from the barista at the counter of the Honey Bean, I whirled around and slammed straight into S, spilling my drink all over his shirt.

"Shit balls! I'm so, so sorry! Let me— I can get—" I lunged at the nearest stack of paper napkins and grabbed a fistful. Madly, I began scrubbing at his coffee-soaked shirt. Gently, he grabbed my wrist. I'd been avoiding his face, but when he did that, I stilled, looking up.

He was laughing and shaking his head.

"Hayley, it's cool. I just got done with a run." That's when I took in what he was wearing, and my stomach did that hot flip-flop thing that makes my fists clench. His workout clothes were simple enough, gym shorts and a gray tee, but his arms and calves were art. *Sculpted and carved and making me stupid.*

"Honestly," S said, "I'm all sweaty and gross. I think you just made me smell better." He was still holding my wrist. "Let me buy you a replacement drink."

So he got me another iced coffee, and I figured he had things to do, friends to see, but he managed to snag two armchairs in a cozy corner and we just . . . talked.

Well, I *talked. He listened. Like, actually listened. Under that steady, gorgeous gaze, I found myself telling him stuff I really only ever tell E. He had this way of coaxing me into honesty. Making me feel seen. Making me feel* strong. *Like none of the shittiness of my life was actually my fault.*

I wanted his number. But I was too scared to give him mine. Still too terrified to be told, Oh, I was just being nice.

But it turned out I didn't need to.

"Give me your phone," he said.

When I did, he put his number in.

"You have my number now. If you ever need anything. Anything. *Call me. Text."*

What if all I want is your mouth on mine? *I felt like asking.*

S gave me a kind smile. A charitable smile. I told myself that he was just being a good person, a good friend.

But then one night I found myself at open mic night at one of the bars in town. P had done something that pissed me off (what else is new?). And everyone else was asleep because it was a school night. I didn't want to bother any of them. Especially E. She had a test the next day, and I care about her grades more than mine.

I was sitting at the bar listening to shitty stand-up and drinking vodka sodas. The bartender liked looking down my shirt, so he never checked for my ID, and I was slowly getting hammered. This wasn't something I ever really did. It'd just been a rough couple of weeks.

I wasn't thinking. One minute, P was screaming at me, and the next minute I was huddled over my second vodka soda.

By the third, I knew I was in trouble.

I needed a ride, but I was too ashamed to call any of my friends. I couldn't do this to them, wake them up because I wasn't handling my shit.

But then I remembered one offer, recently made.

I was already texting him before I had decided to.

If you"re inn th neighborhood I could use a ride. BUT ONY if its on the way. *The screen was blurry, and my fingers felt too big for the buttons.*

Where are you, Hayley?

Just those four words sent a thrill through me.

He was there so quickly, like he really had *been in the neighborhood. I closed my tab and stumbled out into the parking lot, where he was standing, his face dark and serious. When he saw me, and how I needed to lean on the rail to walk, he strode up to me.*

"Hayley, are you all right?"

I tried standing straight, but immediately pitched forward. S caught me, my entire body falling into his.

"No, I suppose you're not," he murmured against my face.

"You came," I sighed.

"Of course I did," he said.

He helped me to his car, nestling me in the passenger seat and buckling me in.

I told him my address and must have passed out, because the next thing I knew, he was easing me out of the car. I kept my arms wrapped around his neck after he pulled me out.

"You're perfect," I whispered into his ear.

"That's the drink talking. Is your mom home?"

"Yeah, but s'probly out cold. We fought, so she Xanax-and-wined." I buried my face into his neck. "You smell perfect."

"Shit, I really don't want your mom to . . . Just be quiet, okay?"

He took my front door keys and let us into the house. While I changed, he snuck to the kitchen to grab me water and even managed to find a bottle of ibuprofen.

I was already in bed when he was back, wearing my sleep shorts and cropped tank. S froze at the door when he saw me, his eyes following the long stretch of my bare legs, lingering on my exposed belly button. He closed his eyes for a moment, and when he opened them, he was all business.

But I had seen the look in his eyes. And, God, I wanted to see it again.

"Lie on your side for me. Put pillows at your back so you don't roll back over. Here's water and ibuprofen. I'm setting it here on

the nightstand if you need it." He knelt down so we were eye level. Moonlight sliced through the blinds, a stripe landing across his eyes, lighting up his gaze.

"Do you think I'm beautiful?" I whispered.

His eyes softened. "I think you're very drunk, Hayley," he whispered. Still, he brushed hair off my face. "Will you text me tomorrow? To let me know you're okay?"

I reached out my hand and cupped his face, bringing it closer to mine. I lifted my head, leaving only an inch between our lips. I could tell he had stopped breathing.

"I want to kiss you," I confessed. "What would you do if I kissed you right now?"

He squeezed his eyes shut and released a harsh breath.

"Hayley." S's voice sounded huskier than before. "Ask me another time. If you remember this conversation."

Of course I remembered.

The next day, I woke up hungover and horrified. I was mortified. Had I ruined everything with S?

I remembered him urging me to text. Telling me to "ask him another time."

When I felt more myself, I texted, asking if I could see him later that day. He said I could come over after school.

I wore a yellow sleeveless sundress with a low neckline. It brought out my eyes and the fire in my hair.

When S opened the door, his eyes went wide. I didn't wait; I pushed past him. I was already trembling from how badly I wanted him.

I walked into his kitchen, put my hands on the counter island, steadying myself.

"Hayley?" S was right behind me. I could feel the heat of his body. I whirled around.

"I'm going to ask you one more time," I said, my voice rough. "What would you do if I kissed you right now?"

S's chest was rising and falling, slow, deliberate. Like he was trying to stay calm. But there was a storm in his eyes.

"It'd be easier to show you," he finally said, and we stepped in to each other at the same time.

When his lips met mine, they were already open, hungry, his tongue tracing my bottom lip, and I opened for him, hoping he would consume me, swallow me whole.

I fisted my hands into his hair, pulling him tight to me. He growled, pleased, and when he licked into my mouth, and I moaned, his strong hands grabbed my thighs and lifted me to the counter.

S stepped between my legs, and I wrapped them around him, keeping him close, slotting him against me.

I pulled back on a gasp when I felt him against me.

"This is what happens when you kiss me. God, it happens when I think *about kissing you." His beautiful face was wild with need. It was awakening something in me that I had never known existed. He ran his hands all over me, grabbing my bare thighs and pulling me closer.*

"You're not beautiful, Hayley," he said hotly, kissing my neck, my jaw, my collarbone. "You're gorgeous."

I was shaking like a leaf. "I need—"

"Shhh," he soothed me, taking my bottom lip between his teeth and sucking. "I know what you need. Be patient."

It started out a small fire, just some warming flames in a circle of stones.

And now it's a conflagration, burning up forests and countries and planets. There is no end to it. Nor do I ever want *there to be. I already know: This will consume me until there's nothing left.*

chapter 11
ella

It's 5:30 p.m. Time for me to blow my whistle, designating a ten-minute adult swim. I give a tight three chirps, wiping the sweat from my eyes, as Seema, who's in the lifeguard stand directly opposite mine, does the same.

The pool where we lifeguard is Olympic-sized, with a short lazy river on one side and a separate kiddie pool opposite with a mushroom waterfall. It was a big deal when it was built, and when I was little, I used to imagine it really was the Olympics, pushing myself to finish each lap, pretending that a gold medal waited for me at the end of each race.

It feels like a lifetime ago, a dream that belonged to a different person.

Now sour-faced kids are climbing out of the side, leaving the water vacant save for a handful of adults carving their way down the lanes.

I make my way over to Seema, who's tapping on her legs, looking at the sky, as if trying to recall something.

"Don't say anything," she snaps before I can speak. "I've almost remembered the conditions that make a sample of uranium supercritical. Well, besides being related to one of my aunties."

I smile sympathetically. "AP Chem?"

Seema sighs, massaging her forehead. "Yup. Big test tomorrow. How the hell am I gonna get into vet school if I can't crack this shit?"

I smile to myself. I happen to know that Seema is brilliant and has an A in AP Chem. But she wants an A-plus. Which I get. Reminds me of a girl I used to know, a girl named Ella whose greatest fear was a B-minus.

"You want some extra time to study? I'm happy to close up by myself tonight."

"Seriously?" She shoots a look at the locker rooms. "Even with that electrician here? You seemed pretty freaked when he showed up."

She's not wrong. It was an unpleasant surprise when right after I clocked in, I bumped into Sean Adams talking to my boss, Kyle, about how the locker room lights have been on the fritz—nothing like trying to get through closing with the locker room lights randomly flickering on and off, horror-movie-style. Sean assured Kyle that it would be a quick fix, and other than a sly wink, he barely acknowledged me.

"Oh, that? It was nothing." I shrug. Sean's not worth explaining to Seema—and honestly, I still can't wrap my head around the fact that he's back in Phoebe's life. "Besides, I'm sure he's gone by now."

Seema frowns skeptically. "Are you *sure*, Ella? Because I can—"

"*Seema*. Don't make me get Kyle to send you home."

"All right, all right." She laughs. A relieved, grateful smile lights up her face. "I'll dedicate my first pair of snipped dog testicles to you, Ella."

"Please don't." I wince.

As soon as the Y shuts its doors to the public for the night, I shoo Seema home and begin my closing duties. Without any lives to guard or Seemas to talk to, there's nothing to keep me from dwelling on the one thing I *shouldn't* be thinking about but desperately want to:

Hayley's diary entry.

It was so much more than I expected. The mere thought of it sends a flush rolling through me. Heat flares in my cheeks even though the sun set a while ago.

I had no idea Hayley and Sawyer's relationship was so . . . intense.

Anytime I remember a line or detail from Hayley's writing, there's a tug behind my navel.

But I'm glad I read it. It's a good reminder. I'd always known that Hayley and Sawyer loved each other, but I'd never seen the *depth* of it. They didn't just have love; they had *real* love.

I'd seen Sawyer do the unromantic things with Hayley. He'd gently hold her hair and rub her back when she'd had too much tequila at a party. He'd gotten her Gmail inbox down from 873 unread emails to zero when she'd been too anxious to see if she'd missed any important deadlines. He was always devoted, fiercely protective, even when they were having their ups and downs. Especially those last couple months before . . . well, *before.*

It's not that Hayley was never sad. Quite the contrary. She called them her little "Ditches of Despair." They'd go off like a flare gun, intense but brief. When she'd thought BTS had broken up, she didn't talk to any of us (even me!) for two days. But on the third day, she was better. "Done with the ditch," she'd said cheerfully.

But this moodiness, this withdrawal of hers before the end had felt a little different. So gradual and quiet I can hardly pinpoint when it started. Sawyer and I would whisper our theories to each other, flailing for things we could understand, could support her with.

As someone crumpling under the pressures of junior year myself, it was clear to me that being varsity track captain and looming AP exams were taking their toll. But Sawyer wasn't so sure. Anytime he went to pick up Hayley from her house, her eyes were always red, like she'd been crying. A few times Phoebe followed her out to the car, still screaming, usually stumbling drunk. When he'd go inside, Sean was always there, lurking in the background, watching Hayley and Phoebe go at it, occasionally joining in.

Anytime I'd ask Hayley about it, she'd only shrug.

"Phoebe's just Phoebe. She'll never change. Eighteen and out, Ella."

I'd keep my mouth shut, out of my depth with my parents having been happily married for twenty years. What comfort could I offer, with my father home for dinner every night and my mother memorizing my class schedules, knowing the names of each one of my teachers?

I didn't know what a broken home life felt like.

But Sawyer did. I never knew details, but that was one thing Hayley used to say. "Sawyer gets it."

With compassion and an understanding I could never offer, Sawyer loved Hayley. And Hayley loved him.

Having finished my closing duties, I realize I've been standing for who knows how long, staring at the pool surface, that still black water. My fingers find the charm against my throat. It's a wisp of a thing, but right now, it feels heavy as a stone.

A grim resolve settles over me. There's no question. A love like that, especially my *best friend's* love, deserves to be honored, preserved. I close my eyes and let out a long breath, the shame of my thoughts so powerful I need to breathe it out.

It's not too late. I can make it right. I've vowed it before, but I really mean it this time.

I'll never speak to Sawyer again.

Still deep in thought, I march into the locker room, my flip-flops slapping echoes on the wet tile. I'm pulling my bag out of my locker when, suddenly, all the lights go out.

I'm instantly swallowed in pitch-black.

"Shit," I yelp, startled. I wait for a moment for the lights to come back on.

They don't.

Of course Sean's work is shoddy. Pathetic. I'm fishing blindly for my phone, wondering what people did before they had flashlights built into their devices, when I hear it. A clattering sound in a distant corner of the room. Then I hear a deep voice swearing.

"Hello?" I call out in a weak voice. "Angus?" Angus is the night janitor. He's an ass, but he's harmless.

All the noises stop.

And then there are footsteps, coming closer and closer.

"Angus?" I call again, but more softly this time. There's no answer and my heartbeat skyrockets. I fumble for my phone once more, but my hands are shaking so badly I can't find it.

At my shoulder, horrifically close, there's a loud metal sound, like a locker door slamming shut. On instinct, I whirl toward the crashing noise, and suddenly, my eyes are stinging from a narrow beam of blinding light.

"It's just me, Ella. Don't move."

Before I can make out whose voice it is, someone's shaking me by the shoulders. I let out a scream, then take in the dirty-blond hair framing a scruffy, handsome face and bright green eyes. When I recognize him, my sense of dread only grows.

Because glaring down at me, his grip on my shoulders so tight I can't move, is Sean.

chapter 12
ella

I said *stop pulling, Ella.*" Sean's fingers dig into my arm. "Unless you've got a death wish."

My heart's beating so fast it's a wonder it's not exploding.

"Look," Sean says, swinging the flashlight toward the end of the row of lockers. There, lying on the ground, is a cluster of wires, spiky copper and black filaments twisted on the ends. One of them sparks. *Live* wires.

"Didn't know anyone was still here." Sean grunts. "No offense, but when it comes to electrical shit, your boss is as sharp as a bowl of Jell-O. Wiring in here's all FUBAR. Basically had to start from scratch fixing it. You see these wires?"

I lick my lips, still shaking. "If—if I'd touched those . . ."

"That's right. Barbecued Ella." He releases my arm, and I huddle in on myself, still shaking. Technically, Sean just saved my life.

Then why do I still feel like it's in danger?

In the halo of the flashlight, the shadows make Sean's face sharp, his smile cutting.

"Didn't mean to frighten you, baby girl," he murmurs. He jerks his head toward the pile of wires. "Looks bad, I know, but believe it or not I'm almost done." He cocks his head, eyes sweeping me head to toe. "You're the last one here? Need a ride home?"

"No," I say, too quickly.

He barks a laugh. "I'll try not to take that personally. I know we don't know each other well, but . . . well, you're an honorary Miller lady. And I take care of my girls."

He's so full of shit.

Or is he? Technically, he's here because he's doing his job, and there's a great chance that without his intervention, I'd have been literal toast.

"Well," Sean says, interrupting my anxious brain chatter. "You ever change your mind . . ." As he says it, his eyes sweep over me once more, lingering on my body. I realize, with a lurch of nausea, that I'm still in my bright red lifeguard bathing suit. Thank God it's my one-piece.

But it's still a bathing suit, and Sean is still staring. Without another word, I snatch all of my things, turn tail, and get out of there as fast as I can.

I sprint all the way to the bus stop. It's an awkward, terrified, flip-flop-slapping, bathing-suit-wearing, wide-eyed run. I'm gasping for breath when I arrive, relieved that there's no one else there.

But that relief is quickly replaced with apprehension.

It takes a few moments for the solitude to feel ominous. It's a remote stretch of road, lit only by a buzzing streetlamp spilling jaundiced, milky light. The quiet is oppressive, broken by the dry scrape of dead leaves blowing across concrete.

Any moment now, Sean will be leaving the parking lot. And for a reason I can't fully articulate, I'm scared to *death* at the idea of his paint-splattered van pulling up next to me where there's not one other soul to bear witness.

Maybe I'm overreacting. Maybe if I'd just taken him up on his offer, I'd already be home, curled under my covers, squeaky clean from a hot shower.

But then I think of the oily way his eyes slicked over my skin, how he made me want to crawl out of my body. Imagined or not, warranted or not, I know what I felt.

I shoot a nervous look toward the Y parking lot. That bus can't come soon enough.

But another ten minutes pass, and still no bus. I'm about to lose my mind when there's a loud honk behind me.

I whirl, gasping.

Bright headlights approach, getting closer.

And suddenly, something in my brain shifts, splitting open. I'm here, but I'm not, because it's four months ago, and I'm in my car, Hayley beside me.

Headlights in the rearview mirror. Like twin furnaces, bright as day.

So bright, I squint.

The road curves left. I turn the wheel left.

But the car goes right. Before I can understand, glass explodes everywhere, there's a shout, and—

"Ella?"

The voice cuts through the vision—the memory?—and I am back in my body. I peek one eye open. There's a car stopped on the street, idling in front of me, the headlights cutting two overlapping circles on the asphalt.

I'm so shaken by the flashback, by what I have to imagine is my first returning memory from that night, I hardly notice Sawyer Hawkins is at the wheel. But when I do, warmth spreads from my belly to my chest. *Thank God.*

"So, are you gonna get in, or what?" Sawyer cocks his head and smiles.

Butterflies dance in my belly, and then I freeze, coming to my senses. *Oh no,* I think. *It's Sawyer.* The butterflies shrivel, turn to ash.

Sawyer's gaze is patient as he waits for my response.

"I'm—I'm waiting for the bus," I say shakily.

He nods, like this is reasonable. Sawyer squints at the bus stop sign and pulls out his phone, typing furiously.

"It should be any moment now," I say to fill the silence.

He doesn't look up from his phone. "Just out of curiosity . . . how long were you willing to wait, Graham?"

"Until the next one gets here."

"Even if that's not for another eleven hours?"

"What?"

Sawyer holds up his phone so I can get a closer look at the screen.

It's our local public transportation app. Where it usually lists the times for next bus arrival, it only has, in big, bold letters, the words:

ROUTE CANCELED FOR THE NIGHT

Unbelievable.

I massage my forehead. Sawyer waits patiently as I process this information. Then he shoots a pointed look at the empty passenger seat and an even more pointed one at me.

I can't.

"Come on. Amenities of this Uber *may* include air-conditioning and a working radio." He makes a face. "Disclaimer: It's stuck on the channel from the local community college. And keep in mind I said 'may.'"

Why does he have to be so cute? With an enormous effort, I shake my head.

"I don't want to put you out. Gas is expensive. I can call my parents—"

A large white van pulls into view, headlights getting brighter upon approach.

Sean.

"On second thought," I squeak, throwing my bag through the window, opening the passenger door, and scrambling into the front seat.

"Graham? You . . . doin' okay there?" Sawyer blinks at me.

"Yes," I say, "just drive." I tug at the seat belt, but it won't move. I pull harder. Nothing. I start to panic.

"All right, all right, just—let me." Sawyer lifts the seat belt from my hands, resets it, and pulls gently. He reaches across my body to click it in.

I freeze.

Sawyer's face is inches from mine. He smells like leather and sweat. The white slash of a scar across his brow is so close I could reach out and trace it with my finger.

He touches my hip as he clicks the belt into place, his voice soft. "See? You just gotta go slow."

The feeling of his breath on my ear awakens something powerful in my skin and belly, hot and honey-thick. I catch a glimpse of something all-consuming, something I want to chase, something that, for a moment, obliterates any thought of solemn oaths and promises to the dead.

When Sawyer pulls back and kicks the gear into drive, I'm trembling, wondering, for a moment, where the real danger is: outside, or right here, in this car.

chapter 13
sawyer

I glance at Ella's profile in the moonlight.

After years of classes together and, of course, the multitude of hours spent in each other's company thanks to Hayley, I can get a pretty decent read on Ella.

She cracks her knuckles if she's impatient. Her mouth twists to the side if she knows the answer in class or has a good hand in poker. She stares at her feet when she's sad. (These days, all she does is stare at her feet.) And when she's scared, her shoulders go high and tight. And when her knee's jiggling like it is right now . . .

Well, that means Ella's losing her shit.

"So," I say, in calm-down mode, "want me to blast some sweet, sweet experimental sounds?"

She turns to me. "Experimental? Sure."

I switch on the radio. After a moment of static and buzzing, the sawing of violins playing discordant notes comes through clearly. The violins come to an abrupt stop, and the low, slow sound of a man crying takes the stage.

Ella stares at the radio like she can't believe what she's hearing.

I clear my throat. "And when I say sounds, I mean *sounds.* It's late and no one listens anyway, so they give this hour to the art majors who want to be the next Banksy."

Finally, the "music" comes to a stop, and the DJ starts to talk. "What you just heard was a piece I wrote called 'The Aftermath,' composed of four out-of-tune violins and a baby's cry that has been pitched down exactly sixteen semi-tones, which is the exact number of hairs that you left on your pillow, Helen. The only things you left. Please come back, Helen. I won't rehearse at home anymore. I prom—"

Ella switches it off, and we look at each other.

At the same exact moment, we burst into laughter.

"That can't be real," Ella says.

"At least this one was short. And sort of had a story. Last week, it was twenty minutes of a piano being tuned."

"You listened to a full twenty minutes of a piano tuning?"

I rub the back of my neck, a little embarrassed. "I kept thinking it was going somewhere. I like jazz improvisations, and I thought it was, like . . . ramping up to some big, wild jazz number." I glance at her sheepishly and am glad to find that her knee has stilled and her shoulders have relaxed.

"Want to talk about it?" I ask.

Out of the corner of my eye, I see her stiffen. "Talk about what?"

I roll my eyes. "Come on, Graham. You looked like a T. rex was gonna come crashing through the trees at any moment."

"Huh. Would have preferred that, I think," she mutters. Ella twists her fingers in her lap for a few silent moments. "The Y's wiring is on the fritz. Guess who was hired to do repairs?"

I clench my jaw, my blood heating. "Sean," I spit.

She nods, biting her lip. "He was fixing the locker room lights. I closed, so it was just me there. Or so I thought. I was gathering my stuff and the lights went out. I got so freaked out and then Sean appeared out of nowhere . . . I panicked, tried to run, but he grabbed me—"

"Grabbed you?"

"—to keep me from sprinting headfirst into live wires, Sawyer."

"That asshole had live wires just lying around a locker room?"

"He didn't know anyone was there, okay? He was doing his job." Her voice is soft, unsure. I try to tamp down my rage, following her lead, giving her space.

Ella presses her face into her hands. "God, I don't know why I'm defending him . . . It's confusing. Like, he was fixing the lights. He *very* technically saved my life. He offered to give me a ride home, didn't push when I said no. He didn't *do* anything, but when he was looking at me, I had this feeling like . . . like I wanted to be a turtle and hide in my shell forever." She turns to the window, leg jiggling again.

Ludicrous thoughts are flooding my mind. Could I design a human shell for Ella that's portable enough to carry around but big enough to include a reading nook? Have any of those assholes at SpaceX cracked an invisibility suit yet, and if they have, how much does one cost?

Would anyone *really* care if Sean mysteriously went missing?

I shake my head. "Ella, I don't know if Sean would have done anything either, but no one has to *do* anything for it to still be wrong. How he made you feel—that's not in your head, and it's fucked up. I'm so sorry he did that."

Hayley had liked protecting Ella when she could. Tried to keep the uglier parts of her life from her. In this case, to Ella's detriment. She needs to know why Sean's bad news. Why it's not in Ella's head.

"Hayley once begged Phoebe to break up with Sean."

"She did?" Ella whispers.

"We only talked about it the one time. You know Hayley—she didn't really like talking about . . . well, anyway. Sean used to stare at Hayley all the time. *All* the time, she said. Anytime she got done showering, he'd always just happen to be in the hallway to catch her walking in her towel."

Ella clutches her stomach, looking as sick as I feel, but doesn't say anything. I continue.

"Hayley told me that the worst part for her was that when she told Phoebe about it, she didn't care. Didn't break up with Sean. In fact, Phoebe's response? 'Enjoy it while you can. You won't have your looks forever.'"

"No. No way. Oh, *Hayley* . . ."

"I know," I say. Because what the hell else *can* I say? I can't bear to tell her any more, to tell her I suspected there was still something Hayley wasn't telling me about Sean, that maybe there were even more reasons she was scared of him.

"Phoebe's taken him back, you know," Ella says quietly.

Now it's my turn to choke "No."

"I know," she whispers.

Fury lances through me at the thought. But why am I even surprised? Phoebe didn't care about what Hayley wanted in life; why would she care in death?

Ella's mouth twists. "Sawyer, I thought Hayley told me everything. Why didn't she talk about what was going on with Phoebe and Sean? I mean, I thought she was stressed about Coach Cud and track!" Ella buries her face in her hands. "Now I'm looking back on those last months and realizing how *stupid* I was. Now I can't help but wonder . . . what else didn't she tell me?"

I try to tamp it down, but it rises within me anyway: a powerful surge of guilt. So I do what I've been doing for a while: I bury and ignore it.

"Ella," I say, switching my focus to comfort her. "Ella, Hayley was the luckiest to have you as her best friend. Seriously. Look. If there was something really important, she—she would have told you."

"I just can't help but feel like I'm missing something," Ella says, sounding unsure. "Maybe it's because I'm missing the day of the accident . . ." Her expression opens for a moment. "Although I think maybe I remembered something. When I saw your headlights, it triggered something. It felt like a flashback. And I think it was from that night."

I drum my fingers on the steering wheel, my heartbeat picking up. "Whoa. Really?"

"Yeah. I haven't remembered anything from that day ever since I woke up in the hospital. I'd honestly given up hope of getting any memories back, despite what the doctors said. But when I saw your headlights coming at me, for a second, it was like I was there." Ella looks down at her hands. "I could feel myself grip the steering wheel and everything."

My hands are getting slippery, so I wipe my palms on my jeans.

"Is that it?" I ask.

"There wasn't much more. I remember seeing bright headlights in the rearview mirror. Which, I guess, is the part of the memory your car triggered? I think it must have been the exact moment I lost control of the car because one minute I'm looking at the lights in my rearview mirror, and the next, there's flying shards of glass everywhere."

I take a deep breath to slow my heart rate.

"But the thing that's driving me nuts right now is I think I'm on the verge of remembering more. Like, there's this unfinished feeling to the flashback. I keep reaching for it, but it's like trying to catch a bubble. It keeps popping when I touch it."

I clear my throat lightly. "Then maybe don't? Think about it, I mean?"

I glance at Ella, catch her frown.

Careful, Sawyer.

"Graham, you've had a hell of a day. And the fact that you've had any part of your memory come back at all is a huge milestone. A step on the road to recovery. But . . . maybe let's walk before we sprint? Give your brain a break?"

I can feel the weight of Ella's stare. Finally, she sighs and shakes her head. "Yeah, you're right. What can knowing more do except bring more pain?"

"Yeah," I say, "yeah, exactly." My heart rate starts to slow down.

"You okay, Sawyer?" I look over at Ella, and now she's the one who's staring at me in concern.

"Yeah. Yeah, of course. Why?" I swallow hard. So much for that heart rate.

"I don't know." She shifts uncomfortably. "I'm afraid . . . I'm afraid talking about Hayley, about that night, upsets you. I don't want to upset you."

I breathe out a harsh laugh. "No, Ella," I sigh. "You're not upsetting me. I mean, don't get me wrong, I'd be lying if I said this was my favorite topic in the world. But as far as you go? It would be pretty hard for me to hate you. Possibly impossible."

But you'd hate me if you knew.

"Possibly impossible? So there's still a chance I could get you to hate me?"

"Possibly."

Ella laughs. "I'll take those odds."

A few minutes later, I'm pulling up at her house. When I turn off my car, she raises a brow at me.

"What?"

"I'm impressed you remember how to get here." She smiles down at her lap. "It's been a minute."

"How could I forget?" I say. "My favorite person ever lives here."

Her eyes widen up at me and hot pink flushes up her chest to her cheeks.

I lean down a little, teasing her in a low voice. "I wouldn't flatter yourself too much, Graham. I was talking about Edna."

She smacks my shoulder. "My cat's name is *Midna*, asshole!"

"Ow, stop! Okay, I'm an asshole." I laugh. She shoots me a glare and crosses her arms. Her cheeks are crimson, and she won't meet my eyes. She's still flushed.

And suddenly, I'm *very* aware of the fact that it's just Ella and me sitting in my parked car. My heartbeat picks up at the sight of the flush spreading down her neck and past her collarbones. It continues down, past her neckline, and I have the sudden, fierce urge to map its path, find out exactly where it ends on her body.

I realize, in horror, that I've been wordlessly staring at her chest. I panic for a moment, but Ella doesn't seem to have noticed at all. She's gazing at my eyebrow.

"Where'd you get that scar?" she asks softly. Then she squeezes her eyes shut. "I'm sorry. That is so rude. I shouldn't have—"

"Stop. It's fine. No sorrys, remember?" I wait until she opens her eyes and looks at me. Even in the dark car, her eyes are the color of bright honey.

I touch the white line that cuts a path through my left eyebrow. "Got it as a kid."

When I don't say more, she frowns, her freckles gathering at the bridge of her nose. "That's it?"

"That's it."

"Was it a bike accident?"

"No."

"Fight with a neighborhood kid?" A tendril of dark hair grazes her cheek when she tilts her head.

"No," I say.

Ella sucks her bottom lip into her mouth, chewing it thoughtfully. *Christ.*

"Got it. You're secretly a banished, fire-bending prince who challenged his father to an Agni Kai." She releases her lip with a pop. "And you lost."

"Something like that," I murmur. Her bottom lip is wet, swollen, and pink from the worrying of her teeth. I can't stop looking. I can't stop imagining.

"Can I touch it?" she whispers. "Your scar, I mean."

My skin feels too hot. The ache in my hips is getting unbearable.

I've stopped looking anywhere but her lips.

She's stopped pretending not to notice.

I can't help it. I lean in.

There's a loud, fisted knock on the window.

Ella and I leap away from each other.

Ella's younger sister, Jess, is anxiously waving at Ella through the window. I turn on the car so I can roll down the passenger window.

"Mom wants you inside now. I'd hurry; she's . . . not happy."

Ella smooths her hair and presses a palm to her cheek, looking a little flustered. "I'm coming, give me a sec." She frowns, as if Jess's words just registered. "Wait, why's Mom mad? She knows I had a late shift tonight."

Jess bites her lip. "That's on me, sorry. She was wondering why you weren't home yet, and I told her to chill because you'd been home for at least ten minutes already, that I could see you parked out here in a car with a boy—"

Ella pales. "Oh no. No, no, no." She scrambles to gather her things and stumbles out of the car. "Thanks so much for the ride, Sawyer—I'm so sorry, Mom's gonna kill me if I don't explain. See you at school!"

She sprints into her house, slamming the door.

Jess waves to me before following Ella, and I'm sitting in the wake of the whole whirlwind, wondering what the hell just happened.

And what the hell *almost* happened.

And that's when I know my answer, about how the hell I am supposed to stay away from Ella.

I don't. I can't. It's that simple.

chapter 14
ella

It started innocently enough, with a text after I talked Mom down and locked myself in my room.

E

Good news! I will not be executed. When Mom understood it was YOU and I wasn't parked with some rando, she asked me to thank you for the ride. And to say hi to your mom and Callan.

S

Glad to hear it. I'll cancel the SWAT team I hired to get you out of there.

And the texts only continued from there. Now I'm in English class three days and countless texts later, and I can't remember the last time I smiled this much or this hard. Underneath my desk, my hands are flying across my phone keyboard.

S

You're joking. You have third period gym? And you never said hi?

E

Please, I know better than to interrupt a man in the middle of a bro-off with Thomas Jones. Esp when said man is losing said bro-off

S

Excuse me, Graham, I take issue with the phrase "bro-off," and Thomas has NEVER beaten me

So wait.

You saw me do pull-ups?

How's my form?

E

Ugh, you're such a guy sometimes. You know exactly how your form is. My opinion won't help in the slightest.

S

Sure. But I want it anyway.

A hand slams on my desk, startling me.

"Aaaaand, look who's back on planet Earth." Seema turns her head sideways. "Man, Ella, if I'd have known you'd be this much trouble, I'd be working on this assignment with Robert. And his sole contribution all class has been to put on a light show with his two new laser pointers." She leans across her desk and taps my nose with the end of her pencil. "Soooo . . . whatcha doing?"

Something I shouldn't be doing.

"Nothing," I say quickly. Too quickly. "Some business I gotta take care of."

Seema's smile is far too knowing for my taste. "Sure, yeah. *Business.* Gotta take care of all your important *business.*" She clears her throat, all innocence. "Tell me, your *business* . . . does he or"—her eyes light up—"*she* or they have a name?"

I sigh in apparent defeat. "Fine. Yeah, he does."

Seema's brows shoot up. "That was easy. Make with the name!"

I only hate myself a little when I say, "Nunya."

"Oh, you little shit." We both giggle when she shoves me hard in the shoulder.

Mrs. Prescott lowers her spectacles at us. "Girls, *really.* I have a headache, and you're supposed to be the good ones. I have enough on my hands without having to deal with— Robert, *put* those laser pointers away, we've all been to the laser show at Stone Mountain, we don't need reminders of the ghastly thing."

"I'm sorry," I say, keeping my voice lower. "I know I've been a little distracted." Seema shoots me a look. "Fine, I've been ignoring you completely."

"Yes, you have. But I'm pretty sure I got a perfect score on my chem test. Between that and your penance of filling out this worksheet by yourself, we'll be square." Seema grins.

"Ugh, you'd be fine in chem without me." My mouth twitching, I start jotting all the rhetorical devices from the poem on the sheet. "What if you need to know this someday?"

Seema snorts. "If I need Pablo Neruda to spay a dog, they'll let me know."

My phone buzzes in my pocket. I scramble for it, smiling as I pull up Sawyer's text. After shooting off a quick reply, I look up.

She raises a brow. "That *business* of yours . . . must be good, hm?"

"Business is *great.*" As I finish with the worksheet with a flourish, my phone buzzes again.

Ever since Sawyer replied to my text that night he drove me home, I've felt as if I was going down a mountain on skis, slowly gathering speed. After each text, I tell myself I should slow down, stop, guilt telling me to take off my skis and get off the mountain. But when my phone chirps with Sawyer's replies, I've lunged at my phone and texted back before I've had any conscious thought. Instead of stopping the descent, I've only leaned into the wind, going at speeds that could kill me if I'm not careful.

I want to stop. Oh, I want to.

I *need* to.

But when I think of Sawyer's low voice, how close his mouth came to mine, and how violently my stomach clenches just from reading a sentence he typed on my screen, my reasons for avoiding him dissolve. Sometimes I even find myself wondering . . . could this be okay?

For four months, I've been playing Hayley's greatest hits on a loop—the Hayley who bear-hugged the people she loved, who threw her head back as she laughed. But the truth is, Hayley wasn't herself in the months leading up to the accident. She'd been erratic and mercurial. One moment she wanted to drive to Tybee Island *right this minute* because she *needed* to watch the sunrise over the ocean. The next, she'd ask if we could just binge-watch Netflix with the curtains drawn, not saying a word for five hours.

I had chalked it up to fights with Phoebe, the instability of her home life, the stress of track . . . but maybe there was something more.

Looking back, I can see it now, how she had started to pull away from Sawyer, how she'd started wanting to hang out without him. "I want it to be just us girls," she'd insist.

I need to break up with Sawyer.

The thought comes out of nowhere, clarion loud, in Hayley's voice. Along with it, an image: Hayley leaning over my vanity, applying lip gloss with a shaking hand. It stops me short. Is it real? Another memory—or just wishful thinking? Something that lets me off the hook each time I smile when Sawyer's texts come through?

But there's something about it that rings true, beyond my wishing it so.

Is this what Hayley had been struggling with? The thing making her moody, contemplative? Had she fallen out of love with Sawyer and was struggling with the idea of breaking up with him?

"Ahem."

I open my eyes to find Seema raising a single brow. "Anything you want to share?"

"I'm just trying . . . to remember something," I say distractedly. Because something's dawning on me: *I think Hayley was going to break up with Sawyer that night.*

What does that realization change? Nothing?

Everything?

I told myself I wouldn't open Hayley's diary again, but this feels important. I *have* to know what my best friend was thinking, if she wrote any clues as to what I just remembered.

"Ella, if you need hel—"

I shoot Seema an apologetic look. "Hold that thought," I say, grabbing a hall pass and marching toward the bathroom, pulling the diary out along the way. There has to be something here, something that will explain what I just remembered. My fingers shake as I open it, flipping a few pages and beginning to read as I turn the hallway corner.

And walk right into a pole.

"Wow, must be a real page-turner," says the pole.

With a gasp, I shove the diary back in my backpack and look up to find that the pole is actually Mr. Wilkens.

"I'm really so sorry, Mr. Wilkens." I rub my forehead. "My mom's always telling me I need to pay more attention to my surroundings."

He cocks his head at me, his eyes sparkling. "Oh, I don't know about that. It's refreshing to see a student absorbed in a book for once instead of a phone. Believe it or not, students bump into me all the time. Usually because they're busy snapping something."

I laugh, surprised. "You use Snapchat?"

He releases a long-suffering sigh. "You act like I was around when the wheel was invented, Ella. Yes, I know how to use Snapchat. If I have any prayer of understanding you guys, I need to learn your communication tools. Which, okay, fine, that last sentence *did* make me sound like I was around when the wheel was invented. Speaking of communication . . ." Mr. Wilkens gives me a searching look. "You got a few minutes to chat in my office? I wanted to check in with you, see how you were doing."

With everything going on, maybe it's not the worst idea to sit down with the school psychologist for a few minutes. It's better than class, at least.

"Pick a seat, any seat." Mr. Wilkens gestures to the array of familiar armchairs as he sinks into his own chair behind his desk. I settle into a soft red chair immediately opposite his desk. I eye the sofa where Sawyer and I had been sitting the last time we were here.

Mr. Wilkens seems to read my train of thought. "I really am sorry about last time. It's part of my job to know when someone's ready to share. I shouldn't have pushed."

"Really, it's okay. I just feel bad I got Sawyer so angry . . ."

Mr. Wilkens laughs. "What seventeen-year-old boy isn't a hothead? I certainly was. If my uncle weren't on the force here, I shudder to think where I'd be now. Either way, definitely not your fault."

We both smile, and then his face fades into something a little more somber. "But I'm glad we're talking, Ella. I know how hard it is to lose someone you love."

"Really?" I sit up straighter.

"It's not the same," Mr. Wilkens says. "Every loss and grief is singular and excruciating. In no way do I want you to think I'm comparing your loss of Hayley to mine, to minimize your feelings. But I remember how alone I felt when my college girlfriend died. We were about to graduate. She wanted to be a social worker. I'd never known I could love someone so much."

My breath catches. I had heard that Mr. Wilkens had a girlfriend who died. Everyone had, in that way that everyone in a small town knows everything about everyone else, but I had never heard the details.

"When she was gone, I couldn't stop thinking, over and over, *What could I have done differently?* I couldn't stop imagining a life where she was still around. That somehow, if I imagined it hard enough, I could go back in time and would know how to keep her here."

That's all gut-wrenchingly familiar. "What made it stop?"

"You're not going to like my answer, but: time. Letting myself feel the feelings. Letting others support me. But here's the good news."

Mr. Wilkens leans forward in his chair, clasps his hands.

"I healed. Eventually, I was able to stand up and keep going. And I was able to find love again. A true and deep love that, frankly, I don't think I would have been capable of had I not gone through what I have."

His eyes are earnest, and I think of the picture I'd seen of his girlfriend. She was stunning, in an expected sort of way—blond hair, high cheekbones, definitely a former cheerleader. I remember Nia and Hayley looking her up once and rolling their eyes at how "perfect" she was.

"Don't give up hope, Ella. There's something on the other side of this pain, I promise you. Life might not be what you had hoped or expected, but it has a way of showing you a door to a place that's better than you could have imagined."

There's a moment of silence between us as I digest his words. Mr. Wilkens has the fervor of an adult begging a kid to take their wisdom. And I can't deny that his story gives me hope. That there is a possibility that one day I won't feel like half my body and heart are missing.

The bell rings, and with a sigh, Mr. Wilkens rises. "I apologize, Ella. I didn't mean to give you a grief filibuster."

I shake my head, following him to the hallway. "No, actually. You gave me a lot to think about."

He stops at the entrance to the main hall, leaning against the door frame while students spill into the hallway. "Let me write a quick note to your last teacher, and I'll send you on your way."

I'm standing patiently while he scribbles, when Scott breaks off from the churn of students and heads our way.

"Ella and Mr. Wilkens, my two favorite grief-group buddies. Let me guess, Ella, you've been curled up in the fetal position on Mr. Wilkens's couch, listening to your Spotify playlist titled 'I didn't get to say goodbye.'"

It stings, his derisive words hitting a little too close to home. "You're an ass," I spit.

Mr. Wilkens frowns. "Guys . . ."

Scott just narrows his eyes. "That the best you can do? You know, Hayley would've said . . ." He stops, shaking his head. "You know what? Never mind."

But he's hooked me, her name lighting my every nerve.

"What would Hayley have said?" I ask, trying to hide how eager I am to hear even his *guess*.

Scott smirks. "Listen to you. So desperate to hear some made-up bullshit so you can pretend that, for a moment, you'll get her back for one new sentence. You really wanna know what Hayley would've said? Too bad. You never will. We've already heard everything she was ever going to say to us."

For just a breath, his face falters. And for one inconceivable moment, it looks like Scott might cry. But then his eyes flash with cruelty. "You made sure of that, right, Ella?"

Tears prick my eyes. But before I can respond, Mr. Wilkens cuts in. "Scott, that's *enough*."

"*Christ*, look at your face! It's not even *fun*, you're so easy to mess with." Scott laughs, ignoring Mr. Wilkens's furious glare.

"You need serious help," I accuse through gritted teeth.

"And you *seriously* need to wise up." Scott chucks my chin. "Thanks for the laugh," he says before traipsing off.

Mr. Wilkens looks at me, his eyes full of concern. "Are you okay? You really shouldn't listen to anything he says . . ."

But I don't hear the rest, because Sawyer's standing on the other side of the hall, watching Scott walk away. And when his eyes find me again, I recoil at what I find there: *fury*.

Startling, black fury.

The final bell rings. Sawyer stalks away before I can catch him.

The only thing in my brain is a single question, clanging in my head:

Why?

chapter 15
ella

It's been twenty hours and four unanswered texts since I last heard from Sawyer. Oh, he saw them. There's that little word, Read, at the bottom corner of every single one. And now I'm in that humiliating position of rereading the pathetic string of messages I sent. There's no way I look anything less than desperate. Especially in that last one.

E

Midna just told me she misses you too. And she's not the only one, *wink wink*

Why did I send that? Why?

I groan, laying my head down on my desk. I can't get my leg to stop bouncing, even when Jackie Nevins, who sits next to me, shoots me a glare. I open my texts again. And *what a surprise*, no change in the last ten seconds.

I haven't heard a word Mr. Moss has said all period, barely registered the school-wide announcement over the loudspeakers reminding students to not park in the bus lane and asking for volunteers to sign up for shifts at the fall festival in two weeks. All that's running through my head is *If Sawyer is mad at me, why? Why, why, why?* I suppress another groan of humiliation. I've become a parody of myself. Hayley and I used to talk about how we would never let any one person and their "imbecilic behavior" (as Hayley called it) take up any real estate in our brains like this. She made me promise that if any guy ever treated me like less than the queen of the universe, I was to never spare them a thought.

And here I am, ignoring all of my classes, binge-texting Sawyer, and willing to do God knows what else to understand why Sawyer's gone not just cold, but positively frosty.

And he's not even "your guy." He doesn't owe you "queen of the universe" status.

But what changed? Was he . . . threatened? By Scott?

It's *Scott*, for God's sake. Not even Scott likes Scott.

My stomach clenches, twin pangs of frenzied hope and despair warring inside me. It feels like such an impossibility that Sawyer could like me enough to be jealous about anyone. Regardless, I feel like I'm being punished for losing a game I didn't know I was playing, one for which I never knew the rules. And what is my crime? Standing next to the wrong person at the wrong time? Possibly overcommunicating?

Frustration leaps in my chest. I didn't *do* anything wrong.

Sawyer did.

When the final bell rings, I'm the first out the door. I find Sawyer at his locker, swapping out books with a sullen expression. As soon as I see him, the flame in my belly flickers. His hair is rumpled. His shirt's so tight I can see the muscles in his arms shift and flex as he rummages in his locker.

But I need an explanation—and he's going to have to give it to me.

Sawyer freezes when he notices me, his hand suspended in the middle of slamming his locker shut. His face is still veiled, giving nothing away.

Heart hammering, I open my mouth. "I—"

Sawyer closes his locker and turns on his heel, walking quickly away from me.

All my uncertainty, insecurity, and hurt melts into something hot and angry. Anger is good. Anger, I can use.

"Hey, Sawyer," I say, "if you want, I can pretend we didn't make eye contact. But that doesn't change the fact that you're acting like a dick."

Sawyer stiffens and, after a few uncertain seconds, makes the call to face me. "What's up, Graham?"

"What's up?" I stare at him in disbelief. "First you glare at me in the hallway, like I kicked you in the nuts or something, then you leave me on read, and then you make *severe* eye contact before just walking away. What gives, Sawyer?"

He opens his mouth, but his phone buzzes, interrupting. And even though we're in the middle of an important conversation, he pulls it out and *checks it*.

"Seriously, Sawyer?"

He doesn't reply, completely absorbed in what's on his phone screen. When he pockets his phone, he looks more stressed than before.

"Who was that, Sawyer?" I ask, hating how Jealous High School Girl™ I sound.

"No one," he says, avoiding my eyes.

Hurt lances through me. "Sawyer . . . why aren't you being honest with me?"

Sawyer's gaze snaps to mine, eyes narrowing. "Look, I'm telling you the truth. I don't even know what 'severe' eye contact is, I'm sorry. I didn't see you. I've got a lot on my mind." He shifts the bag strap on his shoulder. "I didn't have time to reply to your texts. And I don't have time for this now," Sawyer mutters, turning on his heel again.

"Asshole," I seethe. "At least look me in the eye as you keep lying to me."

Sawyer stops short, his shoulders tensing. Finally, he meets my eyes, his gaze cold.

"So you're not a *complete* coward." Part of me feels like I'm going too far. The rest of me wants to wound him at least half as much as he's wounded me. "So tell me: Is it a complete coincidence that you're ignoring me after you see me standing with another guy in the hall?"

Sawyer's eyes turn stormy. He glances up and down the empty hall, then grabs my wrist and pulls me to the nearest vacant classroom and drags me in.

The door slams shut, and we're alone in the dark.

"Does it ever occur to you, Graham, that not everything is about you?" Sawyer raises his voice, his grip tightening on my wrist. "That maybe you're not the only one with shit?"

"Oh, boo-hoo. Yeah, Sawyer, it's called *life.* Of course I know you've got shit outside of here, but that's no excuse to just drop me like hot garbage and then gaslight me about it."

"Drop you like . . . *Jesus.*" He flings away my wrist, pacing in front of me. "Why the hell am I getting the third degree here? Because I didn't respond to your texts within an hour? Why the hell do I owe you an explanation for any of this?"

Sawyer stops directly in front of me. He steps into my space, crowding me, eyes burning.

"I don't. Because *news flash*, Graham, I'm not your boyfriend. Not even close."

I recoil, as if physically struck. It takes several tries to swallow the lump in my throat.

"You're right, Sawyer. You're not my boyfriend. Thank God." I grip the desk behind me, the edges digging into my palm. "Thank *God* you're not my boyfriend, because we're barely even friends, and you still managed to make me feel like shit. Congratulations! You're the bottomless pit I never knew existed!"

"Fantastic," he snarls. "The feeling's completely mutual!"

"Wonderful! So delete my number and get the hell out of my life."

"More than happy to!"

I turn my back to the door, bent over double, hand pressed to my chest. *Not yet, not yet, wait till he's gone.*

I hear the doorknob turn, the door open.

And a pause. I count to three. Then the door closes, unexpectedly soft.

I burst into hot, painful tears, my heart hurting so badly I can't stand straight. I'm trying so hard not to sob, I almost miss the sounds of steps.

A hand falls on my shoulder, turning me around.

Sawyer looks down at me, and before I can fully register that he never left, he's stepping into my space, closer than he's ever been, his hands on my face, and suddenly, his mouth is on mine.

Sawyer Hawkins is kissing me.

He's kissing the hell out of me.

My brain melts. I throw my arms around his neck and kiss him back, pressing the full length of my body against him. He groans in my mouth, a sound that lights up my body, and I respond by tangling my fingers in his hair. Sawyer growls, grabbing me with both his hands and lifting me onto a nearby desk.

He steps between my thighs, his lips never leaving mine.

Sawyer and I are kissing desperately, messily, as if we'll be ripped apart at any moment. I open my mouth, and he moans, pressing his tongue against mine. I've never kissed like this, never knew kissing could be like this, that lips and teeth and tongue alone could awaken such a hunger. It almost frightens me.

My body moves on its own, carried on some deep instinct I'd never known. When I roll my hips against him, he gasps, squeezing his eyes shut and stepping back.

"No, come back," I breathe, reaching for him.

"Ella," he says, his voice in ruins. "Ella, what are you *doing* to me?"

He opens his eyes, and I wonder if I look as undone as him, his eyes black with need, face flushed, lips swollen. His hands hold one of mine, squeezing hard, as if to keep them from reaching elsewhere.

"Sawyer." I run a finger over his lips.

"Stop. I won't be able to—*stop*," he begs, and I see him cant his hips forward, an involuntary movement.

Shaking and panting, he plants his hands on the desk on either side of me, caging me in.

"We shouldn't," Sawyer says as he presses his open mouth to my neck.

"I know," I breathe, arching to give him more access. He traces the tender skin beneath my jaw with his tongue, and when I moan, his hands find my thighs.

"We *can't*," Sawyer says, pulling my shirt to the side and biting my bare shoulder. I writhe against him, and he swears, his fingers digging into my thighs.

"I know," I whisper. In a boldness I've never known, I slip my fingers just beneath the hem of his shirt, hungry to feel more of his bare skin. I scrape my nails across the hard plane of his stomach, following the dip of his muscles, wishing I could see them, hoping one day he'll let me.

My fingers meet elastic and fabric, and when I have the dizzying realization that these are his boxers, the ache high in my thighs sharpens. I dip my middle finger underneath the elastic, running along the edge, and Sawyer pulls off my shoulder, his hand shooting to mine, stilling it. We just sit there for a moment, foreheads pressing, gasping against each other.

"I know," I pant. "I know. We can't—shouldn't—"

"I don't care." Sawyer slides his hands to my lower back and pulls me tight against him. "I don't care, Ella."

I wrap my legs around his waist, arching up for another kiss.

"*Shit*, I've wanted you." His words are hot against my mouth.

"Please," I beg, clenching his shirt with both my fists. Desire has flooded my brain, filling it with nothing but *more, more, more.*

"Shit" is all Sawyer can say before groaning into my mouth, words dissolving into fevered kisses, until all that is left is my mouth against Sawyer's mouth, the taste of his lips, and the realization that I may never be the same again.

chapter 16
sawyer

It was supposed to be just one kiss to get it out of my system.

That seems ridiculous now, but it's true. I had a wake-up call yesterday, seeing her in the hall with Scott and Mr. Wilkens. The rush of anger, the immense guilt, the cold sweep of fear . . . the flood of overwhelming feelings reminded me that I should do the right thing and take a step back. I hated thinking about it, but I also had to wonder what Hayley would have said if she'd still been here to witness all this.

It felt like shit, pushing Ella away, but I figured it was for her own good. And I nearly made it too. I had my hand on the door handle, opened the door, but dammit, I couldn't get my feet to move. And then I heard her crying, and before I knew it, I was turning around and—

Well, I stood no chance.

I never expected her to respond the way she had. To be so ravenous. So needy. I never thought she'd open like a flower under me, cling to me, pleading . . .

Yesterday keeps replaying in my head over and over. Ella blew me away. I've always thought she was beautiful. This sweet, innocent, beautiful thing. All folded hands and straight As and politeness. I knew she'd only ever had one boyfriend, and I was prepared to go slow, simple. But she'd immediately been desperate, and, who am I kidding, I was too. Her hands were clumsy, her lips moving like she was learning, but ever the ambitious student, she was a quick study. And honestly it made it better. It felt like proof that her body was carried on pure need.

It's all I can think about as I walk into the gym. I've been looking forward to this period since I got to school because there she is, walking out of the girls' locker room with Seema. Seeing Ella's bare thighs is doing things to me, especially now that I know how they feel beneath my hands.

As if she can hear my thoughts, her eyes find mine. She tosses her long, shiny hair over her shoulder and gives me a slow smile. I'm struck with the urge to cross the gym, fist her ponytail in my hand, and kiss the smile off her lips.

I squeeze my eyes shut and stretch my quads. I force myself to think of Principal Cantrell, the way spit gathers in the corners of his mouth, and yeah, that does it. My head's on straight again.

Today's arm day, but I'm feeling a very strong pull to work on cardio. Running laps is important too, I tell myself. Never mind that I'll be passing Ella every once in a while.

She catches my eyes the first time I lap her, and I send her a smirk. The second lap, a soccer ball flies in my direction.

"Whoops," Ella says, jogging over to me.

"This yours?" I hand her the ball, but when she clasps it, I don't let go. "You missed the goal by a mile. Need some pointers?" I pull her closer.

"Actually, that's the only time I've ever made a soccer ball go *exactly* where I intended."

When I laugh, it's already rough, husky.

We stare at each other for a few seconds, both of us clasping the soccer ball.

A whistle from Coach Cud breaks our trance.

"Hey," I call as she walks away. "Meet me after school?"

She tucks a strand of hair behind her ear. "Okay."

As I jog away, I hear Seema's fading voice. "What the hell was that?"

Ella's leaning against the brick building after school, texting on her phone. When she looks up and sees me, her eyes spark bright gold.

"Anyone I should be jealous of?" I say, nodding to her phone. She blushes a pleased pink, smiling at the screen as she finishes typing.

"I'm telling Mom I'm spending the afternoon with Seema. Studying."

I raise my brows. "Such falsehoods," I murmur. "My, my, Miss Graham, you are full of surprises."

"Well, Mr. Hawkins, you're a terrible influence." She bites her lip, suddenly shy. "Wanna get out of here?"

"Yeah," I say roughly. "Yeah, I do."

I'm about to reach for her hand, but I snatch it back when I see her eyes flick self-consciously to Nia and Beth, who are talking to Dr. Cantrell near the front door. *Duh, Sawyer.* The last thing we need is the North Davis High rumor mill churning, so I keep my distance as we walk.

But as soon as my car doors shut, free from prying eyes, Ella and I crash into each other. Ella grabs my shirt collar and pulls me in for a kiss. With a growl, I'm immediately pressing her against me. She pulls at my shirt and sucks my bottom lip into her mouth.

"You're gonna need to stop that right about now, Graham," I say through clenched teeth.

"Why?" Ella tilts her chin up, nipping at my lip.

"I keep—I keep wanting to take it slow with you. Just . . . enjoy you." I say this as I press kisses along her jaw. Ella's hands are in my hair, though, and when she tugs on the roots, I attack her mouth.

Things are really starting to feel out of control when a loud honk shocks us apart.

"Who was that?" Ella pants, looking terrified.

I look down at my elbow.

"Me," I say. "When I moved to grab your thigh, I honked."

We stare at each other for a few seconds before dissolving into laughter. But that laughter dies abruptly when Ella goes pale and shrinks in her seat.

I follow her gaze to a white work van at the far end of the parking lot. Sean Adams. He nods at a cluster of junior girls, who giggle as they pass him.

I grip the steering wheel. "Ugh, that asshole still works here?"

"Yeah. Unfortunately. Let's get out of here. Please," Ella says, shaking her head.

"Yeah, let's." I suddenly want to put a million miles between us and this place. "Where to?" I readjust my seat and turn on the ignition.

After a moment, Ella says, "I know a place. It's a bit of a drive."

I flick the gas gauge. "Filled up this morning."

"We'll need bug spray."

I whirl at her. "Bug spray, Graham? You taking me bushwhacking?" Instantly I think of brown recluses, ticks, and yellow jackets and shudder.

Ella pats my hand. "Don't worry, I'll kill any spiders for you."

One supply trip to Publix and a pleasant hour-and-a-half car ride later, I'm pulling into an empty unpaved parking lot at the bottom of a lush, tree-covered mountain. We lost reception about fifteen minutes ago, and I haven't seen another car in a while.

"All right, Graham, fess up. Did you take me out here to kill me?"

"How did you guess?" She laughs and then heads over to a wooden sign with text and pictures of wildlife. There's a map of the mountain, all the trails shown in different colors and lines. I read out loud while Ella snaps a picture of the map with her phone.

"Hemlock Mountain. Three thousand three hundred feet. We climbing this thing?"

"Of course." Ella drags her finger across the map.

I frown at the map. "Yup, you're trying to kill me."

"Are you kidding me?" Ella calls, popping open the trunk. "You run like a million miles a day. Quit being a baby."

Ella takes charge, making sure we are covered in sunscreen and bug spray. She shoves our waters into her school backpack.

"I got it," I say, taking the heavy bag from her.

"You may be a baby, but at least you're still a gentleman," Ella says. "You're a baby gentleman."

"I promise to stop whining if you never call me that again."

As soon as we hit the trailhead, I feel something crawl up my calf.

"Gaaahh!"

I leap away to see it was just a fern leaf brushing my skin.

Ella doubles over, laughing. "Look at you! I had no idea you were such an indoors man. I mean, we used to go on day trips to Amicalola Falls all the time and you weren't so jumpy then."

"That's different. There are wooden stairs, picnic tables, and a toilet that flushes."

Her face falls. "I . . . I did think about having us go there. It's just that . . ."

I know. *It was one of Hayley's favorite places.*

An inconvenient spike of guilt lances through me. *If she knew, Sawyer, if she knew . . .* But I know how to handle this. Shove down. Ignore. In a second, I'm fine.

"You know what," I say, "you're right. Let's try something new. New can be good. Lead the way."

We walk in companionable silence for a little while, enveloped in a green tunnel of oak and elm. The afternoon sun is barely making it through the thick canopy of leaves, golden light sliced by splaying branches. The humidity is gentler in the shade. Sweat clings to my hairline, runs down my neck, but the breeze keeps me cool, and the air smells sweet, like honeysuckle and dogwood. Cicadas buzz, the wind rustles the leaves, birds sing. But it's the sounds I don't hear that begin to stand out.

No constant roar of the highway, no cars, no horns. No people. It's just the gentle crunch of Ella's feet on the forest floor, and the sounds of a Georgia mountain on a summer afternoon.

For a moment, I let something inside my chest unclench.

I look up at Ella, and my heart warms. Her face is flushed and happy in a way I haven't seen in a long time.

"Okay, I get it," I say.

"I knew you would," she says, delighted. She does a little dance-leap onto a small boulder. "My family used to go camping all the time when I was a kid. There was this mountain by a lake that we'd go to in North Georgia. In the mornings, it'd be so cold, you'd see this mist coming off the water. Dad would make hot chocolate and scramble eggs on this little camping stove. He would bring his guitar, and even my mom would sing along."

Unconsciously, I rub my scar. "Must have been nice."

Ella's face softens. "You never went camping, I take it?"

It takes me a second to answer. "Not in the way you did." When I don't elaborate, Ella has the grace not to push for more information.

For a while, the only sound is of our footsteps, cracking and crunching on the forest floor. Then the summit appears out of nowhere. One minute we're in our intimate little forest tunnel; the next, the trees pull away, a green curtain revealing the main event, and we're standing on the edge of a mountain.

"Damn," I breathe.

Ella only sighs, her face soft and peaceful. After the cloister of the forest, this vista makes the world seem infinite. Stretched before us are green-and-yellow rolling hills, carpets of trees, and clouds and sky.

"Can we stay here forever? Please?" Ella whispers, sounding so melancholy my stomach aches.

We're standing side by side, so I don't need to reach far to brush her hand with my pinkie. Ella smiles, hooking my pinkie with hers.

"Sure, but we might have an issue getting Amazon Prime delivered here," I point out.

"That's okay." She gestures to the forest. "We'll shop local."

I nod. "I like it. Fresh, local, organic."

Ella faces me, her eyelids falling. "Where will we sleep?"

I let out a whoosh of air, my pulse already fast. How is it she can activate every nerve in my body just from four little words? I cast a look around the area and find exactly what I need. Dropping her hand, I walk to a large boulder, low and flat enough for me to easily sit. I make a show of examining it.

"This seems comfortable enough," I say. "Only one way to be sure." I hold out my hand. "C'mere."

We've barely touched, and my heart is hammering. I sit down on the rock and pull her onto my lap, sitting sidesaddle.

"What do you think?" I murmur, kissing her neck.

"Good," she says, eyelids fluttering. "But could be better." She scoots back and swings a leg over, so her thighs are now bracketing me. She sinks down on my lap and starts to slide forward.

"Wait," I say roughly, stopping her with one hand on her knee, and the other at my pants. It's a lost cause, though. I'm wearing gym shorts, and if she scoots any closer, she's going to be able to tell just how much she affects me. How, if I'm being honest, she's been affecting me all day.

"What's wrong?" Ella whispers.

"It's—" I clear my throat, embarrassed. "Yesterday, I was wearing jeans. I don't know if you could tell then, but . . . I can't hide *just* how much you—"

Ella's golden eyes go wide. *"Oh,"* she says, before sliding forward and rolling her hips against me.

"Shit," I grunt as we cling to each other. She clutches at my hair, her open mouth pressed against my forehead, panting as she moves exquisitely against me.

"*Christ*, Ella. I've been like this all day."

"All day . . ." The words float out of her on a moan.

I grab her face, bring her mouth to mine. Our lips move against each other, and I lick into her mouth at the same rhythm as her hips. I've got one hand in the back pocket of her jeans, my firm grip guiding her rhythm. I take out her hair tie with my other hand, tangle my fingers in her sweat-damp hair.

"Is this okay? How does it feel?" I say roughly against her mouth.

"Good. Please. Don't stop." She's starting to breathe faster, her jaw slack, panting, her eyes squeezed shut.

With a deep frustration, my hands shoot to her hips, gripping her hard enough to still her.

"Why?" Ella cries, her brows furrowed, an expression of pain.

"I'm so sorry," I choke out, pressing kisses to her jaw. "Let's just say . . . I need a moment. And I think I'm obsessed with the outdoors now."

Ella breathes a husky laugh.

"I'm serious. I'm a changed man." I brush a lock of hair from her face, touch her swollen lips. "I'll make it up to you. I swear."

Ella ducks her head and drags her lips against my mouth. "That a promise, Sawyer?"

"Whatever you want, Ella."

It's terrifying, because in this moment, I mean it. She could ask me to chop off my own finger, and I'd do it, right now, just for three more minutes of her on my lap.

As I sink into her kiss once more, everything else in the world dissolves again. Nothing matters except her wrapped around my body, her tongue in my mouth.

Nothing matters except her.

chapter 17
ella

"They're animals, absolute animals!" Seema rants, bending over to gather the pool floats scattered all along the pool's edge. "Like, are you kidding me?" She frowns down at a row of bushes planted at the edge of the gate. "Why? Why here? Who?" She reaches into the bushes, rummaging, and squeals.

I jump. "What?"

She makes a gagging noise. "That wasn't one of the kiddie pool floats, that was a very colorful, very full diaper. Ugh, give me dog shit any day." Seema stills, turning to me. "Hey, you okay?"

"Yeah." I stop stacking chairs and sit on the edge of the pool. "Why wouldn't I be?"

"Well, for *one*"—Seema marches to the outdoor sink and washes her hands with an impressive violence—"you are not *nearly* horrified enough on my behalf." She wipes her hands on her suit. "And two, you're awfully quiet tonight."

"I'm always quiet."

Seema plops down beside me. "Not true." She nudges my shoulder with hers. "What gives?"

I kick the surface of the water, the ripples glowing a light blue in the gathering dark of the night.

"Long day. Super tired." It's mostly true.

Seema raises a dark brow at me. "Okay, sure. We had a lot of kids trying to play chicken. And then that one guy who you managed to convince couldn't eat his KFC bucket in the kiddie pool. Very impressive, by the way." She frowns. "Remind me to tell Kyle to put him on the banned list."

I swirl my big toe in figure eights on the water's surface.

"Do you remember our secret handshake?" I ask.

"Daaaamn, that's a deep cut." Seema kicks hard in the pool, spraying water in an impressive arc. She watches the spray, looking away from me. "Of course I remember," she says softly.

I hold out my palm, and her hand shoots out, clasping it immediately. As if we were back in fourth grade, our fingers interlock, flutter, and twist around each other in the complicated synchronized dance we invented. It ends with our middle fingers entwined.

"If ya can't keep your mouth shut, you'll be kicked in the butt," we chant in unison.

"Perfect execution. Terrible writing." Her voice softens and she meets my eyes. "You remembered too."

"Yeah, I guess I did." I try not to sound surprised. After a moment, I clear my throat. "Okay, you're sworn to secrecy." I can't look at her for this part. "So. You know . . . Sawyer Hawkins?"

"I effing *knew it*!" Seema does double kicks in the pool. "When you two were grabbing that ball together, it was, like, obviously a metaphor."

I resist the urge to slide into the pool and sink to the bottom.

"So are you two boning?"

I shove Seema hard in the shoulder. "What? Of course not!"

"Ugh, boring. So, what *have* you done?"

I bury my face in my hands. "Too much, Seema. Far too much."

When I feel Seema's hand pat my shoulder, I smile into my palms, surprised.

"Why're you so hard on yourself?" she asks gently.

I sigh. "I don't know if you recall this incredibly salient detail, Seema. But Sawyer is . . . or he *was* . . . very much in love with Hayley, my best friend in the whole wide—"

Seema stiffens just as a voice sounds behind us.

"What the hell are you girls doing here?"

Seema and I whirl around to find Angus, the nighttime janitor for the Y, glaring at us, holding his mop with both hands threateningly.

We scramble to our feet as he keeps yelling.

"Don't you know it's past closing time? My job is damn hard enough without you two treating it like your own private pool."

"We're so sorry, Angus," I say, scooping up my gear as Seema rolls her eyes.

"Let me guess. You still have to do all your girly things in the women's locker room? See, this is why boys are easier. If I could, I'd have it so only men worked here. I'd be in and out in a snap." Angus slaps the mop head down on the tile floor in front of the locker room doors.

"You're totally right, Angus," Seema says, sounding sincere. I shoot her a skeptical look, and she gives me a quick wink. "I'm so sorry. I know that we are such a hassle with our emotions and our periods. I feel bad." She points to the bushes, where she'd left the dirty diaper. "Some dude spilled his wallet over there, and the wind blew his dollar bills and stuff into the bushes, but it was too much work. Just FYI."

Angus's eyes light up. "See what I mean? Lazy. Lazy, lazy. Well, I'll clean up after you like I always do."

Seema and I scurry to the locker room, suppressing giggles.

"That was *so mean*, Seema." I burst into laughter as soon as we're out of earshot.

"Psh, you heard him! He deserved that." She can't stop her crocodile grin from widening.

We hear an angry roar echoing from the pool area.

"Oh God, hurry, he's gonna kill us." I panic, fighting to put my pants on even faster.

Seema waits until we're in the parking lot before speaking again.

"You know, Ella," she says slowly, "*you* were my best friend in the whole wide world."

We both stop walking. She turns to me. "I spent a long time wondering what I had done wrong." Seema's eyes are so sincere. I have a hard time meeting them.

"Nothing. You did nothing wrong." I shift the weight of my bag on my shoulder.

Seema's mouth twists. She kicks at the ground. "Then . . . why?"

I want to say, *Why, what? I don't know what you're talking about. We've never stopped being friends!*

But she deserves better than my cowardice. Way better than that.

"I mean it. You did nothing wrong. Hayley was a . . . *force* to be reckoned with, even when we were kids. At first it was just her punching the boys who were mean to me on the playground. Then her mom started dropping her off at our house on Friday afternoons. And my family loved her, so she'd just *stay* the whole weekend . . ."

Seema looks at me steadily. The cicadas scream, the night pulsing with damp heat and insect cries. She doesn't say it, but I know what she's thinking. That this all sounds like a big, fat excuse.

And she's right.

I cover my eyes with my hand. "Seema, I'm an asshole. You were one of my best friends in the whole wide world too. I'm sorry. I'm really, really sorry. I never, ever meant to ditch you." I drop my hand, meet Seema's eyes. "I'm a shitty friend." My breath hitches. "I don't, um . . . I didn't deserve you. Maybe I still don't."

Seema picks at her thumbnail. "You know, I asked my parents if we could have my tenth birthday at Six Flags. They made me do these insane chores for a month, but"—she shrugs—"they let me."

I tilt my head at her. "You used to hate Six Flags."

Seema throws her hands in the air in exasperation. "I *still* hate Six Flags! I mean, it's like, *Oh yes, let me pay so much money to systematically subject myself to severe bodily torture over and over.*"

"They're called roller coasters, Seema."

"They should be called *hey, let's see what almost dying feels like* machines! Though, I'll admit, it's not quite as snappy." She drops her hands and gets quiet, serious. "I hate theme parks now, and I hated them then." Seema looks up at me. "But you don't."

It feels like a punch in the gut. One I definitely deserve. "Seema, I didn't know . . . I'm so, so . . ."

Seema sighs. "It's fine. I mean, it's fine *now*. It was not then. I emotionally ate a *lot* of funnel cakes that day. Like, we're talking double digits. Pretty sure I frightened my parents." She swings her arms for a minute, chewing her lip. "I didn't blame you, actually. I blamed Hayley. All I wanted was for her to just disappear."

Seema cuts her eyes to me, and for a moment, I see it all. The jealousy, the hurt, the confusion, the fury: the broken heart of a ten-year-old Seema laid bare. It's so potent, it sends a shiver down my spine.

But in a flash, regret takes its place. "Of course, you could imagine how awful I felt when . . . well, you know, after this summer. And then I saw you that first day of school. You looked like a baby deer in a lion's den."

It's so similar to something Hayley would say, I have the sudden urge to throw my arms around Seema's neck.

"It broke my heart. I figured it was time to check in on my good ole karaoke partner."

I groan. "Tell me you don't still have those recordings."

"Hey, just remember. If you ever feel like ditching me again, I have 'Bohemian Rhapsody.' The Ella Edition."

I shake my head, shuddering. "No. The world must never know."

Seema gives me such a vulnerable, crooked smile that I go ahead and throw my arms around her, carried by a rush of fondness. She hugs me back, tighter than I expected.

"I'm sorry again. You've sort of been a lifesaver these past few weeks," I say softly.

"I know," she says. "I'm the best."

We pull away, clearing our throats. Seema looks at the path to the bus stop and looks at me.

"You are not riding the bus right now." She clicks a button on her key fob and the lights on her car flicker with a chirp. "Let me take you home."

"I will *not* argue with you," I say gratefully.

But before we get in, Seema stops me. "For the record, you're not a shitty friend. You weren't then, and you aren't now. In fact, I owe you. If it weren't for you, I wouldn't have found my dream job." She thumps the hood of her car and slips into the driver's seat.

"I'm happy to help, but . . . how exactly—"

Seema's fiddling with the radio, the static rising and falling. "Well, you indirectly helped. See, Baby Seema was a bit melodramatic and took the ending of our friendship hard. She poured her heart into a diary *without* a lock—big mistake—and at a family gathering, my older cousin Dev—excellent beatboxer, terrible human—waltzed in and did a dramatic reading of my most recent entries. 'Dearest Diary, Ella didn't wave to me in the hallway. I am bereft. Doleful beyond consolation.' I'm paraphrasing, of course."

I can barely find the words. "Seema. That's awful. I'm so—"

"Hush, it was hilarious." She pauses. "Eventually, at least. But my parents took enough pity on me to let me choose a puppy from the animal shelter. After that, I fell madly in love with animals, realized I wanted to care for them, you know the rest. And besides, every aunty and uncle in the room roasted Dev that night. My nani wouldn't stop booing until he left the room."

Despite myself, I burst into a laugh. "That's . . . a lot, Seema."

"That's life, baby." She adjusts her rearview mirror. "Point is, you're not a shitty friend."

"That's debatable," I mutter, thinking of Sawyer and me at the top of Hemlock Mountain.

She shakes her head. "Even with whatever you're doing with Sawyer."

Hearing her say his name stops my heart. She sees it on my face, rolls her eyes, switching the gear from park.

"I mean it, Ella," she says seriously. "Hayley loved you. Obviously. She would want whatever made you happy. It's not like you're stealing him while she's actively dating him."

I cringe as she pulls out of the parking lot. "But . . . there's, like, this girl code, you know? Never date a friend's ex—"

"Oh, come on, boss!" Seema thumps the steering wheel. "Hayley was an open-minded kind of gal. You think she'd buy into that? First of all, this is not your typical scenario. You're not stealing him; she's not hung up on him. Second of all, don't you think, even if she were still around, if she saw you and Sawyer were happier with each other, in the long run, that's what she'd want? Her best friend to be happy?"

I fumble with Hayley's necklace at my throat. I mean, it's true.

Hayley wasn't traditional in any sense of the word. She'd probably think that "never date a friend's ex" rule was patriarchal, an attempt to pit women against each other so we wouldn't notice them lowering the glass ceiling. I smile at that thought.

"Maybe you're right," I say slowly. "And maybe one day I'll believe you."

"Believe me now, Ella," Seema says. "Life's too short. And Sawyer's too hot."

Seema drops me off with another reminder to stop beating myself up. By the time I've brushed my teeth, washed my face, and dragged myself into my room, the full force of the day hits me. I change into my sleep clothes, silk shorts and a camisole, and crawl into bed.

My head's hit the pillow when I hear a rustle from my closet.

"Get out of there, Midna," I grumble, turning over. But then I remember I saw her downstairs when I came in, sleeping on a chair.

She's not the one in the closet.

I sit up with a gasp, Sean's cold, flat eyes immediately coming to mind. My mouth goes dry, my heart slamming against my rib cage.

Just as I throw back my blankets and open my mouth to scream, a figure lunges from the closet, and a large hand covers my mouth.

chapter 18
ella

"Shhh, Graham, you want us to get caught?" The voice is familiar.

I take several deep breaths, my hand coming up to cover the fingers over my mouth. A face appears in the darkness as my eyes adjust: dark, warm eyes and a crooked smile.

The hand slides down from my mouth to cradle my jaw.

"Sawyer?" I whisper, my heart still hammering.

"Sorry," he murmurs, brushing hair from my cheek, "didn't mean to scare you."

"I can't believe you're here. How did you—? When did you—?" I press my palms to his chest, feeling his warm, firm muscles.

He jerks his head at the window, keeping his hot eyes on me. "You should really lock that thing. The trellis just outside made climbing up here easy. The hardest part was figuring out which one was yours."

"The latch is broken," I say, my body responding to his heat, the memory of his hands. I roam my palms all over him. He's wearing a

T-shirt and gym shorts. He smells too good. Like cologne and sunshine. "Why are you here?"

"Why do you think, Graham?" He brushes his lips across my forehead. "I couldn't wait until tomorrow to see you."

His words pulse low in my stomach, high in my thighs. "And now you're in my bedroom."

Even in the dark, I can see Sawyer's eyes grow hungry. His hands drop from my face, slide down my neck to my shoulders. He freezes and pulls back.

"God," he groans. "You wear this to bed?"

A muscle ticks in his jaw as he plays with the flimsy strap of my cami. My breath hitches when he traces a finger where my sleep shorts end, nearly at the tops of my thighs.

"You must get cold." He's already starting to sound undone.

"Not really," I breathe, trembling.

Sawyer runs a slow, hot eye over my body. He pauses to stare at my chest. My skin tightens when I remember I don't have a bra on.

"You cold now?" Sawyer asks in a voice made of gravel.

"I feel like I'm on fire," I whisper. I swallow his groan as I pull him down on the mattress, his body spread on top of me.

Sawyer kisses me, and I dig my nails into his back, frustrated by his shirt. His hands dive under me, palming my rear. He squeezes hard, pulling me tight, rolling me against him.

When I feel how much he wants me, I moan.

Sawyer claps a hand over my mouth, panting.

"Ella," he groans. "Shhh."

Keeping his hand on my mouth, he leans down, licks at my earlobe. I make a strangled sound in my throat, arching up.

"See, that's what I'm talking about," he whispers, licking the shell of my ear. "Be quiet for me, Ella."

I bite my lip hard, trembling with need, wanting more than anything to do exactly what Sawyer wants. He gives me a hungry smile, moving his hands to my wrists, pinning me down.

I gasp. It's exactly how I pictured it, but better. So, so much better.

Sawyer leans down, pressing a gentle kiss to my neck. And then another. And another. I shiver under him, close my eyes.

"Good," he says against my jaw. But then he latches at the juncture of my neck and shoulder, licking, sucking, biting. I want to scream his name, moan with all of my body.

But I don't. Even as he licks up the length of my neck, his hot tongue shooting electricity through my entire body, I bite my lip so hard I taste blood. My heart's slamming and I'm squirming beneath him, my core molten and aching, but I keep my mouth shut.

"That's my girl."

I nearly melt from his words alone. I wrap my legs around him and draw him closer. His mouth drops open, his eyelids fluttering. I slip my hands from his loosened grip and slide them beneath his shirt.

"Take this off," I whisper. There's a moment when he looks lost, like he would give me the world if I asked, but then his smile snaps back onto his face.

"You sure you can handle it?"

I roll my hips against him, sparks flying where we're pressed against each other, and he squeezes his eyes shut, smile faltering. I tug his shirt up, and wide-eyed, he helps me.

A shirtless Sawyer Hawkins is a stunning sight.

I swallow hard, tracing the shape of his muscles, dragging a finger down the flat plane of his abs.

"You're unbelievably attractive." I sigh, not realizing I've said it out loud.

"Nothing compared to you," he breathes, diving forward to capture my mouth once more.

We move desperately against each other, swallowing each other's sounds, the push and pull between us delicious. I rake my fingers through his hair, and when he grabs my thighs, pulling me against him, I tug hard at the roots. At this, he grunts into my mouth, cupping my butt hard. It feels so good, I drag my nails down his back, digging hard.

"God." He pulls back. "That, uh . . . that's too good." His brows are creased with need, and he looks so lost, so undone, it ignites a need inside me I never knew I was capable of. I want to push him beyond his limits.

"Take off my shirt," I whisper, my chest rising and falling beneath him.

He freezes, eyes popping. I see Sawyer's throat jerk with a hard swallow, his eyes dragging hungrily up and down my torso.

He squeezes his eyes shut.

"Ella," he groans, as if in agony. "That's . . . not a good idea."

I roll my hips against him, his eyes shooting open once more.

"Why not?" I pant, and it's my turn to smile.

Sawyer hovers above me, blinking, unsure, desperate.

And I can't help it. The only thing in my brain is this dense, hot cloud of need. My entire body is thrumming. Sawyer's looking at me like he never wants to look at anything else ever again.

My hands go to the hem of my shirt. Sawyer makes a choking sound in his throat.

I tug up my cami and take it off.

With a strangled groan, Sawyer's mouth immediately goes to my bare chest. I arch against his swirling tongue, the nip of his teeth.

"Perfect. *God,*" he mutters, almost to himself.

I never knew. That pleasure like this existed.

I'll never be able to lie in this bed and think of anything else again.

"Sawyer," I breathe, trembling. "Sawyer, there are only two pieces of cloth between us. Take them away and you could just—we could just—"

"Shit," he chokes, and his hand moves from my chest, down my bare stomach, and beneath the elastic of my shorts.

When his hand slips between my thighs, I stop breathing.

So does he.

He lifts his head and looks at me in shock.

"Ella," he croaks. "You're so incredibly w—"

The sound of heavy footsteps outside my door has us leaping apart. The heady spell is broken. Sawyer rolls silently off the bed and crouches on the floor as the footsteps pause for a few interminable seconds.

The footsteps keep moving down the hall, eventually disappearing from earshot.

It feels like an anvil crashed through the ceiling, shattering everything between us. I pull my blanket up to cover myself as Sawyer squirms into his shirt.

Both of us still panting, we stare at each other wordlessly for a few seconds. What the hell was I thinking?

"Probably for the best," I whisper.

Sawyer runs a hand through his hair. "Yeah. Yeah, probably right. I should get going anyway." He moves silently through my room, but when he gets to the window, he pauses.

I'm about to ask what's wrong when he strides back to me, grabs my face, and kisses me hard. Before I can pull him back into bed, he breaks away.

"I just . . ." Sawyer squeezes his eyes shut. "See you tomorrow."

As if he's afraid he'll change his mind, he moves swiftly, and he's out of the window before I know it, leaving me breathless, confused, and all alone in the room.

I've never felt like this in my life. Is it always like this?

I would give anything, *anything*, to talk to Hayley right now. She'd tell me. She would know.

My skin prickles with realization. I may not be able to talk to Hayley.

But I can listen to her. And I need wisdom now, more than ever.

I reach under my bed, drag out my backpack, and pull the diary out.

Just one more time, I think, and lift the front cover.

chapter 19
hayley's diary

I still love him. I do.

What even is love, right? It can mean different things, and . . . I mean, I'm sure Phoebe loved my father once. Sure, it got ugly and raw, and thank God I don't know where the hell he is anymore . . .

Why else would there be those lines, in sickness and in health, for better or for worse? *Those are lines in a marriage vow, right? I don't know, I don't know.*

E would know. But . . . she wouldn't understand this. Her parents have been happily married for God knows how long. She wouldn't understand that sometimes . . . sometimes love has challenges.

The first time S got jealous, it actually thrilled me.

I was wearing that red dress I really love, the one with the cut-out shoulders and the halter neck. S loves to kiss my bare shoulders. He said it felt like the dress was made for him, and surprisingly, I agreed. It felt good that he wanted me that much. That a simple scrap of my skin could make his eyes go dark like that, have him pulling me into his arms.

I was at my locker in between classes when a couple of guys on the soccer team walked by. I've seen them before, when they're playing a home game and I'm training by myself on the track in the offseason. I don't know their names, but we've smiled at each other in passing.

I'd just shut my locker when I heard a whistle behind me. The two dudes gave me an approving look.

"Nice dress. Red's definitely your color," one of them said, smiling.

"Didn't wear it for you, dingus," I scoffed, tossing my hair over my shoulder. I turned around and saw S down the hall, arms crossed, watching me. The look in his eyes! God, when he looks at me with that kind of heat, I nearly melt on the spot.

I bit my lip, walking down the hall, intending to pass him. It was the middle of the day, so we didn't really have any time to do much more than make eyes at each other, silent promises for later. So imagine my surprise when as soon as I was near him, he snatched my wrist, pulling me into an empty classroom.

"What are you doing? Mr. Todd's gonna kill me if I'm late again." He didn't answer, locking the classroom door. Bewildered as I was, my blood was already hot, my skin pulled tight with anticipation.

He whirled around, grabbing me, his hands rough with need. He lifted me and set me on a nearby desk.

"Did you like it?" he growled against my mouth. "Tell me."

"What?" I'd already forgotten the boys in the hall.

"Don't play dumb. You know what." He squeezed my thighs so hard, I gasped. "Those guys. When they whistled at you."

My head fell back with a moan as he ran his tongue up the column of my throat. "I don't care about them."

"Well, they care about you." S's hands slid up my dress, his hands moving possessively over my body. "Next time you tell them to shove it. Tell them you got a boyfriend."

As his fingers moved against me, it became harder to talk.

"Wait," I breathed. "You're jealous? Over me?"

With a growl, he bit my shoulder. My toes began to curl.

"Don't wear this dress to school anymore," he rasped. "Wear it for me and me alone."

I squeezed my eyes shut, my head dizzy with the slow tightening of my body, the anticipation.

"But I . . . I like this . . . dress . . ." It was getting harder to concentrate.

"Then you can wear it for me."

"Mhhm." I bit my lip, my thighs squeezing his hand.

His fingers stilled.

"What?" I cried in frustration. "Don't stop. Please."

"Say it." *His voice was so raw, so dark, I opened my eyes.*

I'd never seen his face look like that. Glowering, intense, furious. My heart skipped a beat.

"I won't wear it anywhere else. Just for you," I whispered.

S surged forward, latching onto my bare shoulder, biting and sucking furiously. His fingers moved once more, faster than ever, and he had to cover my mouth, because when the stars exploded behind my eyes, sparks raining down from within my body, I nearly screamed.

Before we walked out of the classroom, S pulled me into his arms, nipping hard at my jaw.

"Mine," he growled, before releasing me and stepping out of the room.

I pressed a hand to my hot cheek, ran a finger through my hair, trying to slow my breath.

Later, when I was in the bathroom, I saw my shoulder in the mirror. A large purple bruise had formed on it.

"Damn, you're gonna need a whole bottle *of concealer," a girl said, popping out of a stall to wash her hands.*

"Yeah," I laughed, touching it, feeling my core warm at the memory.

I hadn't thought anything of it, really. It felt like role play, dirty talk.

But then, later, he pulled me aside, grabbing my arm.

"Don't use the track when the boys' soccer team is playing."

"What?" I laughed, sure he was joking. But his face said anything but.

"It's not you I don't trust," he said, "it's them. Please." S kissed the corner of my mouth. "I'd feel better if you didn't."

It didn't feel quite like playing after that.

I didn't wear the dress again, but only because it seemed to upset him so much. It wasn't a big deal. I had plenty of other dresses. But bit by bit, those weren't okay to wear either.

There was one day we were passing each other in the hall, and when I smiled at him, he glared at me. He didn't respond to any of my texts. I found him after school.

"Are you mad at me?" I had racked my brain to figure out why.

He looked around to make sure we were alone, then grabbed my arm, squeezing painfully hard, pulling me close.

"What the hell are those?" He pointed at my boots.

For some reason, my heart started hammering. S looked so angry.

"Boots," I said. "They're just boots."

"They're not just any boots. They're black and leather. And you're wearing a skirt." He yanked at the denim hem.

"I don't understand . . . I love you!" I'd actually picked out this outfit with him in mind. Which was why I'd been so hurt when he'd given me a once-over this morning, looking disgusted.

"Then why are you trying to get the attention of others? I mean, am I not enough?" He sounded broken.

"Of course—of course you are," I said softly. I'd seen him angry before, sure. Who doesn't get angry? But not like this and not at me. I didn't know what to say to placate him. "I don't . . ." I tried touching his shoulder. He shrugged me off. "I don't want anyone else. Ever."

He looked up at me then, his eyes an open wound. My heart broke at the pain I saw.

"Swear it, Hayley. Swear you want no one else."

"I swear it," I whispered, kissing his eyelid, kissing his nose, kissing his cheek, kissing his mouth. He wrapped his arms around me, his breaths coming stilted and shuddery.

The next week, P was out of town and we had the house to ourselves.

"Hey, let's go do something this weekend," he said, coming up behind me as I cut up fruit. "Just me and you. We can take my car." S slid his hands up my shirt, pulling me back against him. I shuddered at the feel of his body.

"God, I'd love to." I dropped my head back onto his shoulder. He kissed my neck. "But I can't. E and I have plans to do a movie marathon."

S stiffened against me. Immediately, I felt my stomach drop. I licked my lips nervously. "I think . . . I think I told you . . . didn't I?"

S didn't say anything. He just stepped away from me. I turned around slowly. He had his hands braced on the island counter. When he lifted his face to me, I recoiled at the cold fury in his face.

"Do you know what I have to go through to make time for us?"

"Yes, I know, you have a lot going on, but—"

"And can you not watch stupid movies at any time ever?"

"I can, but I just thought—"

"Am I not the most important person in the world to you?"

He was shouting, screaming.

"Yes!" I cried, my vision blurred with tears. "Of—of course you are, I can cancel! I can—"

S grabbed his cup and hurled it against the wall, shattered glass raining down everywhere.

In an instant, I was four years old again, watching my dad upend the dinner table when I told him I didn't want any more of his spaghetti. I was cowering, frightened, helpless.

I ran upstairs to my room. I fled, feeling like a child, exactly like a panicked child. I slammed the door and locked it, shaking so hard my teeth rattled.

What was happening?

Where was the Hayley that flipped off the teacher because he said Ernest Hemingway was the best writer in all of history, despite my well-reasoned and sound argument claiming he was an overrated misogynist?

Where was the Hayley that wore a shirt to school that said, ANYTHING YOU CAN DO, I CAN DO BLEEDING*?*

I sank to the ground, head in my hands, and cried.

I wanted to call E.

But I was so, so, so *ashamed. I was so frightened.*

Yet it wasn't just that.

I felt guilty. Guilty for making S so upset. A part of me wanted to go to him, beg for forgiveness.

Forgiveness for what?

P had begged my dad to forgive me. "She's a stupid kid," she'd said, pointing to my face. But that hadn't been enough to get Dad to stay.

A soft knock startled me.

"Hay?" S's voice was so gentle. "Shit, Hay, I'm so, so sorry. I didn't mean to freak like that. I'm such an asshole . . ." He trailed off.

I couldn't speak, sitting wordlessly on the other side of the door, listening hard.

"I get it if you don't forgive me. But I cleaned it all up. And I ordered some pizza, got you your favorite. I just wanted you to know." S cleared his throat. "I'm gonna go, okay?"

"No!" I leapt to my feet and threw open the door. "Don't go. Please." Before I could throw my arms around his neck, he was kissing me, kissing me everywhere, murmuring promises and vows in desperate whispers.

"I'll stay," he said fervently. "Of course I'll stay."

And isn't that enough?

That he stayed? That he didn't leave?

In sickness and in health.

Isn't that love?

chapter 20
ella

I can't believe I'm about to do this. In no world would I have ever thought myself capable of the deception I'm about to commit. But after what I read last night, I can't find it in me to care. I can't stomach sitting in class right now, and I don't want to be alone.

I knock on Mr. Price's classroom door, poking my head in before I get a response. Mr. Price cuts off midsentence, and he, along with the entire statistics classroom, including Rachael and a bored-looking Scott, turns to the doorway, baffled. Seema, sitting in the back row, looks positively delighted.

"Sorry for the interruption, Mr. Price. But Dr. Cantrell asked me to come get Seema. It's important."

Seema, bless her, doesn't wait for a response to start packing and heading my way. "Well, you heard her, Mr. Price—can't keep the doc waiting." Mr. Price gives us a confused nod as we close the door.

"Dr. Cantrell didn't ask for you," I say as soon as we're out of earshot.

Seema rolls her eyes. "Obviously. You're a lifesaver, by the way. Not sure if you knew this, but stats is my *least* favorite class."

"Seema, *everyone* knows that. I heard you telling the lunch lady last week. C'mon, let's go somewhere we won't get caught."

There's only one spot I know of, and so it's with a pang that I take her to the encyclopedia aisle of the library. I pull out a pack of Sour Skittles that I snagged from the vending machine as we sit side by side on the floor.

"Cute spot," Seema says, looking around. "Smart. You could probably smoke weed back here and no one would ever know." Her eyes light up hopefully.

"Seema," I say dryly, "I didn't bring you here to get you high."

She sighs, shaking her head. "A girl can always dream." She reaches over to pluck some Skittles from the bag. "You gonna tell me why you broke me out of class?"

I tell her the truth. "I just . . . really need to be with a friend right now."

Seema softens at the admission. "Thought you looked a little upset. What's wrong, Ella?"

How could I possibly begin to answer that question?

I lay awake in bed all night, replaying every word of that diary entry in my head, trying to find clues I'd missed in both past and present. I still can't find any. The Sawyer Hayley wrote about is so different from the Sawyer I know. The darkness? The deep well of anger threatening to explode? I can't see it in Sawyer. Now, if she'd been writing about Sean . . . or even stupid Scott, it'd make sense.

But real life is never that easy, is it?

Why didn't you tell me, Hayley?

What else didn't you tell me?

Seema's face is gentle as she sits in my silence. I feel a surge of gratitude at her kindness. It gives me the courage to ask her a question.

"How well do you know Sawyer, Seema?"

She hums. "Well . . . I know he can do at least a hundred chin-ups."

I huff a laugh, and she smiles. But it fades as she grows more thoughtful.

"All jokes aside? I guess, honestly, not super well. I've had some classes with him. Smart, decent student. Not, like, obsessed with school or anything. He kinda has resting bitch face, but on him, it looks all smoldery, which . . ." She cocks a brow. "You should know all about that already."

I nod down at my hands, crinkling the bag of Skittles. "Has he ever gotten, like . . . angry in front of you?"

"Angry?" Seema echoes. "I was walking by the vending machines once, and his KitKat got stuck. He kicked it, but when his food didn't drop, he just stalked off, all broody and—"

"How hard did he kick the machine?"

"Um, like, normal hard? Regular hard? Like, I wasn't sitting there thinking, *Hm, I dunno, that's more of a Doritos level of kick strength, right there.* I mean, Ella, what's going on?" She leans closer, face serious, lowering her voice. "Is something up?"

Yes? No?

How the hell do I answer that?

"I'm so sorry, Seema. I know I'm not making much sense." I close my eyes, digging my fingers into the lids. "I should tell you I got zero sleep last night. Like, literally *no sleep*. Like, I don't even feel human. Feels like I'm losing my mind."

Seema's deep brown eyes soften, and she reaches over to pat my knee. "Hey. You can talk to me, you know." Her mouth twists to the side. "Did something happen? With you and Sawyer? Like, has he been . . . angry? With you?" Seema says each word delicately.

I bite back my immediate need to defend Sawyer and actually think about her words.

Rapidly, I scroll through my memories of him like a photo reel. Bright images of Sawyer through the years flick in my mind: Sawyer dark and quiet after a fight with Hayley; Sawyer yelling, "Come on!" after his favorite team lost. But I could name five more guys in this class who got mopey like that when things didn't go their way.

What about how jealous he got when he saw you and Scott? But it had been more than that, right? Hadn't he thought we should avoid each other? And it wasn't just him yelling at me that day; we'd been screaming at each other in that classroom—*until we were kissing.*

That hadn't been anger, but mutual desire pushed past the point of pain. That had been a dam breaking, and I'd done everything I could to shatter that wall between us.

I groan at the confusion and guilt racking my body, my face buried in my hands.

"Shit, Ella," Seema whispers, and touches my shoulder. "Has Sawyer done something to you?"

I tell her the truth.

"No," I whisper raggedly. "No, he hasn't. To be perfectly honest with you, he's been a dream come true." I shiver as I bat away memories from the night before.

Seema looks at me skeptically. "Uh-huh."

"No, I'm serious. He's been nothing but wonderful. I just . . ."

There's no way I'm telling her about the diary. I can't. Honestly, even *I* shouldn't know about it. I'm tempted, though, to mention Hayley's writings, because I desperately want someone to smooth this all out for me. I'd give anything for someone else to help me match the Sawyer I know with the Sawyer I read about, to help me unfold the corners and edges, tell me how I maybe misread a few things in the dead of night.

But only I can do that.

I swallow hard. "I just can't stop thinking about Hayley. And now *him* and Hayley. And wondering if . . ."

"Ah. All that again." Seema nods in understanding. "You're still beating yourself up about you and Sawyer? Even after our convo?" She takes my silence as confirmation. "And now you're going an entire night without sleeping? Cuz of your guilt."

"It's . . . really hard to put into words." I sigh.

Seema settles back against the bookshelf. "Ella, I mean, I get it. Look at what you've been through. No one's going to have reasonable, rational thoughts about something like this. But a worrywart like you is *definitely* not. It makes sense you're freaking out a little. But that doesn't make your thoughts true."

I thunk my forehead with the heel of my palm. "I just wish I could turn my brain off."

"You can. You want my expert advice? Tell your brain to shut up and go to bed." Seema shrugs. "Sleep deprivation's like an actual torture technique. Don't give me that look—I'm dead serious. After two days of no sleep, some people start hallucinating."

Maybe Seema's right. Maybe I need to reevaluate everything after I've had some sleep and food. I let out an exhale, rubbing my forehead.

"Hold on, Seema, why do you know so much about torture techniques?" I lift a brow.

She grins. "Don't tell me you've never gone down a morbidly curious Wikipedia scroll-hole. I have learned some messed-up shit, my friend. Can't recommend it enough."

I laugh, shaking my head. "Thanks, Seema."

"No, thank *you*. Mr. Price spits every time he says a word that starts with 'P.' And we're covering *p-values*." She grabs the Skittles bag and tips it into her mouth. "Why do you think I was sitting in the back? Seriously, feel free to rescue me from statistics, like, all the time."

The rest of the day is a sleepy, dizzy blur. I'm so exhausted, I don't even have the energy to protest when Ms. Langley badgers me to sign up for the fall festival next weekend, nodding weakly when she says, "How about the s'mores booth, for old times' sake?"

When the final bell rings, my body's immediately nervous, alert. I'm anxious to go find Sawyer. Walking to his car, I take deep breaths, fighting to steady my heart rate. But the buildup turns out to be for nothing. He's nowhere near to be seen.

A pair of arms snake around my belly, squeezing me tight. Lips brush the shell of my ear.

"Got you," says a low, familiar voice.

I gasp, jumping out of the arms, and whirl around to face Sawyer.

"Don't *do* that," I snap.

"I'm sorry! I would never have done it if I'd known—I'm really sorry!" His eyes are brimming with regret. And now I am too.

"It's fine," I say shakily, casting an eye around, grateful no one has seemed to notice us, everyone too glad to be free of school to look beyond their ride home. "Any other day it would have been fine. I just got . . . like, no sleep last night."

Sawyer's face softens. As he unlocks his car, his dark, thick hair falls across his brow, framing his scar perfectly. I could swim in the mahogany pools of his eyes right now. I know this Sawyer. This Sawyer readily agreed to climb to the top of a mountain with me, even though he's terrified of spiders and ticks.

We slide into the front seats of his car. I look over at him, and I can't help it.

I throw my arms around Sawyer, pressing my face into his chest, breathing in his delicious, sunbaked scent.

"Whoa, hey there," he breathes with a fond laugh. His hands are so gentle as they slide around my back that I squeeze him harder. Sawyer presses a kiss to the top of my head.

“Sorry again. I really do feel terrible,” he murmurs into my hair.

“I know,” I say, but I doubt he can hear me, my voice is so muffled against his shirt. *This Sawyer feels terrible when he startles me with a hug,* I think. My fingers fist in the back of his shirt, and there’s a rumble against my cheek, a low humming in his chest.

“So,” he says, and the cadence of his voice shifts, “any particular reason you couldn’t sleep last night, Graham?” I can hear the smirk in his voice.

I laugh into his shirt.

“I’d ask if you’ve tried that banana-before-bed trick I mentioned before,” he continues, “but I think we gave that a shot last night.”

“A *banana*?” I pull back and squint an eye at him. “Aren’t we awfully self-assured?”

Sawyer barks a laugh, his eyes crinkling as they roam my face. After a few moments, his smile falls.

“You really do look tired, Els. Still beautiful, of course,” he adds quickly, “but . . . like you’re stressed.”

His face swims a little in my vision. “It’s apparently possible that if I don’t get sleep soon, I may start hallucinating,” I say.

“Okay.” Sawyer says it like I’ve just told him I’m a little thirsty and need to grab my water bottle. “It just so happens that while my car may be a clunker, the passenger seat is incredibly comfortable.” He leans over me to adjust the passenger seat. “Best naps of my life. Don’t take my word for it, though.”

It’s true.

The passenger seat leans back farther than it probably should, but it makes for a nice bed. Sawyer finds an old cross-country hoodie in his trunk for me to use as a blanket.

“Where will you drive us?” I whisper, my eyelids growing heavy with each word.

“Don’t worry about it.” He brushes a strand of hair off my cheek.

"Mom's home tonight. I don't need to go home to watch Callan. We've got all the time in the world. Sleep as long as you need, Els. Don't worry about a thing." He smiles.

I'm still smiling as I drift off, feeling warm and safe.

When I wake up, it's dark outside. The car is idling, and bright neon lights cast a yellow glow from outside. But Sawyer's not in the car.

I sit up, worried, until I see that he's outside, talking on the phone. I relax. Probably just checking in with his mom.

Which reminds me of *my* mom. With a lurch of panic, I pull out my phone to find I've missed a text from her.

M

Hey, where are you?

I don't even stop to think before I punch in my response.

E

Sorry! I picked up a closing shift at work. I'll be home late. So sorry I forgot to tell you.

I stare at my phone as the three dots blink in the speech bubble, indicating my mom typing a response. It goes on awhile, and I brace myself for a text lecture. But after a long pause, all I get back is two letters.

M

Ok

I feel a terrible pang of guilt and an unexpected grief. A year ago, I would have given *anything* for Mom to ease the pressure off of me, even just a little. It now looks like I finally got my wish. She's eased the pressure *all* the way off. I'm surprised at how painful it is every time I lie to her. But the truth is, I'm not the daughter she thought I was. I'm not the daughter *I* thought I was, either. A brutal lesson for us all.

With a sigh, I look out the window and watch Sawyer pace, his broad shoulders stretching his shirt. Warmth blooms in my stomach when he catches me staring and shoots me a crooked smile and a wink.

A moment later the car door pops open, and Sawyer hops in.

"There she is. How're you feeling?" He grins.

"Starving." It's only now that it hits me, how long it's been since I last ate.

"Well, your timing couldn't be better." Sawyer reaches into the back seat and produces a greasy bag heavy with mouthwatering smells. It's only then that I realize we're in a restaurant parking lot.

"God, I love Biscuits 'N Butter," I groan. "Tell me you got their potato pancakes." I dig into the bag.

"What do you take me for, an amateur?" Sawyer scoffs.

I take a big bite of food and groan. "This is amazing. Thank you."

While I eat, Sawyer regales me with charming anecdotes about him and Callan. By the time I'm done, the warmth of a full belly and an hours-long nap has me feeling like a whole new person. Better than I've felt in a long time, if I'm honest, and completely flooded with affection for Sawyer.

"You know," I say, "if this is the BNB location I think it is, the Y I work at is just around the corner."

"Is it, now?" Sawyer's eyes sparkle with mischief.

"Yeah," I say. "It is."

He puts the car into drive. "You up for a little adventure?"

Butterflies flood my belly. "What kind of adventure?"

"Buckle up," he says, "and I'll show you."

I'm feeling a little less sure as we pull into the near-vacant parking lot of the YMCA.

"The night cleaner is still here." I point to Angus's car. "And he is *not* a nice man."

"Then we better not get caught." Sawyer leans in as he says it, nipping at my bottom lip. My body lights up at that small contact alone. I hardly notice when Sawyer gets out of the car, his movements coiled and panther-like as he makes his way to the gate of the outdoor pool.

"Oh *God*," I mutter, heartbeat picking up, as I slip out to follow him.

"I bet you know the code." Sawyer smirks, jerking his head at the glowing number pad on the black wrought-iron gate.

My mouth goes dry.

"I do," I say, looking up at him. He tilts his head, his crooked smile pulling at my navel. "If we get caught," I say, breathless, "it's worse than me losing my job. It'll be trespassing. Like, cops are called."

He leans in, his teeth grazing my earlobe. "But you're so good at keeping quiet, Graham." I close my eyes as every nerve in my body lights up. "We won't get caught. I'll make sure of it."

Without another thought, I punch in the code, and we sneak into the pool area.

All the lights are off, including the underwater pool lights. Even with our eyes adjusted to the dark, it's hard to see much more than outlines and shapes.

Which is really a pity, because it looks like Sawyer is shedding all of his clothes except his boxers.

"What are you doing?" I whisper-shout, even though I know *exactly* what he's doing.

"Hurry up, Graham," he hisses as he lowers himself slowly into the deep end. "A little birdy told me this is a highly covert mission, and you're just standing there, out in the open."

With shaking hands, I strip down to my panties and bra, scooping up our clothes to hide them in the bushes. I slide silently into the water, and it isn't until Sawyer's hands are on my bare lower back that it hits me.

I'm alone in a pool at night with Sawyer Hawkins.

And we're basically both naked.

"Do you have any idea," he whispers, pressing kisses to my neck, "how irresistible you are? Ella, I can't think of anything else but touching you."

My water-slick arms slide around his neck, and I marvel at the feel of him, of so much of his bare skin slipping against mine, his thigh against my thigh, the press of my chest against the hard plane of his muscles.

All of a sudden, there's no one but us again, alone in the world.

"This feels so good," I say wonderingly, "moving against you in the water." Nearly of their own accord, my legs wrap around his waist.

"God," Sawyer groans. We bob in the water as we move against each other. For a heated moment, I hardly notice the way our faces occasionally dip below the surface. With a gasp, Sawyer grabs the concrete edge of the pool with one hand. "See? I'd rather touch you than breathe."

"I can hold my breath underwater for ages," I say, teasing his neck with my tongue. "I'm practically a mermaid." I seek out his dark eyes in the shadows, gripping the elastic of his boxers with one hand and sliding the other down his stomach. "We can do things in the water others can't."

"In that case," Sawyer growls, shifting me so I'm clinging to his neck, lying back in the water, "I need us to pick up where we left off last night." He keeps clinging to the side with one hand, but the other hand . . . the other hand is everywhere.

It runs up my stomach, dips underneath my bra, exploring, squeezing.

"I'd never seen anything so beautiful," Sawyer pants against my mouth, "as you lying beneath me like that."

His hand slides down my stomach, dips below my waistband.

"And when I felt you . . . I couldn't believe how—how much—"

"How much I want you?" I whisper, arching against his hand, trying to show him.

"Yeah," Sawyer breathes. He slips his hands into my panties, and drops his head when he feels me there, swearing violently. "Ella," he whispers, moving his fingers against me. "You're so perfect, Ella."

I've never felt anything like this. This mounting pressure, this sensation of a promise being made, the knowledge that if I cling on, it'll get fulfilled.

"Sawyer," I whisper. It sounds like I'm about to start crying. "Please."

"Please what?" His voice sounds rougher than I've ever heard it.

"I don't know," I whine, a sound that makes him press his teeth against my jaw. "I don't know, just *please*."

He's breathing harshly, and his hand speeds up. I squeeze my eyes shut, red and gold flashes exploding behind my lids, muscles in my body slowly tensing, like the windup to a punch.

"You're so beautiful like this, Ella." Sawyer's starting to sound needy himself. "Come on, Ella. I wanna be the one. Come on. For me."

If there were any space in my brain for words, I'd ask him what I was supposed to give him. As it is, there's a bright balloon expanding in my entire body, getting bigger and bigger, going to pop any moment.

I don't know why, but I want it to pop. Need it to.

My heartbeat is impossibly fast, rattling my rib cage. My left leg's starting to shake, my fingers curled painfully. Vaguely, I register that a high, desperate sound is starting to leak from my throat.

I have the urge to call out to Sawyer, because there is only Sawyer, my body, and this impossibility he's creating with it. And he needs to know. That wherever we were going, I'm about to step off the platform. I'm looking down at the roller coaster tracks, I'm about to plummet. Cover your ears; the fuse is lit, and the spark has finally reached the firework.

"*God*, Saw—"

A hand claps over my mouth, and I'm suddenly whirled around, Sawyer pressing my back against his chest as he lunges toward the corner of the pool.

My eyes shoot open, but I can't see anything in the tarry black. I try to break free from Sawyer's grip, but the hands on my face only tighten. I grab Sawyer's arm, pulling, wanting an end to my confusion. His grip is too strong.

I start to panic. I thrash against him, kicking as hard as I can. Sawyer grips my torso with his thighs, surprisingly strong, holding me down so I can't move. My heartbeat is still hammering, but of course, now for a completely different reason.

I dig my nails into his chest, and that's when he releases me.

"Shit, shit, Els, you okay? I'm so, so sorry—"

I shove him off me.

"What the hell, Sawyer?!" I cling to the concrete.

"The night man came out," Sawyer says urgently. "You didn't hear him because you were . . ." He clears his throat. "But he came out here, and I didn't want you to get fired, and I panicked, okay?"

I can barely make out Sawyer's face, but even in the dim lighting I can see how wide and horrified his eyes are.

My body is still sensitive and trembling, both from residual panic and from the memory of Sawyer's hands. A wildly confusing, heady mix.

But I still feel a little wary.

"I was really scared, Sawyer."

His entire body sags. "Of course you were. I'm *so* sorry, Ella. I just didn't know what else to do." He looks over his shoulder. "I think he's gone. Listen, I'll take you home, okay?"

Sawyer's face is miserable with guilt. When he swims to the edge of the pool to peek over the edge, he keeps a respectful distance, giving me a wide berth. He looks like he means every word of regret. And then some.

And the truth is, I'd been caught off guard but had never been in any real danger. And getting caught by Angus would've been a disaster.

Sawyer saved us both, and he still felt so genuinely sorry.

"You're sure he's gone?" I ask.

Sawyer nods. "Definitely."

I wrap my arms around his neck, pressing my lips to his.

"Ella?" I'm close enough to see water droplets catch moonlight as they cling to his long lashes.

"It's not over," I whisper huskily.

His throat jerks on a hard swallow. "You sure?"

I move my body against him to show Sawyer *just* how sure I am.

He groans and whirls me around to press me against the side of the pool.

"Ella," Sawyer rasps against my neck as he picks up where he left off, and I'm surprised to find my body responding eagerly. Surprised to realize that maybe our interruption didn't dampen the sensations but, in some twisted way, heightened them.

Because it's not long at all before golden sparks fill my body, Sawyer muffling my cries with his mouth as I nearly weep in ecstasy. Once more, I care about nothing else in the world. There's nothing else that matters besides Sawyer, his artful fingers, the showering stars filling my vision, and his name, over and over, on my lips.

chapter 21
sawyer

I stop to get some gas after dropping Ella off at her house.

"Look at you," Ralphie says, leaning forward on the counter. "You're smiling again."

"Am I?" I do a little skip-hop in front of the small basket of junky toys Ralphie keeps near the packets of gum.

"Yeah, you are. Cut it out, you're gonna scare my other customers," Ralphie harrumphs, twitching his white mustache.

"You don't have any other customers," I say cheerfully, unable to take my eyes from the jumble of crappy toys. I've never spared this basket a thought before, but something catches my eye today. I pluck out a toy, a metal jeep, painted clumsily to look like a safari vehicle.

I peek my head beneath the plastic barrier, rolling the little toy back and forth.

"How much is this, Ralphie?"

He runs a bloodshot eye over it. "Five."

"Cents?"

"Dollars. You idiot." He takes a hit from his vape, filling the air with grape-scented smoke.

"Fine." I slap my debit card on the counter. "I'll take this piece of junk, and twenty bucks on four. Card reader out there's messed up, FYI."

Ralphie looks at me like I'm losing it. "Really? Just like that? No bargaining? No digging in your car seat for pennies? No yelling at me for extortion?" His purple-veined fingers slide my card under the partition.

I shrug. "I dunno, Ralph. I think things are on the up-and-up." I shut my eyes. Ella's too incredible to mention to Ralph, so I change the subject. "You ever been to the Atlanta zoo, Ralph?"

He grumbles, poking at the register one button at a time.

"Yeah, me neither. And neither has Callan." I roll the safari car back and forth on the counter. "He's gonna love it, though. You know what?" I point to him. "Mom's gonna love it too." *And so would Ella.*

Ralphie grunts and hits a final button, the cash register ringing, high and musical. I pocket the card and drum the counter before striding to the door.

"Have a beautiful night, Ralphie!" I call over my shoulder, laughing at his bewildered stare.

I'm still whistling when I walk into the kitchen. Mom's standing at the kitchen table rummaging through her purse, her back to me.

"Well, if it isn't my wonderful mother." I give her a big hug, squeezing her from behind. "Question. Which do you think is more fun, gorillas or pandas?"

"Sawyer," Mom says.

"You're right. Too hard to choose." I grab her hands and twirl her to my side, a dance move we used to do together as a joke. "Other question: Which snack is better to eat while watching the elephants? A snow cone or an ice cream sandwich?"

"Sawyer—"

"Again, you're right, too hard to choose!" I turn her to face me. "But guess what, Mom? You won't have to choose! All my tips are now going to go toward *fun*! Or, hell, maybe I can just join cross-country again. The options are *endless*!" I let go of her and pull the toy safari jeep out of my pocket. "Listen, let me know when you get your offer letter. I wanna be there when you tell Callan. I'm planning this whole fun little surprise speech with this stupid little thing . . ." I plunk the toy on the dining room table and send it rolling into a folded Waffle House apron.

I blink. It's Mom's old work uniform, next to her packed purse and a freshly made thermos of coffee.

"What's this? Did you agree to give them two weeks? You know you don't have to, Mom. Especially since your new job's probably gonna start—"

"I didn't get it, Sawyer." Mom says it so quietly, I'm sure I misheard her. I brace myself on the kitchen table.

"What do you mean you didn't get it? You're perfect for it. You juggle all three of our schedules and three jobs. One stupid CEO's schedule would be cake. Anyone could see that. Anyone." I dig my thumb into my scar.

"I didn't tell you, but I hadn't heard from them. I was starting to get nervous, so this afternoon, I called Betsy, who works their front desk." Mom takes a shuddery breath. "She said she's really not supposed to say, but . . . they gave the position to someone else. They liked me, she said, but they said they really needed someone . . . who had a college degree."

"No, Mom. *No.*" I start pacing the kitchen, my blood on fire. "This is ridiculous."

"Sawyer, keep your voice down, Callan's asleep." Mom's voice is sharp.

"Mom, come on. We have to do something." I grab her hands, and I'm shocked to find that mine are shaking.

"Sawyer," she says, and her voice cracks in half, her swollen red eyes spilling over. "I get it. I really do. But it's the way the world works, baby."

"Mom."

"It's gonna be fine." She sniffs. "We'll just keep on keepin' on. It's okay, Sawyer. It's gonna be okay." Mom reaches up to wipe my cheek. When had I started crying? I recoil from her touch.

"No," I say, backing up. "*No.* This is not okay." I can't stop shaking. "This? This is *bullshit.*"

Mom's eyes turn hard as flint. "Watch your language, Sawyer Hawkins."

I whirl on her. "But it is! You can't—you can't just take this, Mom. I can fix it. I swear. Give me the number to their office. I'll go in person, tomorrow. I'll convince him. I'll tell that asshole everything you've been through, why you couldn't go to college. I'll tell him how it's me—how it's my—"

"You'll do no such thing," Mom snarls. "This is life, Sawyer, and throwing a tantrum doesn't make a lick of difference. I didn't get the job, and that's that." She shoulders her purse and scoops up her apron and coffee. "If having that job meant I'd never have had you, well . . . screw it, then! No job's worth that. You hear me, Sawyer Hawkins? Nothing matters more to me than you and your brother."

She takes a moment to fix me with a steely stare.

But all I see are the purple shadows under her tear-swollen eyes. There's a grim set to her mouth that wasn't there before. I see the decades of three-job, rent-stressed exhaustion stretched in front of her. My sweet, courageous mother. After all she's endured? This is her life?

Something inside me breaks.

"This—is—bullshit." With each word, I bring my fist down onto the kitchen table. Pens, lipstick, and Advil bottles go flying with each slam.

On the last word, there's a terrible cracking sound, and the table sags on one side. The leg Mom and I repaired has splintered.

Something ugly and bitter howls through me.

"So we just deserve this?" I shout. "Broken tables, nothing more?"

I catch sight of the shitty little safari jeep rolling on the uneven table, and feel a surge of self-loathing so potent, bile rises in my throat. I snatch it up.

"And screw the zoo, right? Weekends and sleep and basic human needs? Screw all the bullshit?" I throw the toy against the wall, where it shatters into tiny pieces.

"Saw-Saw?"

Inches from where I flung the jeep is Callan, clutching his toy monkey in sweaty hands, his eyes as wide and terrified as I've ever seen them.

What the hell did I almost do?

"God, Callan," I choke. "Callan, I'm so sorry."

His face is crumpling, and his eyes are filling.

"Buddy," I say, reaching out a hand. "It's okay, c'mere . . ." But when I take a step toward him, he bursts into tears, sprinting down the hall away from me.

"Wait!" I start to go after him, when my mom lunges in front of me, putting an arm up to block my pursuit, and screams.

"Stop! Dan, don't!"

I freeze.

Mom's eyes are swimming, and it's hard to guess who feels worse in this moment. She doesn't move her arm. She doesn't try to explain herself. I don't need her to.

I sprint out of the kitchen, out the front door, wishing I could run forever, never stop. But this isn't a truth I can outrun. I need to face it.

My worst fear has come true.

Dan is the name of my father.

And tonight, my mother saw him in me.

chapter 22
ella

It happened again, as I was standing in my driveway, right after Sawyer had dropped me off. The doctors said anything could trigger them—the flashbacks, the memories. Maybe it was the state I was in, trembling from the damp of night, my nerves still raw from the evening's activities, that knife's edge of pleasure and fear. Maybe it was the icy light of the full moon, cold and cutting. Maybe it was just *about damn time* I remembered something else from that night.

Who knows? It doesn't matter.

What *does* matter is that one moment I had been watching the taillights of Sawyer's car retreat down the road, and the next I was hurtled into a flashback. As vivid as the ones that came before, I was suddenly back in the driver's seat of my car on the night of the accident.

I'm squeezing the steering wheel within an inch of my life.

Hayley is screaming.

"Drive faster," she shrieks in my ear.

A click. The sound of a seat belt unbuckling.

And now I'm sitting at the desk in my room, staring at Hayley's diary lying shut before me. How long have I been in this chair? Twenty minutes? One hour? Six? Wouldn't matter. I'm no closer now to making sense of any of this than I was when I first slipped into the desk chair, having shakily made my way up from the driveway.

My hair is stiff from chlorine, and my clothes are damp. And I can still feel the leather of the steering wheel against my palm. My right ear, impossibly, is ringing. Was that a real memory? Because if it was . . . what had Hayley so terrified?

Gaining a new memory has only created more questions and answered no existing ones. Just like Hayley's diary. Every time I read it, searching for clarity, searching for the peace of mind I so desperately need, I'm only left more tortured than ever.

I pick up the little black book, running a thumb against the spine. There's no doubt in my mind that what I read in here last night is true. Hayley's experience, her pain, her fear . . . that all happened. Believing her was never the issue. In fact, that's the exact problem. Because if I believe her, how the *hell* am I still okay kissing Sawyer or having him in my life at all?

Ella, we are a bit beyond kissing at this point, says a super-unhelpful voice in the back of my head.

I believe Hayley, would never doubt any woman speaking her experience, and . . . well, I believe me too. How I feel. Specifically how I feel around Sawyer. His sincerity, how he cares for me, how lost he looks when we kiss . . .

I shake my head hard. There has to be something *I'm* missing. It's the hope of a desperate fool, but I have the thought just the same:

Just one more entry, Ella. Maybe the answer's right in front of you.

That unhelpful voice is starting to make a little sense. After all, what if Hayley explains that Sawyer was just going through a rough time? He doesn't talk much about the details of his past to me, but maybe some old traumas had arisen?

Maybe he secretly did intense therapy and amended his ways? Maybe she mentions something that can shed some light on the memory I just had? Maybe I'm full of shit?

I squeeze Hayley's diary to my chest and hop on my bed.

There's only one way to find out.

chapter 23
hayley's diary

See? See? *He was just going through a rough moment. It was a bad day. Everyone's had a breakdown during a bad day. Jesus, even E's had a moment or two. Remember when over the summer she was reading that romantic thriller? E was sitting next to me on the couch while I scrolled Netflix, and she screamed suddenly, scaring the* shit *out of me.*

"Three days of reading, three days wasted. *I pulled an all-nighter for this* bullshit*!" She threw the book across the room, scuffing the white living room wall. This was E, who has the heart of a baby Cavalier King Charles spaniel, but I found myself genuinely on edge. When I asked her gently what that book had done to her, she said, "I just read five hundred pages of slow buildup, only to have the only romance scene fade to black right at the very end."*

"Did they kiss?" I asked.

"Once. And before you ask, no, not even any tongue." E's face was red *with fury.*

"In that case," I said solemnly, "let me get that book so you can throw it again."

She threw it again, so hard she knocked down a painting and we had to hear an earful *from her mom.*

Here's my point: If it can happen to E, it can happen to anyone.

Including S.

And things have been better than ever since then. Truthfully, I think it brought S and me to a more honest place. I'd never seen that side of him, never known it existed. But now I know him more completely. Better than anyone else does. We lay in bed together, and I stroked his brow, asking him to show me the ugly parts, the mottled parts, telling him there was never going to be any part of him that I wouldn't love with all my heart.

It took coaxing. It took kissing. It took pledging and professing, but S finally let his guard down and opened up to me.

He told me about how when he was seven, he wasn't strong enough to hold the bedroom door shut against his father when his dad was in a blustering, drunken rage, but how even as a child, S knew that if his father's fists chose him that night, it meant that they were not currently choosing his mother.

He told me that he cannot remember a time when he ever loved his father, that the strongest feelings S ever had for him were fear and hate, and then relief when he disappeared.

And then, ten minutes later, amidst tears, S admitted that it'd be simpler if that were true, but the truth is always so much more complex. That the truth was, he can still remember the leaping in his heart when he was five years old and he heard his father's keys turn in the front door when he came home from work.

There were terrible things. Worse things. Things I needed to close my eyes to hear.

But I listened. And kissed him through it.

"There's nothing you can tell me that won't make me love you more," I promised.

I told him how he made me feel less alone. Our lives weren't the same, exactly. Instead of one terrible father who, for too long, refused to leave, I'd had multiple terrible fathers who refused to stay.

"I want to blame Phoebe," I told him. But I admitted the one thing I barely admit to myself. "If I'd been more lovable . . . there's no way any of them would have left."

"It doesn't matter anymore," S had said, holding me. "You've got me now. You don't need anyone else."

I swear there's some sort of psychic connection between us.

I can't tell you how many times in the past few weeks I'll be lying in bed at night, aching for him, when I'll get a text from S at that exact moment.

Come outside.

I'll slink out the front door, and there he is, leaning against his car, holding a sunflower.

"What are you doing—" But I can't ever get my whole sentence out because he's wrapped his arms around me and pressed his mouth to mine. It's always a close call, scrambling into his back seat before we're all over each other. And when we're finished, panting and sweaty, we've always managed to sit on the flower somehow. I always feel a little sad, cradling the torn petals, but S kisses my collarbone with a smirk.

"I guess I'll just have to get you another one," he says. And he always does.

One time, E and I were at the mall, a long-awaited shopping trip for just us two. S had felt so terrible about his outburst that he'd nearly insisted I plan a girlfriend excursion with E.

I'd found a few skirts and shirts I wanted to try on, so while E kept browsing the shoes, I went to the fitting rooms. A few seconds after I slipped off my shirt, the door to my stall opened, and someone darted in, covering my mouth before I could scream.

"Shhh, don't worry, it's just me, Hay!" S whispered, his eyes shining with mischief.

My heart didn't stop pounding. "What are you doing?" I hissed. "I'm meeting up with you in a couple hours!"

"I know, but I saw you and couldn't resist. I was picking something up for my mom. I totally forgot you'd be here right now."

He started kissing my neck, and my body leapt into awareness, as it always does around him.

"I can't really think," he said, "since you're standing here in nothing but a skirt, bra, and boots, looking hot as hell."

"I was about to try on some clothes. Want me to model for you?"

"Later," he whispered.

S turned me around so I was facing the mirror. He hooked his chin over my shoulder, locking eyes with mine in the reflection.

"Feel this?" He dug his fingers into my hips as he pulled me back against him. I bit my lip to keep from moaning. "You do this to me, Hayley."

I heard the slow unzipping of his fly. "Don't take your eyes off the mirror," he whispered. "I want you to watch how beautiful you are when I make you fall apart."

And I did. I didn't look away for the slow, delicious entirety of it. He had to keep his hand pressed tight against my mouth, otherwise we would have definitely been arrested for public (extreme) indecency, but once more, S had shown me an avenue of pleasure I'd never known existed.

I definitely felt a hot dose of shame when I slunk out of there to find E, and all she said was "There you are! I guess it was a really tough decision. Did you like any of the clothes?"

So, see? Life with S has been nothing but sunflowers and kisses and then *some, ha! He keeps me pretty busy. Between him and school and squeezing in E, I find that I don't worry about all of Phoebe's bullshit. What a relief that is!*

I actually have to cut this short because S just texted me. He's outside, and we're gonna go grab a bite to eat. More later!

I'm so ashamed.

I'm so humiliated.

I'm so lost.

What is my life that all I have to turn to is this diary at a time like this?

I mean, everything I wrote before is true. S has been perfect. Happy. I literally wrote about how great things were in here just like a few hours ago.

Here's how it happened.

When I ran outside to meet S, I could tell he was in a mood. Who doesn't get in those? Besides, I know him pretty well at this point. I have a decent idea of how to cheer him up.

"You okay?" I asked when I got in the car.

"I'm tired," he said. "Long day."

"Poor thing," I said, meaning it. I leaned in to kiss him on the cheek. Unfortunately, this was at the same exact moment that he turned his head toward me to check his blind spot before backing out of the driveway. So I ended up accidentally slamming my nose into his cheek.

"I'm sorry!" I squeaked at the same time that he screamed, "Can you just, for once, stop being such an annoying pain in the ass?"

I nodded, heart beating fast. It hurt, of course. It always does when he gets like this. But I know he doesn't mean it, and even though this time it was an accident, he's not wrong.

I totally can *be a terrible pain in the ass. On occasion, quite intentionally. Not anytime recently, of course, but . . . well, there's a time and a place.*

These are the things I was chewing on as I stared down at my lap during the drive. I was trying to pay very close attention to S. I'm not great at predicting it yet, but sometimes I can tell what category of storm we're dealing with. A category five means the evening is basically shot. Try again tomorrow. A category three can go either way, but it's most likely salvageable. Category one or two means he just needs a little bit of polite silence to calm down and then everything's fine.

Honestly, I don't even remember the category ones or twos anymore.

I remembered not to hum and bounce my knee, which took some concentration. The drive was longer than normal, since we wanted to try the new Burger Shack a few towns over. The long drive was good for S, though—by the time we pulled into the parking lot, I could tell some of the tension had left his shoulders.

"Shit, Hay," he said after putting the car in park. "I'm the biggest asshole in the world. I'm sorry. Today blew. I took it out on you, when you're literally the only good thing in my life." S leaned over and kissed me. "You're never a pain in the ass," he murmured.

A category one, then.

Or so I thought.

I kissed him back, telling him that of course I understood, and he shouldn't be ridiculous, I was definitely a pain in the ass. The truth was, the predominant thing I felt was relief. Relief that, perhaps, the evening wasn't a bust after all and maybe I could relax a little.

We walked into the restaurant, his arm wrapped around my waist and my head on his shoulder. Things were fine then. Waiting in line, observing the menu, standing in his arms. All felt right with the world.

"I can take whoever's next!" S was all cozy and sweet as we placed our orders.

I waited for the food while S went to find a table for us.

I hummed to the song on the radio, swaying as I waited, trying not to think too hard about S and how he had snapped in the car. When our order number was called, I grabbed our tray. As I plucked ketchup, mustard, and salt packets from the condiment station, I noticed we were missing an order of fries. I went back to the food counter.

"Hey," I said to the guy behind the counter, "no biggie, but I think there are some fries back there with my name on them."

"That would be impressive," he said, scooping fresh fries for me. "Burger Shack stopped doing custom fries back in the nineties." He set an extra-large portion on my tray.

"Well, I'm secret Burger Shack royalty—don't tell anyone. Thanks for the upgrade."

"Anytime," he said, giving me a smile.

I didn't think anything of it. As soon as I turned around, I forgot about the guy behind the Burger Shack counter.

But I hadn't even set the tray of food down in front of S when he grabbed my wrist, yanking me from our table.

"We're leaving. Now."

"What? But our food—"

People turned to watch as the tray clattered from my hands, spilling fries and a vanilla milkshake across the table. Thank God no one here knows us, *I thought, tears of humiliation pricking the corners of my eyes. I was wearing flip-flops, so I couldn't really keep up with S as he dragged me out the door.*

Category five, category five, *sounded the alarm in my head.*

I racked my brain, wondering where I'd gone wrong. These were the hardest moments. When I thought I'd done everything I could, remembered all the things he'd asked of me, respected his boundaries, and still managed to upset him.

"Please," I begged. "What did I do?"

S didn't say anything until we reached his car.

"Don't play stupid. You know what you did." He threw open the passenger door and shoved me in. S didn't say anything else until we were back on the road. He threw me a disgusted glance as he took in how I was huddled, how I was trying to hide my tears.

"I just really don't understand. Please, tell me so I can fix it."

As S stepped on the gas, his fury echoed through the roar of the engine.

"Who was that guy you were flirting with?" S finally yelled.

I pulled at my hair. I had no idea who he was talking about, but that would make no difference to him. Not that there was any winning in this scenario. If I knew who he was talking about, I was confirming his paranoia. If I didn't know, I was lying.

Damned either way, I only had the truth.

“I know you won’t believe me,” I said slowly, my voice wobbly with tears, “but I swear on all holy things I don’t know who—”

“Whatever you said, he gave you free food. What’d you promise him, hm?”

With a shriek of tires, we pulled up in my driveway.

“Wait, the counter guy?” *It was so ridiculous. It was beyond ridiculous.*

This whole thing was this terrible, grotesque absurdity. A comedy of errors.

The fry guy?

S actually thought I would risk a category five for an extra handful of fries?

I burst into dark laughter, half sob, half mirth. Hot tears poured from my eyes.

“Stop laughing,” S snarled, glaring at me.

“I—can’t—” I gasped between painful breaths. And I couldn’t, I really couldn’t.

“Stop laughing at me,” *S shouted.*

And when I didn’t, he reared back his arm and backhanded me across the face so hard, my head slammed into the window.

Pain exploded on both sides of my skull. And even then, I didn’t understand what had happened.

S hadn’t hit me. He wouldn’t do that. That’s not something that happened to girls like me.

Did I laugh so hard I knocked my head against the glass?

Bewildered, I touched a hand to my face and felt something wet. I looked down and saw a small dot of blood on my fingers. I tasted copper on my lip.

I looked over at S, expecting to see contrition, horror, for him to scramble over himself saying he’d been possessed . . .

But he was glaring at the ceiling, still racked with cold fury, jaw clenched, but if anything, a little more . . . relieved?

It all sort of washed over me then. How I'd remembered the little salt packets he likes. The way the vanilla milkshake had spread across the table. How I'd really *been looking forward to some fries. The sound my skull had made when it cracked against the windowpane. The sharp headache that was already slicing into my temple, growing worse as I sat there.*

Choking on a horrified sob, I opened the car door, stumbling onto the asphalt. I ran to the front door, fingers shaking violently as I tried to slot my keys into the lock.

By the time I had locked the dead bolt, fled to my bedroom, made sure all the locks on my windows and door were secure, I had eight missed calls from S. Terrified, I switched off my phone and threw it in my closet, as if he could crawl out of the device itself.

And now here I am, sitting here, writing this horror show down for no one to ever read. I just checked my face in the mirror. It's not as bad as it feels. My lip is split, and there's a reddish splotch where his knuckles hit my cheekbone, but I don't think it'll bruise. There's a little bump forming where my head hit the window, but that's under my hair, so no one will be able to see it.

What I don't understand is how embarrassed I am. How ashamed.

Not that I'd ever imagined something like this happening, but before, whenever I watched movies or read news stories about piece-of-shit guys doing this to women, I'd feel so consumed with rage, I'd have to stand up and pace my living room.

I'd never let someone do that to me, *I'd preach to E.* I'd kill them. I'd kill all of them.

And now? Now I want to crawl under my bed, excise this memory from my brain so that I'll forget it happened, blot it from existence so no one ever finds out.

Why do I feel this overwhelming need to say I'm sorry *over and over? Not to S. Well, maybe to S. (That is the very fuck of it.) I don't know. It's more like a general apology. I'm sorry to every person ever this has happened to. I'm sorry that most have had it worse. I'm sorry I'm a coward. I'm sorry I judged you.*

I'm sorry I can't tell you, E.

I want to tell you the most. But I just . . . can't.

How did I get here? How do any of us get here, that our only hope lies in scraps of secret paper that will end up in a landfill, unread?

What do I do, diary? What the fuck do I do now?

chapter 24
ella

I have to snap the book shut before any more of my tears smear Hayley's words. Cross-legged on my bed, staring in horror at the dark—I want to throw this book into the closet, just like Hayley did with the phone. These words are too horrible, the guilt too immense. But how can I do anything but clutch it closer?

"Hayley." I press the diary into my belly, the corners digging in the soft space beside my navel. "I'm so sorry. I'm so sorry."

Hayley was terrified, lost, and so, so, so alone. How did I have no idea? She probably came to school the next day and sat there listening to me while I whined about how I had a seven-page paper due the same week as a big swim meet. It's staggering, the things that used to keep me up at night.

My morning alarm goes off, and a new horror overtakes me.

Sawyer.

How the hell am I supposed to face Sawyer now? My lungs squeeze painfully, and it suddenly feels like I can't get enough oxygen.

Hayley was so worldly. Wise in a way no seventeen-year-old should be. I felt like a tadpole, and she was one of those gorgeous Amazon rainforest frogs whose stunning colors showed you how brilliant and deadly they were. She always had the answers, and she always assured me that no matter how naive I was, she'd take care of me.

I never saw her scared, heard her voice uncertain. And I had no idea about Sawyer.

Next to Hayley, there was no one who made me feel safer than he did. Even amongst my doubts, at certain moments, if he'd asked me to walk off a bridge last night, I would have.

There is no comfort in realizing that it wasn't just me.

Sawyer had us all fooled.

A knock on my bedroom door startles me, and I shove the diary under my mattress.

"Ella? Why are you still in bed?" Mom flicks on the bedroom lights and frowns when I wince at the brightness.

Midna sprints from the hallway, bounding onto the bed with a chirp. I scoop her up and bury my face deep into her warm, soft fur.

"What . . ." Mom turns around when she hears me sniff. "Goodness, Ella. What's wrong?"

Midna purrs, and I cry harder.

I feel the mattress shift and a hand on my leg. "Are you sick? Did something happen?"

With another sniff, I lift my eyes to Mom. She looks worried, confused. For a moment, I imagine the relief I would feel to unload this burden onto her. To hand it to an adult, then curl up and sleep for a million years.

Mom squeezes my ankle, half encouragement, half insistence, and I consider it for a fleeting breath. Telling her everything. But she wouldn't be able to get past what I'd done with Sawyer. The sneaking around, the things we'd done and *almost* done. She's already so disappointed in me.

But most of all . . . why would I burden her with the horrors of a dead girl's diary?

I release Midna's sleek, soft body. She headbutts my hand and curls up against my thigh.

"Nothing happened, Mom," I say, voice hoarse. "I don't feel well. I'm not sure if I'm going to school today."

Or ever again.

Mom presses the back of her hand to my forehead. "Well, you don't have a temperature." She furrows her brows, piercing me with her gaze. "Babycakes, what's really going on?" My childhood nickname and the urgent thread in her voice tempts me into spilling my guts again. Because that's the hardest part. She really does want to help.

But she can't.

I close my eyes. "Nothing, Mom. I think I just slept poorly."

Mom would never be able to get past all the ways I'd betrayed her trust. Violated that idea of the little girl I once was. My parents would—

My eyes snap open.

I can't go to my parents. But there is another adult I could go to. One who can still remember what it was like to be young and dumb.

I leap out of bed, startling both Mom and Midna.

"Crap. I just remembered. Quiz in AP Gov today. I can't stay home." I rush to my closet to change.

Hurt flashes across Mom's face. But only for a second. She stands, nodding, smoothing wrinkles from her blouse, her face shuttered once more. "If you're sure you're okay . . . The bus is coming soon."

"Yup," I say absently, shimmying into jeans. She doesn't need to worry, though. No way I'm missing the bus. It's the only thing between me and someone who'll know what to do.

I GO STRAIGHT to Mr. Wilkens's office as soon as I arrive at school. His door is cracked open, and he's sitting at his desk, typing on his laptop, music playing on his speakers. Thank God he's by himself.

With a shaking fist, I rap on his door. Mr. Wilkens looks up. He begins to smile, but it drops the second he takes in my face.

"Ella, what happened? Are you all right—"

"No. *No.*" And what a relief it is to tell him the truth. "I'm really pretty far from all right."

His eyes soften. "Oh, Ella." Mr. Wilkens rushes to shut the door.

I'm curled over in the chair, arms wrapped around my middle, trying to swallow the more violent of my sobs. He grabs a box of tissues from his desk and sits in the armchair beside me.

"Here," he says, and I take the offered tissues. "I've got a ton of those boxes, so please, snot away."

I hiccup a laugh and proceed to cry harder. Not once do I feel like I'm taking too long to cry, that I'm not getting to my words fast enough. Mr. Wilkens sits there, a patient and gentle presence. His eyes never leave me, but it feels less like he's judging me or trying to read my mind, and more like he's the family German shepherd. He's there to protect me, just making sure I'm okay.

It hits me that, finally, I don't have to hold anything back. No secrets. This is a safe space. I have a surge of gratitude for Mr. Wilkens that is so strong, I have to suppress the urge to hug him.

"You know," I say thickly, "you're really good at this."

"Hm?"

I gesture vaguely around the room. "I don't know. This. Listening."

Mr. Wilkens laughs, a warm, fond sound. "Remind me to have you do my next performance evaluation." His eyes are intent on mine. "Seriously, though, are you okay?"

"I've been—sort of hooking up with Sawyer." It feels like pushing a diamond up my throat.

"Okay?" Mr. Wilkens blinks at me. Whatever he'd expected, I don't think it was that. He shakes his head, recovers. "Okay," he says again. "I'm assuming you feel . . . guilty? Because of Hayley."

"You assume correctly. Massively. I'm the biggest asshole friend in the entire history of all assholes and all friends." This part feels good to say. Like I'm in a confessional booth.

"All right, I hear that you feel incredibly guilty, Ella. But there's no reason to say such awful and, objectively, impossible things about yourself." He shakes his head. "That being said, it's perfectly understandable to feel guilt. But let's break—"

"He hit her."

"What?" This stops him short. "Who hit who, Ella?"

"Sawyer hit Hayley. I had no idea. *No* idea. He's been so wonderful to me, honestly, like, my dream guy, but I read her diary and *he hit her*—"

"Ella," Mr. Wilkens says, his voice slow and serious. "Slow down. Back up. I believe you. I believe Hayley. But these are serious accusations. How do you know Sawyer physically abused Hayley?"

"Hayley kept a diary." Hot tears leak out of my eyes. "I know I shouldn't have—shouldn't have read it. I just missed her so much, but then she started writing about how Sawyer got all controlling and jealous and then—and then he hit her so hard he made her bleed!"

Mr. Wilkens blanches. "Sawyer did this?" he whispers.

"I know." I press a fistful of tissues against my mouth. "I feel so stupid."

"Don't." Mr. Wilkens stands up, pressing his fingers against his temples. "Don't you dare feel stupid, Ella. This isn't your fault or Hayley's fault—no one's fault but Sawyer's."

"All these years I've known him and thought he was just the most wonderful person . . . How could he have hidden it so well?" I tuck my legs tight against me, propping my chin on my knees.

Mr. Wilkens sits down beside me, fixing me with sad, warm eyes.

"Unfortunately, Ella, this is pretty common when it comes to abusers. During my master's, I worked with victims of domestic violence on one of my rotations. It was typical for friends and family to be shocked when they found out their loved one had been in an abusive relationship. They'd lament about how charming and wonderful they thought the abuser was. 'But he loved her so much,' and 'But he was so nice and funny!'"

Mr. Wilkens swallows hard, looking nauseated. "I know it's no one's fault, but if anyone should have recognized Sawyer for what he was, been a support system for Hayley, it should have been me." He rakes a hand through his hair. But after a moment, his face smooths out.

"Sorry, Ella. That's not terribly professional of me."

"Don't apologize," I whisper. It's touching, how much he cares. "It's nice that someone other than me cares like this. Even though Hayley's gone."

He nods, staring at the floor. "I care about all my students, past or present." After a moment, Mr. Wilkens's head snaps up. "Ella, has Sawyer hurt you?"

"No," I say, a shudder rattling my spine. "Not yet."

"Thank God. Does he know you have the diary?"

"No one does," I say. "Except for you."

"Good." He rises, pacing behind his desk. "It's safest that no one knows for now. It's the closest thing we have to evidence. If . . . it can be considered evidence at all." He frowns. "Without Hayley, I'm afraid it would hold very little weight in court."

"In court?" I sit up, panicking. "Wait, Mr. Wilkens, you want to send Sawyer to jail?"

Mr. Wilkens stops pacing, and when he sees my face, his eyes soften.

"Ella," he says gently, walking over to place a hand on my shoulder. "I can't imagine how difficult this has to be for you. You've not only been friends with Sawyer for a long time, but . . . I'm sure you've been feeling much stronger feelings for him as of late."

I squeeze my eyes shut. I have to voice this traitorous thought or let it rot inside me.

"Mr. Wilkens," I whisper. "I trust Hayley with all my heart. She was my best friend in the entire world. But this feels so hasty . . . what if . . . Is there any chance . . . any remote possibility that . . . there's some kind of misunderstanding? That—that I messed something up or read something wrong or—"

"Ella." He squeezes my shoulder, his voice so full of understanding that my heart breaks. "I get it. Reconciling the Sawyer you know with this ugly, hidden truth about him . . . that's an impossibility anyone would have issues accepting. You're not alone in that. So many people out there know the confusion and hurt you feel. It doesn't make you a bad person. In fact"—he reaches over and hands me the tissue box once more—"I happen to think it makes you a very good person. You want to see the good in everyone, despite being faced with ugly truths."

Bile threatens to rush up my throat. I swallow it down, along with this horrible reality where Sawyer hit Hayley and I yearned for his touch.

"Ella, you're a very smart girl. Brilliant, according to Principal Cantrell. But in this instance, you need to trust the professionals. We may not have been able to help Hayley, but we can stop this from happening to anyone else. During my rotation, another thing I learned was abusers like Sawyer don't change their ways. Unless some kind of miracle happens, Sawyer will do this again. He will even do it to you."

I fight the urge to shut down, to curl into myself. No one else can do this for me.

I couldn't save you, Hayley, but I can save others.

With a hard swallow, I lift my chin. "What should I do?"

Mr. Wilkens nods, grim but proud. "You have a good hiding spot for the diary?"

"In my room, yeah."

"Good enough for now. I'll reach out to my uncle Rick at the police department. I know absolutely nothing about how these laws work, what can be done, if anything *can* be done, especially while Sawyer's under eighteen . . ." He shakes his head, frustrated. "I'll pick his brain, let him know what's going on, see if there's anything that the school or law enforcement can do . . ."

"What if he trespassed at the Y pool after hours?" I blurt.

Mr. Wilkens raises a brow. "Do you have proof?"

Shame heats my cheeks. "Nothing that won't implicate me."

He stares at me steadily, considering, then shakes his head. "No need to throw a wrench in your own future. I'll figure something out. You just stay strong and do whatever you can to focus on school." He pauses. "Ella, I'm sure I don't need to say this. But you need to keep away from Sawyer from now on. Your safety is the priority."

When I flinch, Mr. Wilkens drops back in the chair beside me. "You've been so strong. What you've been through would have crushed most people. You should be proud of yourself."

"Thanks," I say miserably.

He tilts his head. "Is there anyone at home you can turn to for support? Any other friends? Or—or relatives? Or . . ." He trails off when he sees the truth on my face.

No one. I've got no one. My parents would yank me out of school and send me across the country. Jess is impossibly innocent and young. I've already been a huge burden to Seema. Besides, she's preoccupied with the upcoming deadline for UGA's early acceptance application.

There was only one person I could have turned to. But we know this already, don't we?

"Here." Mr. Wilkens digs into his pocket, pulls out his phone. "Look. Type in your number." I do, and he calls it. I can feel the buzzing against my thigh.

"You've got my number now. When you start to feel alone or confused or scared, use it." I touch the phone through my pocket. It feels like a lifeline now. A parachute. I'm dizzy with relief.

Mr. Wilkens holds me with a fervent, warm gaze. "Keep yourself safe, Ella."

It's such a simple statement, but right now, I don't know how I'll ever feel safe again.

chapter 25
ella

In any other lifetime or universe, tonight would be perfect. It's unseasonably cold for a late-September night in Georgia, and the scents of fresh-spun cotton candy, hay, and hot apple cider are carried on a crisp autumn wind.

It feels like the whole school has shown up for the fall festival. Most of the staff is milling around. Ms. Langley gave me a quick hug at the start of the night, her bangle bracelets jingling as she thanked me again for showing up. Mr. Wilkens gave me a bolstering nod from his place at the ticket counter. Nia, Beth, and Rachael gave me perfunctory hugs before they set off for the corn maze, and Seema waved from the cotton candy stand. Jess and Kelly bought s'mores from me before joining their friends in the crowd. Everyone is laughing and happy, even Scott, who held up the teddy bear he won at the ring toss like it was the Stanley Cup.

I couldn't be more miserable.

I hardly notice the live bluegrass band playing across the field, people clapping along to the twanging banjo and jaunty fiddles. The rumbling tractor of the hayrides, the splashes of the apple bobbing, the shrieks of glee sounding from the corn maze . . . it all fades into the background.

The only thing I notice right now is Sawyer, a couple stalls down across from me, selling candy apples.

I walked out of Mr. Wilkens's office the other morning in a daze. It felt like wrestling a bear, grappling with this newfound fact that Sawyer was dangerous, and my safety depended on keeping as far away from him as possible.

But now, after hours of peddling bags of graham crackers, marshmallows, and chocolate and keeping a wary eye on Sawyer, I feel like I'm losing my mind. I've been staring at him while pretending to organize my change drawer and I just—can't—see it. He's not smiling much tonight, which means when he does, the effect is heart-stopping. He's soft-spoken and polite as he sells the candied apples, and it's hard not to melt, watching him interact with the kids.

Right now, Sawyer's leaning over his wooden counter as a little girl, clutching her mom's hand, is pointing shyly at the candy apple she wants. His face is open and fond, his mouth curved and twitching, as if holding back a laugh.

He plucks the brightest red of all the apples, reaching down to give it to her. She grabs the stick eagerly, but it's heavier than she expects, and the heft of the apple tips it out of her hand, plopping into the dirt and hay of the ground.

Her tiny face is a ruin of despair as she looks from her mom to Sawyer, then back to her mom. Her mom bends over, and I can't hear what she's saying, but when the little girl bursts into tears, it's clear she's not getting another apple.

Sawyer looks back and forth, checking to see if any teachers are watching. When he sees it's safe, he grabs two apples and hands them to the mom. Presumably one for each of them. He waves off any attempt at refusal by the mom, and he leans forward, smiling as he murmurs something to the little girl. I can imagine him telling her in that warm, velvet voice of his that the apple is heavy for him too, but if she uses two hands, she'll be more than strong enough.

I turn away from him, unable to bear watching anymore. One more second of seeing the adoration in that tiny girl's eyes and I'll forget everything Mr. Wilkens has said. And I need to be strong.

Especially when I see who is strolling up to my stall: Sean and Phoebe. I cannot believe they're here. But why am I shocked? It's become more and more clear that Phoebe's only ever done whatever she wants—*screw* how anyone else felt.

Phoebe's mouth is twisted in a wry smile, and she sways with every step. She looks . . . well, she looks drunk—but she also looks beautiful. Her auburn hair is slicked back in a low ponytail, and her floral dress hugs her curves. Her nails are done, her makeup flawless. She looks almost overdressed next to Sean, who is wearing a beat-up jean jacket, Timberlands, and the same kind of watch Scott has, which I'm surprised he can afford. Phoebe approaches while Sean hangs back, leaning against a pumpkin display while smoking a cigarette, his eyes watching me carefully.

As Phoebe leans on the counter of my stand, I can smell the cloying scent of alcohol on her breath.

"Two s'mores, Ella girl," she slurs.

I can't help but wrinkle my nose as I open a new bag of marshmallows.

Phoebe raises a brow. "You know, you keep frowning like that, you're gonna get wrinkles. Who will want you then?"

Again, I shouldn't be surprised. But bitter anger rises in me so fast, I accidentally snap the graham cracker in my hand. "If someone reduces the worth of a human to the smoothness of their skin, I want nothing to do with them. In fact, it makes me want wrinkles sooner so I can start weeding them out."

Phoebe cackles. "What's that quote? 'Youth is wasted on the young'? Call me when you're pushing sixty and you've been alone for decades. Tell me how much you love your wrinkles then."

Behind Phoebe, Sean snorts. My blood heats, and I glare at him. "I'd rather be alone for my entire life than be with *some* men," I mutter.

Phoebe follows my gaze and shrugs. "Who, Sean? Sure, he's no saint. But neither am I. We get each other."

I think of everything that Sawyer told me about Sean, about how he had watched Hayley in her towel, how Phoebe knew but didn't care, and something inside me snaps. "Hayley deserved better than you. And you never deserved her at all."

Phoebe rolls her eyes. "And I deserved better than my mom, and on and on—it's the oldest story in the book, kid." She laughs. "Believe it or not, this is one of the happier endings. Hayley's spared the pain of life, and I get a second chance at it."

All the air leaves my lungs. I think of Phoebe sitting in her kitchen, too broken to even set foot in Hayley's room. I'd been so shocked at her devastation. But I think of my lola's words on love, how nothing is ever so simple as that twisting, complicated river, how some are tranquil, some treacherous.

And now, I can see, some rivers become throttled by dams, built by those who, in the end, decided that love was never anything more than a burden.

I hand Phoebe her s'mores, then draw myself up. "If that's all you're buying, I'm gonna have to ask you to leave."

Phoebe stiffens, her face sharpening with fury. *This* is what she gets upset at?

"I'm not going anywhere," she spits. "I don't take orders from a little—"

"All right, that's enough." Strong hands gently take my shoulders and move me back, and Sawyer steps in front of me, his face black with fury. "You're drunk. Please leave."

Phoebe sneers at Sawyer, just as Sean appears at her shoulder, tense and alert. Phoebe's gaze shifts between me and Sawyer, understanding lighting her features. She turns to me when she speaks.

"Such a little hypocrite," she says. "Hayley's not dead six months and you're wearing her jewelry and bending over for her boyfriend—"

I can't take her words anymore. I step out from behind the stand, hoping to flag down one of the teachers to escort Phoebe off the premises. I notice Coach Cud a few stalls down, handing an apple cider to one of the junior girls on his track team. Perfect.

"Oh no you don't, you are *not* getting rid of me." Phoebe's drunken voice rises, and before I can call out to Coach Cud, she takes a lurching step toward me. I shrink back with a gasp.

Sawyer leaps in between us, and Sean puts his arms around Phoebe, pulling her back with an amused expression.

"I'd love nothing more than to watch you two go at it, but now is not the time or the place," Sean says as Phoebe struggles in his arms.

He leads a swearing, slurring Phoebe away, attracting glares from students and parents alike. Scott, who's just broken away from a crowd of senior guys to watch, stares after them, his mouth slightly open, an unreadable look on his face.

Before Sean and Phoebe disappear from sight, Sean looks back at me one last time and winks.

chapter 26
ella

For a moment, Sawyer and I stand there, panting and baffled.

"That . . . that is a horrible woman," Sawyer says after a moment. "Are you okay, Ella?"

"Yeah," I say in a small voice.

When Sawyer lifts his face to mine, I'm startled to see the dark shadows beneath his eyes, the weariness in his expression. Eerily, he mirrors exactly how I feel, like he hasn't slept in days. But what, exactly, is keeping him up?

"Well, I hate to say it, but I think this is just another Thursday night for Phoebe." Sawyer lets out a breath. "I'm glad you're okay. Haven't had much of a chance to talk to you the past couple of days." He laughs lightly, but I can tell there's a question behind it. "I missed you." He reaches out to brush hair off my cheek, and involuntarily, I flinch.

For half a second, Sawyer's face crumples. He looks so hurt. So confused, and *God*, he's not the only one.

"Sorry." I wrap my arms tight around my stomach. "I'm still shaken from the things Phoebe said."

Sawyer's fists clench. "Don't be sorry. They were awful."

The sounds of the fall festival winding down fill the space between us. The chugging of the tractor's gone, replaced by the farmer yelling for his sons to stop throwing the hay so carelessly from the wagon. The bluegrass band's all packed up. The murmur of the crowd is deeper, more adult, now that most of the children have gone home.

"Hey, so, I get it if you're not up for it, but . . ." Sawyer reaches into his pocket and pulls out two tickets to the corn maze. "I got us a couple of these. Our shift is basically done, so . . . I thought maybe you'd want to, I dunno . . . get lost in a field of corn together?"

A clear, cold wind kicks up, carrying his delicious smoked leather scent across the counter. In a visceral flashback, I'm reminded of how potent and singular that scent is when I'm pressing my face against his neck, how it tastes as good as it smells when it mixes with the salt of his skin.

It reminds me that not so long ago, all I would have wanted was to get lost in any kind of labyrinth with Sawyer Hawkins. And now, even thinking of all the things Mr. Wilkens had said, the diary . . . there's a war inside my chest.

"Ella, you sure you're okay? You look green."

I nod. "I think . . . I think I just need to sit down for a second."

Sawyer darts around to look for any kind of a chair for me, his motions anxious and jerky. He comes back carrying one of the huge tree stumps that are scattered around the grounds for thematic seating.

"Here," he grunts, dropping the stump to the ground. "Sit."

"Thanks." I look over at the scattered bags of marshmallows and graham crackers. "I just need a minute and then I'll clean all that up."

"Sit," Sawyer repeats. "I got it." His smile is small and crooked, and the moonlight is turning that scar of his into a silver slash across his eyebrow. *I haven't kissed it yet* comes the traitorous, unbidden thought, and I fall to the stump, clutching my stomach.

I watch, unblinking, as he methodically and carefully breaks down my stand. The pinch of doubt in my chest won't go away. Call me stupid, call me naive, but . . . I need to see it. I need proof. Not just for Mr. Wilkens, for something to possibly be done.

But I realize I need it . . . I need it for me.

What more proof do you need? You read the diary. You heard Mr. Wilkens. What more do you need? A hospital bill?

A proof more permanent?

"Done!" Sawyer says, and I try to hide my jump. But his eyes are sharp. "Sorry. Still twitchy? Maybe . . . maybe we won't do the corn maze, then?" He looks longingly over his shoulder at the giant stalks of corn lining the horizon. "We can always come back next year . . ."

"Ella!"

Seema walks up to Sawyer and me, wearing a burgundy sweater-dress. She's flanked by a group of friends I recognize from the school's lacrosse team. Seema holds up tickets to the corn maze.

"Me and the gals were gonna squeeze in a maze run before this place shuts down. How about it?" Seema jerks her head at Sawyer. "Chin-Ups can come too, of course."

Sawyer raises a dark brow at me. *Chin-Ups?* he mouths, crossing his arms.

I squirm on the stump, wiping sweaty hands on my jeans. Maybe it'll be okay in a big group of people. Or maybe I'm the biggest idiot in the world.

Seema groans. "Come *on*, Ella." She steps close and pats my head. "It's the best night of the year so far, and you look like you're watching

Coach Cud take a dump. Plus, I heard about what went down at your stand earlier." She softens as I groan, embarrassed the gossip's already made the rounds. "Forget about them. Let's end the night on a good note."

I sneak a glance at Sawyer. He's looking at me, his wide cocoa eyes hopeful.

I need proof.

"Okay," I say, nodding.

"Awesome!" Seema claps her hands. "But maybe act like I'm taking you to have some fall fun with your friends, not like I'm leading you to the guillotine?"

Sawyer sidles up to me as we walk to the entrance. I make a conscious effort not to flinch when his pinkie grazes mine, an unspoken request. I've got to tamp down the suspicion if I want to get any answers tonight, so I thread my fingers with his, a move that has Sawyer visibly relaxing.

Seema's making cursory introductions as we walk into the maze, but after a few seconds, she shuts up.

"Whoa," she says, giving voice to our thoughts, "this is creepy as shit."

With most visitors gone, the silence is palpable. The towering walls of corn block any other sound or light from the festival outside. In here, it's just the moonlight and the occasional rustle of dry stalks as a cold autumn wind whistles through the leaves.

My heart starts to hammer.

"Well, this maze isn't gonna solve itself, ya chickens." Seema marches down the long corridor, where we reach our first fork. There's a plaque in the center with a trivia question.

"'If you know your Georgia trivia, you won't be lead astray. Choose the correct answer to go the right way,'" Seema calls back to the group. "All right, you Georgia folk better know your stuff. This first one's tough. 'Which river is the deepest and fastest running in all of north—'"

"We go right," I say quietly, stomach churning.

Seema frowns at me. "I'm not about to get lost on the first one, Ella, so make sure you're super sure—"

"She's right. We're sure." When Sawyer tugs my hand, I don't have it in me to shrink away.

It takes Seema a moment. "The Silver River? The one that's just down—*oh*." I've never seen Seema look so awkward. "Right. Yeah. We go right. Sorry, Ella."

The next few forks are easy trivia, ones the other girls in the group can weigh in on easily. I keep a careful eye on Sawyer, wondering what I can possibly say or ask to gently prod him to make any revelations. Seema and her crew are chatting at least, keeping the foreboding dark and quiet of the cornfield at bay. But then we reach a plaque that stumps us. The questions have been simple enough that we haven't needed to weigh in so far, but after Seema and her lacrosse friends stare at the plaque silently for a few seconds, she turns around.

"All right, we need your big brain. 'Amicalola Falls is the highest waterfall in the state of Georgia. How tall is it?' If it's seven hundred thirty feet, we go left. If it's nine hundred forty feet, we go right." Seema growls. "How the hell is this a fair question?"

"We go right," insists one of Seema's lacrosse friends, tossing her blond hair. "I went there once this summer with my parents."

We're about to follow when Sawyer's soft voice stops us.

"We go left," he says. "We—I used to go all the time."

I can feel my hands go clammy. Seema looks back and forth between Sawyer and her friend.

"Okay . . . but how sure are you two?"

"I'm positive," the blond girl says. "Plus, it's the tallest, right? I mean, seven hundred thirty feet doesn't really sound that impressive."

"I'm positive too," Sawyer says. "I've read the brochure for this thing a million times."

Seema sighs. "I'm going with Kaley. We're in a big group, and I'd rather keep moving anyway." She frowns when she sees we aren't following them. "You coming, Ella?"

My heart's racing as I look from Seema to Sawyer.

"Ella." Sawyer shakes his head in disbelief. "I mean—don't you trust me?"

If only I knew how to answer that question.

I look up into Sawyer's eyes, searching, picturing diving into the deep brown and excavating truths. Surrounded by Seema and her friends, there's been no chance to do any digging, to find answers to any of my questions.

"I'm going left," I say, keeping my eyes on Sawyer. His eyelids flicker, and he lets out a breath.

"Whatever you say," Seema calls back. "I'll send a search team to find you if you don't make it out."

Without the ambience of Seema and her friends, the silence begins to feel oppressive. I twist the hem of my sweater in my fingers as we walk side by side. We reach our next crossroads, but before I can read the clue on the sign, Sawyer speaks.

"Wait." Sawyer stops walking. "Ella. Are we good?"

"What?" I take a shaky breath. "Yeah. Why—why wouldn't we be?"

He shoots me a disappointed look. "You tell me. Ever since the night at the pool, you seem . . . off. Did you not . . . do you regret what we did?"

I squeeze my eyes shut. "No." I confess the terrible truth. Even now, my shameful, traitorous truth is "I'll never forget it as long as I live."

Immediately, Sawyer's on me. His large hands cup my face, his bangs brushing my brow as he ducks his head. I'm enveloped by him, his warm, spicy scent. I hear a faint whimper and am humiliated to find it's me.

"Why, then?" he whispers urgently, his lips brushing mine. "Why've you been so cold?"

My fingers tremble as I bring them to his wrists, not pulling them off me but not encouraging either. I'm a needy, guilty mess, doing everything I can to fight off instincts I hate myself for having. Several times, I nearly give in, my mouth aching for his.

But I can't. I won't.

I manage to pull back. Ignoring the naked hurt on his face, I ask, "Sawyer, is there anything you've been hiding from me?"

He stiffens against me, and I immediately regret opening my mouth. "What's that supposed to mean?" His voice is as soft and cold as snow.

I lick my lips. No going back now. "If you had . . . *stuff* going on. You know you could tell me, right? You can trust me? That you can tell me anything?"

The skin around his eyes tightens. "What *stuff* do you think I'm hiding from you, Ella?"

"You just . . ." I lick my lips, scrambling for something to cling to. I think of the purple shadows beneath his eyes, the weariness. "You just seem off tonight, is all."

Something hot flares in his expression before his face shutters tight. I'm becoming increasingly aware of how the only sound I hear is Sawyer's feet crunching dry straw as he paces irritably. There's no light beyond the half-moon above. Not a sound of another soul.

Sawyer lets out a harsh breath, toeing at a bale of hay nestled against the wooden sign. "Guess my poker face isn't as good as I thought." He stares at me, considering. "I got pretty bad news after our night at the pool. Still a little thrown from it. I thought I was keeping a better lid on it."

I wait for him to elaborate, but he keeps his mouth shut. What news?

"That's awful," I breathe. I push as gently as I can. "I'm so sorry that happened. This news . . . Is it anything I can help you with?"

Sawyer sighs. "Not unless you've got a slick job with benefits in your back pocket. Mom was perfect for this job she was up for. Could have been a real game changer." He kicks at the dirt. "They gave it to someone else."

"Your mom didn't get a job . . . that's what you've been upset about?" I don't mean to say it like that or sound so relieved, but Sawyer whirls on me.

"Yeah, that's what I'm upset about. Not a bad enough reason for you? My mom works *three* jobs. You know what that's like?" His voice is rising.

"Sawyer, I didn't mean—"

"All because she doesn't have this expensive piece of paper saying she's in debt the rest of her life . . ." Sawyer presses his fingers into his eyelids. "It's so unfair. And . . . it's not just the news that's eating me up. I reacted . . . poorly."

I go on high alert. *Poorly?* "What do you mean by that? Poorly."

"I was upset. I was angry. I just thought we were gonna finally catch a break, but of course we didn't, and it was so *crushing*, and . . ." Sawyer falters. "It all sort of exploded out of me. I didn't *mean* to . . ." He buries his face in his hands. "And now Callan's scared of me. He's *still* scared of me. He's tiptoeing around me, and it's killing me."

The words are out of my mouth before I can stop them. "Sawyer, what did you do to Callan? Is he all right? Is your mom all right?"

Sawyer's head shoots up, and his face is white as a sheet. "Is Callan . . . all right?"

"I only mean—Sawyer, I know that you'd never mean to hurt

anyone you love . . ." When wounded fury blazes in Sawyer's eyes, I realize how very grave my mistake is.

"Ella, do you actually think I could hurt my mom? My baby brother?"

"No, Sawyer, no! Of course not! You'd never mean to—you'd never want to—"

"So you *do* think I'd hurt them, if I'm angry enough, if I'm upset enough?" He takes a step toward me, horror flooding his face when I flinch.

"It's not your fault, Sawyer. It's not your fault—after everything your dad did to you, of course you have—of course you'd struggle with—"

Every time I speak, it's as if I've slapped Sawyer across the face.

But the last thing I say makes his face go blank.

"What did you say?" Sawyer asks, voice deadly quiet. "Why'd you mention my father? *Why?* I'm not my father. Understand? I'll never *be* my father." Something ugly flashes in his eyes. "How do you even know? I only ever told— Did Hayley tell you?"

I'm crying hot, panicked tears, scrambling desperately for the right thing to say. "I d-don't remember, I swear, Sawyer, I don't, I'm sorry! Maybe she told me, or I read—"

Sawyer stops, staring at me. "Read? Read what? What the hell does that mean?"

"Nothing, nothing. I don't even know what I'm saying. I didn't bring it up to hurt you, I just— There are ways to heal what he did. I can— If you wanted to talk to someone, Mr. Wilkens has helped me recently. I trust him, and I can take you to him, I can—"

"Ella, are you *kidding* me?" Sawyer is pacing furiously, face twisted in an ugly snarl. "After all I've— You have me. You have *me* to talk to!" He whirls toward the sign, both hands fisted in his hair, yanking. "And you go to *Wilkens*?"

"Sawyer," I plead, taking a step back. "I didn't— I'm sorry that I— Please stop shouting."

But he's too lost in his anger to hear me. With a dark growl he pulls back his leg and kicks the bale of hay so hard it breaks apart. The air fills with stiff, golden straw.

"Sawyer," I plead through a sob. "Sawyer, you're scaring me!"

He freezes. Shakily, he turns to face me, staring down at his body, his trembling hands and legs, as if he doesn't know whose they are. When he raises his stricken face to mine, his eyes are wild and black.

"Ella," he rasps, taking a halting step toward me.

But before he can take another, I turn on my heel and *run*.

Hot tears blind me as I sprint down the eerie, gnarled corridor of the cornstalks. My heart slams, my lungs burn, and the pieces of hay clinging to my sweater pierce like splinters.

I can barely stand the sorrow filling my lungs and throat. I can't help it.

I take one last look back over my shoulder before he disappears in the night: Sawyer's still standing there, just as I left him, staring at his hands, a stiff black silhouette underneath the frigid moonlight. He looks strange in that moment, unlike anyone I've ever known, and I wonder, heart breaking, if I ever even knew him at all.

chapter 27

hayley's diary

I feel like I'm losing my mind. After that terrible night weeks ago, S felt horrible. He told me he understood if I didn't want to see him again. That it had opened his eyes to how fucked up he still was about everything that had happened with his dad as a kid. How his damage made him do these terrible things, things he would never and could never have imagined he was capable of doing.

S said he had hated his father, despised him. And now here he was, still carrying the wounds and poisons of his childhood, letting them turn him into a man he didn't want to be. How the anger seizes him, how he wishes he could purge it.

I had been so touched—these aren't easy things to admit for anyone, and, I know, especially for guys. Toxic masculinity is a hell of a thing, and having to fight the socially enforced rules of what it means to be a man is hard for S.

I mean, no guy wants to admit that deep down, he's sensitive and hurting.

When I thanked S for being honest, and mentioned that his behavior had really scared me, that sent him into a new spiral. "You're the one person in the world I've ever been this honest to," he said, "and the first thing you do when I choose to open up is to knife me right where it hurts the most!"

I felt so guilty. I know he's trying to be a better person. Working on yourself is one of the hardest things anyone can do. It causes you to have to dig in, reopen wounds for close inspection. It's excruciating, like rebreaking bones to make sure they heal properly.

This process has left him vulnerable, so I must be so careful around him. It's not his fault he's emotionally covered in third-degree burns. It takes time to heal, so I've had to be sure that all I do is apply aloe, make sure I don't graze him, accidentally sending him into a howling spiral.

He's a good person working through difficult things that make him act in ways he doesn't want to or mean.

So why am I scared? All the time?

And why, lately, do I feel a sense of foreboding so potent I'm constantly nauseous? I'm worried, so fucking worried, and it feels dangerous to carry that worry. So I try not to think about it, and it's easy to pretend it's not there in front of others.

It's getting harder, though. These days, it's tough to smile at S so convincingly that he can't tell that behind my eyes, I'm screaming. This constant feeling of dread, once like a background noise, a rumble in the earth, is growing louder and louder.

I want to ignore it. But, if my greatest fear proves true, there will come a point where no one can ignore it.

God, thinking about it alone is making my stomach fill with acid.

I won't think about it. Won't even write about it. I can't.

I can't even risk thinking about it. I'm afraid that any kind of thought around it may somehow make the nightmare come true.

chapter 28
ella

S

Ella—I'm so sorry about the other night. My dad's a touchy subject. It's not an excuse, I know. I want to make sure you're okay.

Can we talk, please?

Ella?

I would have opened up to you about the shit my dad put us through eventually. Promise.

Ella, if Hayley didn't tell you, can you please just tell me how you found out?

It's strange being on the other side of this. I think about deleting all of Sawyer's texts but decide it doesn't hurt to have a little hard evidence. If for no other reason than to remind myself of Sawyer's true capabilities.

The other night, I texted Mr. Wilkens as soon as I got home, telling him everything. Even though it was late, he responded immediately. Even over text, his presence was calming. I could hear his warm, gentle voice as I read his words.

W

Thank you for telling me. I know what you went through was terrifying. You're very brave. Get some rest, stay away from him, and we'll make sure you stay safe.

And then last night, after reading Hayley's diary entry, I texted him again, even later. Once more, his replies had been near instantaneous.

W

Don't apologize, Ella. You're not bothering me in the slightest. This is my job. It's what I'm here for. I'm so sorry you're going through this. Come to my office tomorrow after school so we can go over some of this in person.

I've been fending off anxiety attacks all day, but I've finally made it to the end of seventh period. Once more, I'm watching the clock, counting down the minutes until the bell rings. My phone's at least stopped buzzing. Instead of bringing relief, the silence fills me with dread.

Sawyer must know about the diary.

It's my fault if he does. My stupid slip of the tongue.

The bell has hardly finished its first knell when I lunge out of my seat. I scurry to my locker, swap out my books, and half walk, half jog toward the front of the school, where Mr. Wilkens's office is.

I'm nearly there when Sawyer steps around the corner and blocks my path. I gasp so loudly, a few students turn their heads in our direction.

He looks *terrible*, like he hasn't slept since I last saw him in the cornfield. His eyes are bloodshot and red-rimmed, his face pale and shadowed.

When I take a step back, Sawyer's eyes close. "There's that look again. I'd hoped it was a nightmare." He opens his eyes. "What do I have to do to make sure you never look at me like that again?"

My eyes flash to Mr. Wilkens's door. Safety is just steps away, but the idea of talking about Sawyer while he stands just outside the room makes my stomach twist in fear.

Sawyer follows my eyes to Mr. Wilkens's door, and he shoots up, suddenly alert.

"Ella, don't." His eyes darken. "Just talk to me. You *have* to talk to me." He takes a step toward me, and I duck under his arm, dashing down the hallway and outside with the stream of students, never once daring to look behind me.

THIRTY MINUTES LATER, I'm sitting on a bench at Hollow Grove Park, waiting for Mr. Wilkens. It was nice to not have to lie to Mom for once. She seemed glad when I called her to say I was spending the afternoon with the school psychologist.

I've never been to Hollow Grove Park before, but it's beautiful. There are a few paved trails looping through a modest field of tall, browning grass and oak trees beginning to lose their color. Women chat as they push strollers in pairs; people are jogging and walking their dogs.

A pair of college-aged girls jogs by, and slows down to give someone a near-vulgar once-over. When I look up, I'm not surprised to see who they're ogling: Mr. Wilkens. And I can't exactly blame them. He's in a gray Georgia Tech T-shirt and black jogging pants. His usually neatly combed hair is now a ruffled chestnut mess.

He lifts a hand to wave and then frowns at my face.

"What's the matter?" He looks down at himself. "Did I grab my shirt from the dirty pile again? I'm headed out for a run after this, so, you know, two birds, one stone."

I shake my head, feeling my cheeks heat. "No, no. I just haven't seen you in . . . non-teacher clothes. It's, um. Weird."

After I made it outside of the school, I texted Mr. Wilkens to tell him what happened. He suggested we meet here, where Sawyer wouldn't see.

"I had no idea this place existed," I say. "It's so beautiful."

"It's new," he says. "It just opened toward the end of the summer, and it's my go-to place for running now." He gestures for me to follow as he heads toward a forest trail lined with oak and elm trees.

"You know, when I first saw construction vehicles, tractors, and the like around here . . . I got upset. I grew up in Cedarbrook, and I still remember when everything was miles of untamed forest. Just trees and brush as far as the eye can see."

I gesture at the wild berry bushes crowding over the path, the towering trees. "Not tree and brush enough for you?"

He laughs, shaking his head. "No, that's the perfect amount. It's more than that . . . Like, I'm talking more about how I used to feed corn to a family of deer in a little meadow that is now a Chick-fil-A. I once read comic books in an abandoned tree house in the woods that's now a parking lot for a bank. My first kiss was under a thirty-year-old weeping willow."

My heart sinks. "I take it they didn't spare the tree?"

He shakes his head. "A Chipotle," he says sorrowfully. "Which is extra painful because I love their burrito bowls."

I laugh, kicking at a few fallen leaves on the path.

"Change is hard. It's a form of loss, which, as you know, is devastating. It seems silly. The deer, the tree house, a ninth-grade memory . . . but seeing it completely replaced by something else—"

"Made it feel like it never existed at all," I whisper, my stomach squeezing painfully. "It's the worst form of loss . . . when a place, a *person* that's part of who you are, helped make you who you are . . . is just *gone*."

Mr. Wilkens stops me gently, understanding in his eyes.

"Come over here, Ella." He guides me to a thick patch of green, pointing out a vine of honeysuckle. He plucks a yellow flower and places it in my hand. "Right now, there's nothing in the world but this flower. Notice the smell. Is it sweet? Are the petals smooth? Is each petal identical? Is it the color yellow, or is it made up out of a bunch of different colors?"

He stops talking, and I do as he says. I close my eyes, breathe in the scent, sweet as sugar, the thready stamen tickling my nose. I think of its days in the forest shade, the hundreds of tiny insect feet dancing on the velvet petals.

When I open my eyes, I'm the calmest I've felt in days.

"Better, right?" Mr. Wilkens says, watching me.

"Yeah." I nod, looking wonderingly at the petals in my hand.

"Good." He gestures us back to the path to continue our walk. "This park is beautiful. And it wouldn't be here if they hadn't redeveloped the fields where I used to pick blackberries with my grandmother." He looks at me meaningfully. "Sometimes change can give us good things."

We walk for a few minutes in silence, until we're far along the trail, surrounded by trees. The only sounds are of birdsong and the wind playing the leaves like chimes. No one else is around, but unlike the corn maze, where the isolation felt claustrophobic, out here, I feel like I can breathe.

"Ready to talk?" Mr. Wilkens asks, his tone low pressure.

I nod and begin telling him all about the fall festival.

He listens carefully, nodding at all the right parts, shaking his head darkly at others, and even clenches his fist when I mention Sawyer's outburst at the end.

"I'd never seen him like that. I actually still had my doubts. Even up until the very end." I rub the inside of my wrist, where his thumb dug into my muscle when he tugged my arm.

"Did he leave any marks?" Mr. Wilkens spares a quick glance over and touches where I'm rubbing.

"No," I say. *No physical ones.*

"Thank God," he says grimly.

"I'm scared," I confess to my wringing hands. "I thought I knew Sawyer. Hayley thought she knew Sawyer. Even now, I can't believe how wrong we were." My voice breaks. "I've been so stupid."

Mr. Wilkens stops walking and faces me. "Hey. *Hey.* Ella, listen to me. What's happening with Sawyer? Is no one's fault but Sawyer's." He gives my shoulder a reassuring squeeze, leaving my skin tingly and warm.

I try to hide the tremble his words incite in my limbs, how much they're affecting me. I know he's just being a good school psychologist. Maybe going the extra mile because he doesn't want something happening to me on his watch, like it did with Hayley.

But that doesn't stop his words from meaning something to me, from lighting my bones from within like golden sparks.

"Thank you," I whisper, hoping he knows just how much I mean it.

Mr. Wilkens shakes his head, falling back into step along the path. "I'm just telling the truth, Ella. I don't deserve your thanks. I don't deserve anyone's. You think *you* feel stupid? This is literally my job. I failed Hayley, and I'm currently failing you." Even though he's walking ahead, his back to me, I can still hear the grim determination in his next words. "That'll never happen again."

Just then we round a corner and the trees thin out, revealing a single-lane road that runs parallel to the trail.

"This place seems familiar," I muse.

"We might be near an older county park. They've been trying to make little connecting trails between all of them. It'll be nice, having so many paths to choose from."

It's not long before I realize the real reason this stretch of road is familiar. There's a curve in the trail, and when we round the bend, I stop breathing.

"Oh. Shit, Ella. I didn't realize . . ." Mr. Wilkens turns to me, his face pale.

Up ahead is the Silver River Bridge. How had I not noticed the sounds of rushing water before now? The crashing against wet boulders and sharp rocks? The steel railing still isn't repaired, the mangled metal curling and gnarled like claws from where my car had barreled through the barrier into the embankment below.

I'm keeping it together relatively well. After all, I'd never seen the aftermath. I hardly remember this place as it is, and now that I'm seeing it, I'm stunned I survived at all. Even the two weeks I stayed in the hospital no longer seem like overkill. Even after I'd mostly recovered from my broken ribs and concussion, they insisted on keeping me for a week longer. The monitoring felt . . . different after that. Judgmental. Cold. Ironically, I think they were trying to make sure I was doing okay mentally, but they had *made* me feel like I was losing it.

No matter how many times I insisted I'd only had one beer, that I had been sober, that I don't understand how all of this had happened, the doctors would nod, lips in a tight line. No one believed me. And eventually, neither did I. After all, why else would they keep me for so long?

But now, seeing this place, how wrecked it still is nearly half a year later, hearing the power of the rapids below us, I'm surprised they didn't keep me longer.

I'm surprised I'm standing here at all and not wherever Hayley is right now.

It's a thought that nearly buckles my knees. And then an anguished sound escapes me, because there, on the other side of the road, is a large white cross, covered in shiny plastic roses.

I've never seen this, her little memorial. I saw pictures of the enormous pile of flowers and candles on social media, right after it happened, right before I deleted all of my accounts. But this is much more modest, more permanent. This marker will stand here, memorializing what I did to her on that night forever.

She would hate it, I realize. She hated plastic. And plastic flowers above all. She called them "a macabre display flouting nature's creation."

I don't even realize I'm sprinting across the road until I hear Mr. Wilkens calling after me to stop.

I ignore him. I'm hell-bent on getting rid of those disgusting flowers.

So hell-bent, in fact, that I don't notice the pickup truck coming around the curve. At the last second, I leap out of the way, the truck's horn blaring, its brights on, furious and flashing. I lift a hand to shield myself from the punishing light, and then I'm transported to this bridge once more, but six months ago.

"What are you doing?" I cry, flooring the gas.

Hayley's undone her seat belt and twisted in her seat. I need both hands on the wheel, so I can't pull her back down.

"Oh God—he's trying to kill me," she shrieks.

She turns to me, her eyes terrified.

"He's gonna kill us."

"Ella, it's me. It's okay. It's me. Calm down."

I open my eyes to find Mr. Wilkens's white face looking down at me. I'm on the ground and I can't move. It takes me a second to realize Mr. Wilkens has me locked in a tight embrace.

"You were screaming. Thrashing on the ground. Luckily, I got here before you tumbled over the edge." His voice is shaky. Gently, he helps me sit up but doesn't remove his arms from me, as if nervous I'll have another fit.

"I remember what happened that night," I rasp.

Mr. Wilkens's arms tighten around me, his blue eyes flying wide. If possible, he grows even more pale. "You do?"

"Hayley was screaming. Right before we crashed, before I lost control of the car . . . she said—'He's gonna kill us.'"

I'm shaking so hard my teeth are clicking. Mr. Wilkens pulls me tight against him, trying to still the tremble in my limbs.

"Mr. Wilkens . . . who would want to kill us?"

He looks down at me, face ashen. Fear flits across his gaze before it hardens, determined. We both know there's only one answer.

Sawyer.

chapter 29
hayley's diary

My nightmare has come true.

I'm pregnant.

Question: Is there anything more miserable than squatting over a toilet and a generic-brand pregnancy stick in a Walgreens bathroom while trying (and failing) to keep pee from splashing on the mood ring you got from Dave & Buster's?

Answer: Yes, yes, there is. There is squatting over a toilet, over a Walgreens-brand pregnancy stick and soaking your mood ring in pee, when you have to turn suddenly and puke in said toilet.

As my head hung over the toilet, I looked over at the test gripped in my fist and saw that my mood ring had turned blue. It's a good thing no one else was in there to hear my unhinged laughter, the way it all dissolved into sobs when the second pink line appeared.

I didn't have much money, but I used it all to get more tests, all different brands. The old man at the counter, Cleave, certainly recognized me this second go-around. He eyed each test as he scanned them with careful, shaking fingers. I could feel his judgment, and it turned my blood to lava. I would have asked for a pack of Marlboros if I'd had the money left over, grabbed a pack of Bud Light if I'd had a fake ID, just to see the scandalized look on his face.

When he finally met my eyes, all the wind went out of my sails.

"Darlin'," he said. "Are you all right?"

"No," I said, lifting my chin. "Not even remotely."

It occurred to me in that moment that Cleave, quite possibly, knew me better than any other human being on this entire planet.

He nodded his ancient head gravely. "That's what I thought."

After hitting a few buttons and scanning a badge he pulled from a drawer, Cleave read me my total.

"That'll be a dollar fifty."

"What?" I snapped. It was supposed to be at least forty times that amount.

"One dollar and fifty cents, darlin'. What're they gonna do?" He shrugged. "Fire me? I'm eighty-two."

Oh, Cleave.

I burst into tears. I'd never felt so overwhelmed with gratitude and love, the kind act such sharp relief from the rest of my life. I was split between asking if he'd adopt me or run away with me. He did let me reach over the counter to hug him before shooing me away, not keen on drawing too much attention from a manager.

And thirty minutes later, voilà: five different tests confirming the same thing.

My doom. My downfall. My pregnancy.

Why don't I sound scared? Because I'm so past the point of scared, I've reached a new threshold: a numb, liminal stage where I'm on the absolute brink of losing my mind.

I have this memory of Dad chasing me around the house when I was four years old. I'd screech and laugh as he'd pretend to be a dinosaur, hot on my tail. My heart would pound, and as he got closer and closer, the mirth turned to fear. Terror. And when I was certain I would be caught, I'd fall to the ground, roll in a tight ball. "Don't eat me, don't eat me!" I'd squeal, actually terrified. And while I lay there, I'd go numb, curling tighter and tighter.

Sometimes that's what this feels like. But I know I've got to fight through this. I need a plan. Because there's no scenario where things just play their course and everything is even remotely okay.

Something very, very *bad is going to happen.*

Can I be honest? Until recently, I hadn't realized just how much danger I am in.

It's like those old, vintage Bugs Bunny cartoons. You know, the ones where he thinks he's getting inside a relaxing, hot bathtub in the middle of the forest? It feels so good, the water. He doesn't notice the carrots, the chopped onion being added. And then, my God, mmm-mmm, *what smells so delicious?* Wabbit stew, *says Elmer Fudd. And for a moment, Bugs Bunny thinks,* Well, that sounds mighty good. *But then, of course, Bugs Bunny realizes what's happening and screams.*

It happened so slowly to me; I didn't realize the mouthwatering smell was my own charred flesh. I didn't realize that when S, the light of my life, the guy I adored, told me he loved me, his love meant control, his love meant mine. *And what do I do when I feel like I added the carrots and onions to my own broth? When I once* liked *how protected he made me feel? How a part of me found the idea delicious, that someone could covet me so much they never wanted to let me go, never wanted to let anyone so much as look at me?*

Did I bring this on myself?

Regardless, it's all over. No more balancing on a Hattori Hanzo sword. My being pregnant is going to tip that blade over, and that sword's so undeniably sharp, I'm getting sliced either way.

One route I can see: S loves *me being pregnant. It'll be insurmountable proof that I'm his—literally inside and out. He'll have his hand on my belly when he's driving, when I'm filling my cup with water at the kitchen sink, while I pump gas in my car. He'll put himself in charge of everything about my life (which, what's even left?): what I eat, which bottled water I'm allowed to drink, what positions I should sleep in . . . Why, he would only be doing what's best for me and the baby.*

He'll use the pregnancy as a way to own me, irrefutably. Body and soul.

And that would just be the pregnancy. What would happen after I had the baby? Imagine a child raised by S. Two futures robbed, just like that.

Another route: S doesn't like sharing.

Not even with his own baby. I could see him being wildly jealous at the idea that anything could justifiably take precedence over him in my life. Oh, how torn he'd be! On one hand, it's his progeny, his DNA, and on the other, he'd have no choice but to be dethroned as the most important person in my life.

There's only one choice for me—and it's a choice I know he'd never allow.

I want an abortion. It's the only thing I want right now.

Sure, I want kids someday. But not his. *And not now. Not when I'm seventeen. Not when I've decided I want to study abroad in Germany, live in at least three different countries before I turn twenty-five. Not when I want the freedom to spend twenty-four hours straight on Archive of Our Own if I want, whenever I want. Not when I'm too scared to even own a goldfish.*

I can't have a baby right now. For a million reasons. It would end my life. It wouldn't be fair to the child.

And it wouldn't be fair to me.

I won't have a baby. I won't have his *baby.*

But how?

Even if S weren't ruling every moment of my life, having an abortion now feels impossible. I'm broke, and is there even somewhere in this whole state *I can go? And if I Google . . . will S find my search history? My hands are actually shaking from terror at the very thought of him finding out that I want one.*

There's no way that he won't blame me for all this. Even though he's the one who doesn't like wearing condoms and didn't like how moody I got on birth control.

The walls are closing in. I feel like I'm slowly suffocating.

Oh God. What do I do?

What the fuck *am I going to do?*

chapter 30
ella

I feel bad that Seema's here in my bedroom wasting her Friday night on me. We're supposed to be stuffing kettle corn in our mouths, nearly finished with *Scream*, prepping for *Scream II*, but with as many times as Seema's had to pause the movie on my laptop so I can get up to go cry in the bathroom or go back thirty seconds because I was completely zoned out, the only people who've died so far are Drew Barrymore's character and her boyfriend.

Seema's been very patient so far, sitting cross-legged at the foot of my bed, but I can tell it's starting to frustrate her. I feel terrible. It's supposed to be a celebratory Friday night. Seema submitted her application to UGA before the early action deadline, and she'd asked me earlier this week if I wanted to celebrate with a horror movie marathon and sleepover. At the time, I was actually excited. It occurred to me later that this would be my first "friend" hangout since Hayley. The thought was bittersweet.

But, you see, that was before I'd read Hayley's most recent journal entry. I was an idiot and read it before Seema came over, and now I'm a mess.

I excuse myself to go to the bathroom once more. I want to be alone for a few precious moments while I try to grapple with everything I've learned.

Hayley was *pregnant*. She was pregnant, had nowhere else to turn . . . and didn't tell me. Why, oh, *why* didn't she tell me?

But then there's the other realization. A darker one.

Is her pregnancy the thing that did it? That pushed Sawyer to the edge? The reason he ran us off the road?

I need to figure out what else happened that night. I need to remember more.

If I can remember, then maybe I'll have evidence that will allow us to bring justice to Sawyer. To avenge Hayley.

Tears start to well up in my throat once more. God, I'm so sick of crying.

But probably not as sick as Seema is of me crying.

When I excused myself to go to the bathroom just now, I caught Seema pinching the bridge of her nose in frustration.

I don't blame her.

When I walk back in my room, my laptop is shut, and Seema's standing in the middle of my bedroom, arms folded.

"Ella," she says, "do you not want to hang out?" She falters, her face showing an uncertainty I've never seen. "Do you not want me here?"

"God, Seema, that's not it at all! Honestly, I don't know what I'd do without you. Now and for the past few months." I sink to the bed with a deep sigh. "You've been a lifesaver."

"All right . . ." Seema sinks into my desk chair, brows

furrowed. "Then what's up? You haven't had your eyes on the movie *once*; I threw popcorn at you twice and you didn't flinch. In fact, it's still in your hair."

I reach up and, sure enough, pull two kernels of kettle corn off the top of my head. Midna trots into the room, hopping on my desk, giving Seema a raspy meow. Seema's eyes soften, and she leans forward to press her forehead to Midna's.

"Hey, sweet girl," she murmurs. "They giving you enough tuna? You call me if they don't. I'll have words with the boss." Midna purrs louder, curling up on the desk so she can press her head against Seema.

"Ella," Seema continues, softer now. "Clearly something's up. Talk to me, tell me what it is. If you don't want to, that's fine. But then if we go back to watching movies and having a fun horror-movie sleepover, we're doing *that*. Nothing else. No staring at your phone or sneaking away to cry. If you have to do that, I get it. But then I'm going to go."

Seema's eyes are open, vulnerable. She's scratching Midna's head, ducking to kiss between her ears once or twice. Her kindness, maturity, and tenderness break me open.

I swallow hard.

"Seema," I say. "If I tell you something . . . will you promise to keep it between us?"

Seema rolls her eyes at me and glances at Midna. "You hear this? It's like she doesn't know me at all. She thinks I'm some kind of narc?" She turns to me, lifts a dark, beautiful brow. "I'm all ears and no lips, Ella."

So I tell her.

I start off by telling her the details about Sawyer, about how he started off as a dream guy. She nods, listening intently.

"He even seemed incredible at the beginning of Hayley's diary when they first got together—"

"Hold up," she says. "What are you talking about, Hayley's diary?"

"Er—well, I know it's not great. I didn't want Phoebe or anyone else to read it, so I took it to keep it safe."

"Uh-huh." Seema cocks her head. "And how's that going?"

I hold up my hands in protest. "Hey, I didn't want to. But I had to, okay? You don't know what it's been like. I'm scraping the barrel here, trying to remember as much about her as I can. And it's a good thing that I've read her diary, because I've learned some important information, and maybe it will help me remember what happened the night of the—"

"Stop." Seema's voice is as cold as I've ever heard it. "Did you just tell me it's a good thing that you're reading someone's diary?"

I clear my throat. "I— No, Seema, that's not what I was saying. It's . . . These circumstances are different . . ."

"Really? Enlighten me. How do you justify opening someone's diary like it's a goddamn romance novel and just going for it?" Seema folds her arms. Midna looks between the two of us and hops off the desk, scurrying to hide in the closet.

"Okay, *wow*, it wasn't like that at all." My blood's starting to run hot. She's missing the point. "First of all, you have no idea what it's like. One day, your best friend in the world, in some ways, your *only* friend, is just suddenly *gone*. And you'd give anything for just a little—"

"I do, actually."

I blink rapidly. "What?"

"I do know what that's like. In fact, I don't think *you* know what it's like. You don't know what it's like to move to a new place when you're eight. Knowing *no one*. Being the only Indian girl in a small town in Georgia. And then finally meeting a girl you can connect with, who knows sort of what it's like to be the odd one out, and becoming best friends with her. And you think, *Okay, I'm finally not alone.* Your best friend in the world, as you like to say. And then, one day, *poof,* gone."

Seema stands, her eyes shining. "Except it's worse, Ella. Way worse. Because your best friend isn't taken from you by some sheer, horrible act of God. She *chose* to be gone. She wanted it."

I open my mouth to say something, *anything.* Nothing comes out. Seema tilts her head.

"Yeah, Ella. All those things I just said? Didn't have anyone to talk to about it. So I wrote it down. In my, you guessed it, diary. Which, ten-year-old me thought, thank God no one was gonna see this shit, this private agony." Seema's voice hitches. "Joke's on me, right? But it's okay, because Dev was stupid, he got booed away, I got a puppy, and everybody clapped, right? I left out the rest of the story. The part where I was so humiliated I couldn't stop crying for weeks. My family didn't know how to talk to me, so they just . . . didn't. For months, I talked more to the dog than my dad." Her jaw clenches. "And *you* don't think any of it's a big deal."

I clutch my stomach, nauseated from guilt, shame, and, confusingly, anger.

"Seema," I say, "if I could take it back, I would. I wish I'd stayed friends with you. I'm so sorry that happened. But it's not like that . . . I'm not reading her diary for fun, okay?"

"Unbelievable." Seema shakes her head in disgust. "Read the room, Ella. I'm not your audience if you're looking for someone to support your secret diary book club. Not really into the whole violating-trust-and-privacy thing. I know what it means to be an *actual* good friend."

My anger boils over. "Jesus Christ, Seema, I was ten years old. I was a kid. A *child*. Like, how many times do I have to apologize? I'm sorry, I'm sorry, *I'm sorry*. Okay? This isn't even about you! This is about me trying to learn more about that night, the night of Scott's party, and Hayley's diary is my only option—"

"Wow." It's the quiet of Seema's voice that shocks me into silence. "Ella," she says, "even after all these years, you don't see me. I was at Scott's party that night."

That stops me short. "I— That's . . . Seema, obviously I wouldn't *know* that. I don't remember anything—"

"So you've said. But did it ever occur to you to ask me about it? Talk to me? What's Seema good for, hm? Tampons and pep talks. But when it comes to important shit, like getting back your memories, like remembering the night of your life-altering accident? Your 'only option' is a dead girl's diary."

I press my hands to my head. "Seema, that's not even close to true. But I seriously can't deal with this right now—"

"Of course you can't. Because it's all about you. You know, you were a *shit* friend then, and you're a *shit* friend now!"

"*Ugh*, I get it, I'm the worst friend in the world—"

"The *planet*—"

"So then *why are you still here*?"

"Good question!"

We're both screaming at each other. Hot, angry tears are leaking down my cheeks. Seema's face is blotchy, her eyes wet. She's gathering her things violently, slamming her bag into my desk, my drawers, my table lamp wobbling dangerously.

She puts her hand on the bedroom doorknob, and I thrust out a hand toward her.

"Seema, wait."

She turns around, eyes wary. Distantly, I know it's shitty, to ask this of her while we're fighting, while she's crying. But I'm crying and hurt too. And there are bigger things at stake, things I need to know.

"What . . . do you remember? From the night of Scott's party?"

Seema shakes her head in disbelief, laughing bitterly under her breath. "Man. Even when she's dead, she's got me beat." She closes her eyes. When she opens them, they're blank. Cold. "You and Hayley didn't really hang out together. I didn't talk to either of you, so I don't know if you were fighting. I just know that Hayley kept taking shots. She seemed sort of . . . I don't know. On edge, I guess. She disappeared upstairs for a little bit. I thought she was banging Sawyer, but when she came down the stairs, it was Scott following her—"

"Wait a minute. *Scott?*"

"Ella, let me just get this out so I can go home. Yeah, Scott. He was super drunk. But it was weird. I don't know the dick, but I've never seen him upset like that. It was like . . . he kept trying to talk to Hayley, but she kept brushing him off." She shrugs. "And that's it."

"Wait—that's *it*? Did—"

"I'm done, Ella." She looks at me somberly. "Really done. I'm leaving. Don't call, don't text. Done." Her lip wobbles. "Goodbye."

Mom finds me sobbing in bed. "It's nothing, Mom." I curl onto the mattress, tuck my knees into my chest. "I think I'd like to just go to sleep now."

"Ella," she says, sitting next to me, "Ella, what's going on? You finally bring a friend home for the first time in months . . . I guess it didn't go well?" I feel her touch my hair, and it's a gesture so unbelievably tender from her, especially after the distance between us, that for a moment I'm tempted to spill everything.

But I can't. I've already shown her I'm not the perfect daughter they thought I was. The daughter they wanted. I can't stand making it worse. Telling Mom everything would also mean telling her that I've been sneaking off with Sawyer, lying to her, reading Hayley's diary. I can't take seeing the look in her eyes as I reveal just how awful their daughter *really* is.

"It's just stupid boy stuff, Mom," I say finally. Midna appears next to me on the bed, headbutting my cheek.

"Midna's worried about you," Mom says.

"She just wants me to feed her." I press my face into the bedspread, muffling my words.

She clears her throat. "Want to come down and watch a movie with Dad, Jess, and me? I could use your vote. Otherwise, it'll be *Godzilla* again, and I am very sick of Mothra."

"It's true." Jess is leaning against the door frame, arms crossed. "I'm obsessed with Mothra's tiny twins. Can't say no to their songs. But." She shoots me a small smirk. "If you come down, I'll consider the first *Lord of the Rings*."

Mom's eyes fill with fear. "Please, no extended edition. I beg of you."

I snort a wet laugh. Tempting. But I meant it when I said I just wanted to go to bed. I'm suddenly so very exhausted.

"Rain check for tomorrow. That okay?"

"All right, Ella." Mom gets up. "Coming, Midna?" Midna just yawns and curls up against me. Mom smiles softly before exiting. Jess lingers a moment before finally murmuring a quiet "Night, Els," and shutting the door.

I can't stop thinking of everything Seema said.

I wish I could say she was being harsh, cruel.

But maybe she's right. Maybe I'm a terrible friend. Thinking about it is giving me a headache. I turn my face so that I'm pressed against

Midna's soft, warm side. She purrs, the most soothing sound in the world, and I'm asleep in no time.

I THINK I hear Midna growl. At least, that's the sound I think woke me up. But Midna never growls. I blink sleepily, my jaws cracking from a wide yawn.

Midna's crouched next to my head, her tail flicking back and forth.

"Oh, Midna, for the last time, it's not a bug." I flop on my back with a groan. There's a scuff on the wall that she has been trying to catch for *years*, certain it's a moth.

A sudden slam to my right has me diving under my covers, gasping. When I peek my head out, I realize it's the wooden shutters of my window crashing against each other in the wind.

I sigh in relief. It was just the wind—

But then I freeze. I didn't leave that window open.

Horrible dread fills me. Why is that window open?

Midna growls again.

And then she's hissing.

With a burst of adrenaline, I throw off my covers and sit up. There, at the foot of my bed, where Midna's currently spitting, is a tall, dark figure looming over the edge of my mattress. He makes a sudden move, arms outstretched, but when I scream, he shrinks back.

And I scream and scream, so loud I feel my throat tear.

I trip as I go for the light. There's crashing in my room, a frantic scrambling. My parents burst into the room just as I get the light on, but the figure is already gone.

"Ella, Ella, what the—"

"Call nine-one-one," I say, voice quaking. I point at my open window, the now-ripped curtain still fluttering. "Someone broke into my room. I woke up and they were standing over my bed."

My dad swears and pulls out his phone, and my mom makes the sign of the cross. I can see Jess hunched in the hall, her eyes wide as baseballs. And now I see the state of my room. It's torn apart. Clothes are thrown from my closet, and every drawer I have is open.

"I thought this was a safe town. I thought that only happened in big cities." My mom is shaking, her hand on her mouth.

But this wasn't just people. This was someone looking for something.

Someone who has used that very same window to get into this room before.

And that's what I tell the police when they arrive ten minutes later.

"I know who broke in," I say. "It was Sawyer. It was Sawyer Hawkins."

chapter 31
sawyer

They've been letting me sweat it out in this windowless room for about two or three hours now by the time the door opens.

A stout man in his fifties wearing the Band-Aid-colored sheriff's uniform struts into the interrogation room. He's got thick glasses and a handlebar mustache, and looks like he gets his styling tips from a shitty seventies porno flick. I bite back the urge to tell him so.

"Whew," he says, taking off his wide-billed sheriff's hat and fanning himself with flair. "It's hotter than Satan's house cat in here! You all right, there, son?"

For an answer, I stare at him. Silent, unblinking, not bothering to wipe at the rivulets of perspiration flooding down my neck, the sides of my face.

My silence doesn't faze him in the slightest.

He runs a hand through the entire length of his greasy dirty-blond hair. "You want a Coke? Just sit tight."

The door slams as he pops back out, and I take a deep breath.

Shit. *Shit.*

I'd just gotten home from a long shift at the restaurant when the banging started on our front door. Mom had opened it to find three cops crowding the entry. I knew how this could go. If I refused to submit to their questioning, they'd do whatever they could to get a warrant. Wouldn't take much. I'd seen it enough times with my dad when I was younger, before Mom managed to get us out, move us to Cedarbrook.

And then there's the fact that Ella, jewel of the community, gave my name to the cops.

My saving grace is they've got nothing on me. Nothing concrete.

So I told them I'd go, let them ask me whatever they wanted. I don't have to answer shit. It'll buy me time, keep me out of cuffs until I can figure a way out of this. So I stepped around Mom, shushed her protests, her insistence that I would *never* do anything like what they were accusing me of. I told her it was fine, I'd just go, clear the whole thing up.

Now I close my eyes, clench my jaw so hard it pops. That look on her face. Red and blue lights swirling in the dark horror of her eyes. Like for a second, she wasn't sure who was standing in front of her: her son or a stranger.

We'd both apologized to each other after the other night. But it had been quick, stilted. I was coming in from school and she was leaving for work. It was a cursory hug in the hall, her halfway out the door. The tension's still there. Callan barely wants to be in the same room as me.

I have the urge to text Ella, but there's no good outcome of that at this point. I just need to play it cool, keep my mouth shut and see what exactly these idiots know and, hopefully, what they don't.

The door opens and the officer from before comes in, arms laden with cans of Coca-Cola, Sprite, and bottles of water.

"That damn vending machine's the most ornery thing in this building," he grumbles. The door swings shut, and he spills the drinks onto the steel table before me. "And lemme tell you, since that's including the chief, that's sure saying something."

I stop a Coke can from rolling off the table as he plops down in a seat beside me, pulling a handkerchief out of his pocket and wiping his brow. He waves at the array of cans and bottles, then opens one for himself.

"Don't be shy, choose whichever. My doc wouldn't take too kindly to me having sugar. A1c and all that. I tell you what, the better something tastes, the angrier my doc gets."

My throat is parched, but I know how this works. He plies me with soda, he convinces me he'll be the dad I never had, and next thing I know I'm signing a confession saying I'm the Zodiac Killer. Doesn't matter if I never so much as got a speeding ticket. That piece of paper would put me away for life.

Or worse.

I stare at him steadily, the only sound in the room the tiny pops of carbonation in the open can. He eyes me for a moment before smiling softly and offering his hand, palm up. "I'm Rick, by the way."

I don't move a muscle.

When I don't take his hand, Rick leans back, his chair creaking. "You know, you look young enough to go to North Davis." He scratches his chin. "They've got a damn fine football team. *Damn* fine. Went there myself. Won't tell you what year, though. Just saying it out loud'll make me sadder'n hell." He sighs. "Where does the time go?"

Rick checks his watch, drums a little beat on the table, and stands up with a groan. "Christ Almighty." He winces, pressing a hand on his back. "I'mma take a leak, son. You hungry? Need a snack? Just let me know."

He leaves without waiting for my answer. I take a huge exhale when he steps out, reaching for a bottle of water. I know that there's definitely someone watching me through the two-way mirror, but I don't care. I guzzle down the entire bottle before he can get back.

My heart is hammering. Despite appearances, it was tough not answering Rick. His friendly chatter, his seemingly kind offers to help—it's a trap.

It's all a trap. Because I know exactly how precarious my situation is, and I know exactly who Officer Rick is: Mr. Wilkens's uncle. For the first time, I'm grateful for small-town life, that everyone-knows-each-other perk. My fingers twitch near my pocket. *God*, I want to text Ella. But like I said. I need to figure out how much they know first.

Hours go by. It's hard to tell how many. I'm starting to sway in my seat, my eyes getting heavy. I resist the urge to fidget, to run my finger along the scar on my palm, to do anything that makes them look at me the wrong way. Because this is part of it. The trap. Can't let them do it.

Finally, Rick comes back into the room. He looks like he may have caught a short nap somewhere in the station, looking as bright-eyed as ever. He smiles at me, and in his arms, he's carrying a file of papers and a small book.

I sit up straight, cracking my knuckles.

Here we go.

"Sorry to keep you waiting, Sawyer. Sawyer. Good name, good name. I always liked Tom Sawyer more than Huckleberry Finn myself. Course, it helps my high school sweetheart was named Becky."

Rick slaps the pile onto the table, sliding into the seat across from me this time.

"Sawyer Hawkins . . ." He pushes his glasses up his nose and flips through the folder. I stretch my neck but can't see anything in the file. "Now, hear tell you're quite popular with the ladies. You reckon that's true?"

I must make a face because he laughs. "Aw, don't be so modest, son. Ain't no surprise to me. Tall, dark, mysterious. Very, *very* mysterious, if I say so myself. Tell me. Is it true you've been hanging around lately with a little gal named Ella Graham?"

Keep. Your mouth. Shut.

Officer Rick licks his fingers and turns a page in the folder. "That was more of a rhetorical question, son. Just testin' you, is all. I won't bore you with details, but what I think you'll find interesting is that someone broke into Miss Ella's bedroom while she was sleeping. And as soon as I got there, she ran up to me, and before even so much as a 'howdy-do,' she told me that it was you, Sawyer Hawkins, that had broken into her room. Now what do you think about that?"

My entire body is clenched, trembling with the strain. Officer Rick leans in, his hazel eyes narrowing.

"You all right, there, Sawyer? You look so angry that you're fixin' to bust. Got a vein popping out of your neck and everything. Why, some might even say you look downright *murderous*."

I close my eyes so I'm no longer tempted to slug him across the jaw. I feel like a tiger in a cage, being poked and prodded. First with blunt sticks and now with needle-pointed pitchforks. I need to prepare for the lit torches, for sharpened swords, for far more painful things. Because no matter what, I cannot snap.

I know what happens to the tiger that snaps.

Officer Rick leans back and sighs, taking off his hat and scratching his head. "Course I don't blame you for being angry. We didn't find any evidence in her room that you were there tonight." He shrugs. "Course, you don't got an alibi. 'Drivin' around to clear your mind after work'? Well, just between you and me, that sounds mighty suspicious, son. But that don't mean you were there tonight.

"It ain't right, how they punish us guys for nothing. You look at her friend too long, you don't text her back fast enough, you don't thank her enough for that shitty meal she made out of a damn box . . . and they take that as a sign to hit the nuclear option! After all we do for them!" He shakes his head. "You've got every right to be angry, Sawyer. There you was in the kitchen with your poor, tired momma, and now you've got to come all the way down here on your Friday night because Ella's got it in her head to sic the police on you."

I focus on the way he says "police." Like it's two words, slapping that first syllable hard. *Poh-leese.* It keeps me from opening my mouth, saying something really stupid.

Officer Rick's eyes are hazel ice picks, chipping away at my veneer. But he's not gonna get me to crack. He won't.

He *can't.*

When I remain silent, he nods, and I sense he's a little impressed.

"Yeah, you're right . . . maybe that ain't it. Ella wouldn't do that, would she?" He scratches his chin. "She did say something mighty interesting. Said you was looking for something. Some kinda . . . book or some other?"

My ears prick up, my heart pounding. This does not sound good. But so far, I've given them nothing. It'll all be for nothing if I break now.

Officer Rick's eyes narrow, scanning me like laser beams. But I just give him my best impression of a stone statue. After a beat, he goes on. "I'll be honest, son. Didn't take you much for a reader, which is why it didn't make sense that you'd climb into a second-story window for a book . . . or maybe it's not a book. A diary?"

My heart stops.

He holds up a black clothbound book. “This diary?”

It takes everything in me not to explode from my chair, to flee. I hadn’t been sure . . . but now that Officer Rick’s waving it in my face, it feels like the walls are closing in.

I can’t think of all the implications right now. I need to focus on maintaining the best poker face of my entire life.

“You know what, I’ve been grilling you pretty hard, Sawyer. And I’ll admit, you’re a hell of a tough nut to crack. But I’m tired. Let’s take a break. My dad used to read me bedtime stories. Your dad ever do that?”

Ha.

“Didn’t think so. Well, I’ll read to you now, son. Let’s have a little bit of story time, shall we?” Officer Rick looks positively jaunty as he licks his index finger and opens the diary. “Oh, and since you didn’t ask, I’m gonna assume that you already know that this here ain’t Ella’s diary. It’s Hayley’s. And she’s got some mighty interesting things to say about you in here.”

I stop breathing. Do long division in my head. Anything to keep my face from mirroring the thunder that’s gathering in my chest.

“Let’s see . . . Oh, here’s one. ‘S grabbed his cup and hurled it against the wall, shattered glass raining down everywhere.’ That’s not great . . . but, eh, that’s not terribly interesting either. I mean, who hasn’t thrown the good silver during a family meal once or twice?”

I’m digging my thumbnail into my scar hard enough to break skin. I try not to blink.

“Ooh, this one’s juicier. ‘He reared back his arm and backhanded me across the face so hard, my head slammed into the window.’”

Unspeakable fury and fear are crashing into my body in mountain-tall waves. I swallow against the roiling in my gut and fight the urge to squeeze my eyes shut.

Rick's eyes rake over my face, a muscle ticking in his jaw. I'm starting to piss him off. I cling to his frustration, his failure.

"Hard to hear, ain't it?" His voice is quiet. "Makes a grown man want to cry, don't it? Well, don't worry, I only got just one more for you . . . ah, here. Last entry in the entire book." He turns a page. "'This is it. Shit, is this really the only way? Doesn't matter. I've run out of time, and I can't think of another way to keep me and everyone I love safe. The hardest part will be keeping it from S. Easier said than done these days. But I've got no option. And I cannot let him find out. It's a matter of life and death.'"

Officer Rick gives a performative shiver. "That little ex of yours sure had a way with words. I mean, sure, she warn't terribly consistent in her entries, and it's a helluva cliff-hanger. Not too many people'll be pleased about that. But it still paints quite the picture, don't it?"

I fight the urge to snarl at him. Any opening of my mouth dooms me. There's no good outcome. As of right now, all they have is a book where Hayley talked about an "S" and the allegations of a frightened teenage girl in the middle of the night. They've got nothing. They can't hold me.

And as I look Officer Rick dead in the eye, I realize: He knows that.

He drops the sweet-Southern-cop act, and his face contorts with rage. *There's the bastard.* He leans forward, his splotchy face inches from mine.

"You little piece of trash," he snarls, seizing my shirt.

And this last little spit of anger nearly breaks me. I'm about to open my mouth when the door swings open.

"Maybe take a break, Rick." A tired-looking officer leans against the door, hand on the knob.

Rick doesn't break eye contact with me. He gives me a little shake by my collar. "I ain't done."

Another officer fills the door. Square-faced and stern.

"Rick, you take a walk." I feel the timbre of his voice in my chest.

With a violent swear, Rick drops me. He marches out of the room, the door slams, and I'm suddenly by myself.

I take a huge breath. I'm dizzy from exhaustion and hours of adrenaline rippling in my muscles. My palms feel wet, and I look down and see amongst the pools of sweat there are blood-dappled half-moon crescents from where my nails dug into my skin. It nearly killed me, but I kept it together. On the outside, anyway.

Inside, I'm still screaming.

But at least I know I'm good. For now. I whip out my phone and type out a text to Ella.

S

Ella. I'm not mad. I just need to know where you are. Please. Tell me where you are.

It's a huge Hail Mary, hoping Ella will answer me for the first time in days. But I just need to make sure she's at home with her parents. Not anywhere else. Not *with* anyone else.

The thought fills me with such sudden anger I thump my fist on the table. My eyes shoot to the two-way mirror, the door, the camera's blinking red light in the corner of the room. *Come on, Sawyer. Keep it together. You're almost free.*

Then I can just check on Ella myself.

I still haven't gotten a text back when Officer Rick, flanked by two other cops, comes back into the room. *Finally,* I think.

But then I see Officer Rick's face.

He looks smug. Really smug.

My phone buzzes, and I can't help but pull it out to check if it's Ella replying. My heart leaps when I see that it's Ella, but I only catch a glimpse of the text, the words fine and Mr. W, before my phone is yanked from my hand.

"What the hell?" I burst out.

"Emergency warrant, son." Officer Rick unfurls an official-looking document in front of my nose. "Means we can take it, go through it. You play ball real well, Sawyer. But I really can't stomach having girl-beaters walking free in this city, and the judge just so happens to agree with me."

I seethe as he scrolls through my messages.

"Damn, son. I leave the room for ten minutes and you're already harassing Ella? And, hell, looks like you've been harassing her for a few days! Now, don't you know when a woman don't answer, she ain't interested?"

"Am I under arrest?" I ask, my heart beating like I'm running a marathon.

There's a thunderous silence.

"I would have thought that'd been obvious. Yes. Yes, you're under arrest," says Officer Rick.

"Then I get a phone call," I growl.

There's a beat. "He isn't even done reading your—" begins one of the other officers.

"Phone call!" I demand. "By law I get a phone call!"

There's another fraught silence. Then finally, "Goddammit, I'll read him his rights along the way. Take the little shit to get his phone call."

There may be a way out of this yet.

chapter 32
ella

I hardly notice morning sneak up on me. My parents didn't sleep either, pacing the living room as I sat motionless on the couch, knees tucked up into my chest, staring vacantly at our cold stone fireplace. "Why did you think it was Sawyer? What did you mean he'd come through that window before? Please, Ella, talk to us."

Their voices barely reached me through the fog pressing at me from all sides. He'd actually been in my room. That tall, skulking shadow. I'd never felt so scared in my life. But after the police had left, the weight of my accusation felt like a stone in my stomach.

It was one thing to go to Mr. Wilkens with my fears, to tell him my theories about Sawyer. It was another thing entirely to have handcuffs clapped on his wrists. Should I have asked questions first? Given him a chance to explain himself? I can barely handle picturing it: the police knocking on his door, adding yet one more misery to his mother's life, to Callan's.

Sawyer's under arrest, and it should be relief, but somehow, it's not. I remember my dad once saying, after his own father had spent half a year in hospice, unable to walk, speak, or see, that he couldn't wait for my grandfather to die, how the agony of his loss would not be greater than the agony of his father's suffering, the agony of having to bear witness to it all.

I'm safe now. I know it. I can feel the way I carry that knowledge in the looseness in my shoulders, how deep my lungs can now pull, no longer squeezed with constant fear. The relief is of a tornado survived, but accompanied by the grim resolution of staring at the splintered home you thought you'd grow old in.

"Hey." A small hand touches my shoulder. Jess. "I sent Mom and Dad to the kitchen to take a lap. You good?"

I reach for her hand, squeezing it hard.

"Thanks, Jess. I owe you one." I swallow down the trembling in my voice.

She shrugs, studying her toes as she curls them in the carpet. "I gave Midna extra tuna, by the way. She earned it."

"Give her as much as she wants," I say thickly.

Jess's smile catches the peach light of the dawning sun. It's the first moment that I think maybe it's all going to be okay.

But there's still a terrible restlessness inside my chest. The idea of staying cooped up in this house, this house where Sawyer made me feel things I never had before, where Seema had declared our friendship over, where Sawyer invaded my room, prowling in the dark . . . let's just say I need to get the hell out of here.

Jess has been watching me carefully. "Mom and Dad will never let you leave."

"What? Why do you say that?"

"You've got that look on your face—the one you had when you had mono and couldn't leave the house for weeks." She smiles at her feet. "It's actually nice to see it. The stir-crazy face."

"Why?"

"Well. You spent the entire summer in bed. Didn't get stir-crazy once. I worried . . . I was afraid that you'd be that sad forever."

I take her hand. "I know I've been a mess. And I'm sorry. You're the best sister."

Jess nods. "I know. Because I'm gonna cover for you. Go on your walk, do what you need to do. I'll tell them that you need to sleep or something, that you're locked in your room. I'll make sure they don't go in. Take as long as you need."

"Jess . . ." I can barely talk, I'm so touched. "I seriously don't deserve you."

She gives me a soft smile. "I know. But what are sisters for?" I'm hit with the staggering realization of just how much Jess has done for me since Hayley died. And, honestly, even before. Jess has always been here, my secret safe harbor. My heart aches from gratitude and love.

I give Jess a huge hug, grab my purse and phone, and sneak out the back door.

That's how I find myself walking aimlessly around Cedarbrook on a clear, cool October morning. The first few hours feel good. Moving my body. Feeling like I'm going somewhere, that I'm leaving all the bad shit behind.

But then, after a while, I start to feel overwhelmed again. Alone. Scared. And not only that: I'm lost. I'm in a neighborhood where none of the houses look familiar. I stop walking, weighing my options.

I could call Mom and Dad, send them my location, have them come get me. But I'm not ready to go home. Not even a little. Besides, I'd be grounded for a million years, and worse, so would Jess for helping me.

And then it hits me. I pull up Mr. Wilkens's number in my phone and hit the call button. I feel a pang of uncertainty. It's a Saturday morning. His off day. Maybe I shouldn't . . .

Mr. Wilkens picks up my call immediately. "Ella? Are you all right?" A wave of warm relief falls over me.

I tell him everything: about Sawyer breaking in, about what I'd read in the diary. I tell him that I don't want to go home yet, how he's the only one who knows everything, who understands what I'm going through.

"If you need a safe space," he says, "you can come to my house for a few hours, until you're ready to go home."

"Please," I say, and text him my location, overwhelmed with relief.

While I'm waiting for Mr. Wilkens, I feel a buzz in my pocket. I pull out my phone and stop breathing when I see a text from Sawyer.

S

Ella. I'm not mad. I just need to know where you are. Please. Tell me where you are.

I chew on my chapped lip, pacing on the sidewalk. Not mad? I can't believe that Sawyer is so far gone. He still thinks he's taking care of me, watching over me. I move my thumb to delete the text, to block his number, but I pause.

For my own closure, I want to send him one last text. I need to say goodbye.

E

I'm fine. Safe with Mr. W. Please don't contact me again. Goodbye, S

Then I hit send and block his number.

MR. WILKENS'S HOUSE is *beautiful*. Nestled in the woods, it's a charming ranch-style home that pops into view when you turn onto his street. It's painted a blue so dark it looks like coal, but the twining ivy that hugs the siding softens the modern feel. He parks in the driveway and taps a series of numbers into the keypad at the front door to get in.

"Welcome to Casa de Wilkens." He toes his sneakers off, wipes a hand down his face. He looks as exhausted as I feel. "Make yourself at home. I'm just going to make us some coffee."

While he ducks into a hallway around the corner, I shift nervously, intimidated by the wide, beautiful space stretching before me. The ceilings are tall and slanted. A set of leather couches is arranged around a large fireplace, the red and gray stones of the chimney running all the way up the wall. I can see the opening to the kitchen, tile floors and the edge of a marble counter, just beyond the living room. On the opposite side of the house, in place of a wall, there are a pair of large glass sliding doors, opening up to a view of a lush backyard ensconced in a forest of oak and elm.

It's easy to picture Mr. Wilkens here with his girlfriend, her feet propped up on his lap as they read books in quiet camaraderie by the fire.

I slip out of my tennis shoes, setting them neatly by the door, and drop my bag right next to them. His carpet is soft and expensive, the color of a rich cream. His house smells like fresh pine and sunshine.

I pad across the space, running a hand over the butter-soft leather as I pass the couches and press my forehead against the cold glass overlooking the garden. I bet he slides these doors open any chance he can get. Lets them stay open, making the forest itself his living room. It reminds me of the pictures of cottages I see on Instagram or the ones on the covers of those travel magazines with thick, glossy covers.

Mr. Wilkens pops around the corner. "Are you hungry? I can make breakfast too."

A hummingbird flits to the glass door. A small red feeder I hadn't noticed is hanging from the awning outside, swinging just above my head. The tiny, jeweled body glints in the sun, searching for sugar water from the empty feeder, tiny wings faster than sight.

I feel a pang at its beauty, at the absence of its food. Hayley hated empty bird feeders. She'd probably already be digging through Mr. Wilkens's cabinets for pots, intent on boiling water for syrup.

"So, I've been meaning to go to the grocery store . . ." Mr. Wilkens closes his fridge, face apologetic. "Let me see if I have any pancake mix or something." He opens a cabinet. "How do you feel about blueberry muffins— Oh wait. This mix is expired."

"I'm okay with coffee, Mr. Wilkens. I promise. You've done so much for me." I look shyly at my feet. "I don't know how I'll ever thank you."

Mr. Wilkens smiles and launches into a deep dive on the art of coffee making. I nod and smile as he tells me about the different types of roasts, the merits of grinding your own beans fresh, always checking the roast date on a bag before you purchase it, how everyone should throw out their single-serve and drip coffee units.

While he talks, I look at the series of framed photos on the walls. Most are artsy shots, black-and-white landscapes, a dramatic shot of dark forest pushing into an otherwise empty sky. At the end of the wall, closer to the living room, are two framed diplomas, one for undergrad and one for his master's.

I squint at the ornate text, the glossy, golden hue of the words, and read out loud.

"'This document certifies that Andrew Samuel Wilkens the *Third*—'" I turn to him, eyebrows raised. "You're a third? You sound like royalty."

He pulls a face. "Not even remotely. I hate my first name. Every iteration. Drew. Andy. Classic Andrew. Reminds me of my dad. It was my college girlfriend who suggested that if I hated it so much, I should just start going by my middle name."

"I like that," I say, remembering how I'd briefly pondered going by Anna and leaving all the baggage that went with being Ella behind. It makes me feel like reinvention is possible, even after all this.

Mr. Wilkens tells me about the coffee he's chosen, how he found it by chance while driving around Montana on vacation. I like listening to him talk, the passion in his voice, the way he's such a grown-up. And I like perusing his house, his art minimalist and Eastern-leaning. Terra-cotta Buddhas and singing bowls next to stone incense burners. The sticks of sandalwood smell strong, even unlit. A smattering of houseplants is tucked around in corners of the house, on shelves, on tables, so in the backdrop I hadn't noticed them before.

"I'd say you should water your plants"—I point to a browning button fern—"but we might need to call it."

Mr. Wilkens doesn't look up from pouring coffee beans into the grinder. "Yeah, I know. I keep meaning to get rid of them." He pushes the button, and the roar of dozens of beans being pulverized by tiny metal blades drowns out any other sound.

I head to a large glass display case filled with sports memorabilia. I catch my smiling reflection in the glass. Mindfulness and meditation on one side of the room, Cracker Jack and peanuts on the other.

Mr. Wilkens doesn't seem to have a loyalty to any one sport, but every team is from Georgia. There are Braves baseball cards, each one on a tiny display stand, a tiny blue helmet sporting the giant red *A* of the Atlanta Braves. But there's plenty of Atlanta Falcons gear as well—a glossy, mint-condition program from a Super Bowl game a few years back, a carefully folded jersey. The crown jewel, however, is a Braves item: a shiny wooden bat with an autograph on the side, *To Sam*.

The grinding finally stops. I look over, grinning. "So you're one of those sports guys. I wouldn't have guessed."

"What can I say? I contain multitudes." Mr. Wilkens pours the grounds into the French press. He's quiet as he clicks off the electric kettle. "It was the only time my dad and I could share a space without a fight breaking out between us. We didn't have a great relationship, and he wasn't around much after I got a little older. But when a game was on . . . we could talk."

"Sounds tough," I say softly.

He pours the steaming water into the French press, and the dark, cherry-chocolate smell of coffee blooms around us.

Between Mr. Wilkens's smile and the morning light from the large glass wall dappling the space, I'm remembering there's a way to live where dread doesn't sit in my belly, heavy as a brick. Where there's a future full of hot, cinnamon-spiced drinks on cold, autumn-leafed mornings. Bare feet in the kitchen and the promise of pancakes. A life where loss means misplaced keys and not my heart, my love, ripped away over and over. That life exists, I remember.

Not now, not here, but someday.

In this soft-lit kitchen, watching Mr. Wilkens work, the sunlight turning his hair chestnut, I think of all he may have lost. What he spoke about during our walk, the agony of loss and change. But what about loss of things that could have been? The things he never had? Clutching a well-worn baseball instead of his father's hand. And yet here he is, humming in the kitchen, smiling softly to himself. Happy despite it all.

I tap the glass display, seeing all the items in a new light. "I'm sorry it was like that with your dad. I appreciate you sharing with me."

"Vulnerability is the point of connection, Ella. Don't forget that." He gestures with a white mug he plucks from a shelf.

I wrinkle my nose at a basketball on the top shelf of his display. "You like the St. Louis Cardinals?"

"Hm?" Mr. Wilkens follows my gaze to a small white-and-red basketball with a logo of a little red bird perched on a bat. "Oh, that. *Ha.* A funny little keepsake. I've just always thought it was hilarious that a basketball would be advertising a baseball team." He sets a timer on his phone and sighs. "It's gonna be ten minutes before the coffee's ready. Want a tour?"

"Sure," I say and follow him outside. The most stunning thing about his backyard is the quiet. Leaves rustle and robins sing and brown thrashers chirp, but there are no cars, no highway rush.

"God," I sigh. "This is my dream."

He preens at the compliment. "This is my little paradise."

His garden is eclectic, composed of small, well-tended plots of plants of all varieties. He has herbs: fragrant lavender, spindles of rosemary, green bursts of basil. A small thatch of tomatoes ripen on fuzzy stems. A cluster of flower bushes host a flock of butterflies, landing on yellow and pink blooms. Towering sunflowers make my heart clench.

"Multitudes," I say. "You are also secretly an expert gardener."

"Hardly." He smiles at a white butterfly dancing before us.

The wind catches the scent of lavender and grass, threads it through my hair. He makes this life look so easy, so perfect. I decide I would want strawberries in my garden, along with a large row of basil and lavender, sprigs of thyme and rosemary.

And sunflowers. Rows and rows of sunflowers.

I'm about to ask how difficult it is to grow them when I see a few ceramic pots by the door. But all that's in there are water and ocean-blue marbles. A really familiar shade of ocean-blue marbles.

"That's so funny that you do that," I say, pointing to the pots.

"Ah yes." He laughs. "My bee hydration station. It's the secret to my gardening."

I hear a single crow caw. I hear the brush of leaves dancing in the wind.

For three seconds I hear nothing at all.

"Sorry." I blink rapidly at Mr. Wilkens. "What did you say?"

"It's a place for bees and other insects to land and drink water without drowning." He shrugs. "No bees, no garden."

As I stare at the cobalt-blue marbles, gears grind to a halt in my head. I think of Hayley's porch, of the fetid pots with the same blue marbles, and for some reason, I remember a time I had a fever so terrible that I kept thinking my mother was with me in my bedroom. I was delirious with thirst and imagined my mom was leaning forward, offering me a cup of water. Over and over, I reached for it, tears pricking from the need to quench the fire in my throat. I'd never been so confused as when my fingers snapped on empty air, again and again.

I'd never imagined I couldn't trust my own eyes, my own brain.

I feel the same as I watch Mr. Wilkens walk to his plot of herbs. He stoops to pluck stray weeds from between the basil. As he bends over, I catch a gash on his palm. It looks fresh.

"What happened to your hand?" I ask.

"Oh?" He stands, frowning at his palm before tucking his hand in his pocket. "I cut it on some tomato stakes this morning. Careless of me."

I nod mechanically, brain whirring, brain clicking.

Wooden stakes. *Wooden like the trellis outside my window?*

Mr. Wilkens smiles, brows creased. "Is everything all right, Ella?"

"I guess it just hit me," I say. "All these nights without sleep, the stress of it all."

"Of course. God, I can't imagine. That coffee will set you straight. In fact, it should be ready by now. Let's go in."

I can't seem to stop blinking, a malfunctioning machine. I'm a page that won't reload, a spinning circle. I need someone to reset me. Shut me down. Unplug, replug. I stand in front of the glass display case as Mr. Wilkens strides into the kitchen, chatting.

But I'm not listening.

I'm staring at the baseball bat. Specifically, the inscription.

To Sam.

Everything except for the letter "S" fades into the background.

All sounds stop; the oxygen in my lungs is sucked out, violent and sudden.

I forget how to breathe. It's not working right. Sounds are distorted, stretched and pulled like taffy, the world shifting beneath me like the deck of a storm-tossed ship. There's a small flash of yellow shining off the display glass. In the pane in front of the little St. Louis Cardinals basketball is a reflection from the garden outside: two perfect, beaming sunflowers.

It's all right here. Everything Hayley meticulously recorded in her journal.

"I have to go to the bathroom." I stumble to the hallway, ignoring how he calls after me. A moment longer and it would all be written on my face.

I try a few doors and finally find the bathroom, shut and lock the door behind me.

I turn on the faucet, my hands braced on either side of the sink. The face in the mirror does not belong to me. It belongs to a girl with black circles for eyes and bloodless lips. A girl who fell asleep amongst lambs and has awoken in the den of the lion, carcasses scattered all around.

"Ella?" A gentle knock on the door nearly makes me scream. "You okay in there? You seem . . . unwell."

"Fine," I say, sounding anything but. "Felt sick all of a sudden. The stress. I'm almost done."

"Okay. I'll be out here if you need me," says Mr. Wilkens.

Says Sam.

Says *S.*

After some cold splashes of water, I steel myself.

Be brave, Ella. We can break down later.

The bathroom door makes no noise as I open it slowly, peeking my head out for any sign of him. There is none, so I make a break for it, rushing to the front door.

"Is everything okay?"

I'm a few steps from the door when Mr. Wilkens stands from the leather couch, his face a portrait of concern.

"Yes," I say as he approaches me. "No, I mean. I'm not well. I need to get home."

"That's terrible. I'll get my keys. Let's get you home."

"I'll walk." I slip my feet into my shoes, grab my bag. I take a step to the door.

"Ella, that's ridiculous." He purses his lips, his tone slow and patient, as if dealing with a toddler's tantrum. "That's over twelve miles, especially if you're sick—"

"Thanks for everything, I really mean it." I put my hand on the door.

"Ella, please, can you just talk to me for a moment? Tell me what's going on?"

I can see Mr. Wilkens's car through the small glass panel of the front door. Notice a scuff on the front bumper. How dumb I've been. So blindingly stupid.

The same instant I turn the front doorknob, a bruising hand grabs my shoulder to whirl me around.

"Ella," Mr. Wilkens says, "it's gonna be okay."

Then I feel a blow to the side of my head, and everything goes black.

chapter 33
ella

I don't know where I am. There's a sharp, piercing ringing in my ears. My heartbeat is so violent, each pulse swells my tongue, jumping up my throat.

I'm going to die, I'm going to die, I'm going to die clangs in my head, over and over. I fight to steady myself, to form conscious thought. I'm confused why half my vision is dark. Turns out, I can only open one of my eyes, because the other has a ziplock bag of ice pressed against it.

"Thank God, Ella. I was so worried." Mr. Wilkens is seated in a chair across from me, the sharp cold of the bag stinging against the fiery concern in his eyes. The entire left side of my face throbs and pulses, and I have a stabbing pain in my temples.

And then I remember.

The panic is back, full force. My blood is howling with fear, my thoughts incoherent. I try to stand up, shove him away, but only end up falling sideways out of my chair, my legs bound at the ankles, my wrists tied behind my back.

Mr. Wilkens catches me before I hit the floor, dropping the bag of ice. He eases me back into my chair.

"Ella." He looks stricken. "Calm down. I'm trying to take care of you here."

"Untie me!" I thrash, frantic. I swivel my head, screaming. "Please! Somebody! Help!"

"Ella, what are you saying? I'm not trying to hurt—"

"Somebody!" I glance around frantically. I haven't been in this room yet. Low ceilings, no windows. Thick carpet and scuffed leather couches. An expensive drum kit in the corner, two subwoofers as tall as I stand.

I'm in a basement. One that's designed to disguise sounds that could fill a stadium.

"Please!" I scream anyway, unable to face the implications.

"Can we talk, Ella? You'll hurt yourself; you're already not well." Mr. Wilkens—*Sam*—settles back into the seat across from me, picking up the ice pack once more. "I'm going to untie you, but you need to calm down first, okay? Can you do that for me? Calm down?"

I look wildly around the room. Stairs behind Wilkens on my right. Not a goddamn loose panel to be seen, not even a vent or a crack. *Escape, escape, escape.*

I've never been so scared in my life.

Dad told me a story once of a dog he had as a kid. On the Fourth of July they put him in the basement, hoping he wouldn't hear the fireworks. They found him the next day, under the back shed, flanks heaving, both front paws bloodied to the bone, gums shredded, teeth broken. He'd clawed his way through the cellar door, so sturdy and reinforced that my grandfather had marveled that a grown man with an axe would have needed all night to break through the thick wood.

I'd been skeptical, sure it was hyperbole. God, I was wrong.

I want to chew through my wrists. I want to claw an Ella-sized hole through Wilkens, scramble up the stairs, covered in his entrails, to safety.

"Ella," he says, soft as a sigh. "My God, you look terrified. I hate that. Look at me." He nestles the bag of ice against my tender cheek, the cold shocking me into obeying him. "I'm not going to hurt you. I'm keeping you safe from yourself."

It's hard to think around the nuclear pulse of pain in my head. His voice is oil-slick and honey-coated, his words confusing me. I feel like I'm drowning, but I'm all turned around. I don't remember which way I need to kick, the direction of the surface.

I squeeze my eyes shut.

Don't think. Just run.

I renew my fight against my restraints, the thin plastic slicing into my skin. Zip ties, I realize.

Wilkens paces. "Psychotic breaks aren't uncommon after something so traumatic. Of course you're feeling this way. After all you've been through. You lost your best friend, then you fell for a guy who betrayed you, and now he's in jail and you're all alone again. It makes sense that you'd have a break from reality." Wilkens looks at me, desperate, pleading. "I hope you know that's not true, Ella. You're not alone. Not ever. And I really, *really* want you to be okay, Ella. I care about you. Do you hear me? I don't want anything to happen to you."

I stay frozen, my heart threatening to split my ribs and beat itself out of my chest. I remember how long the driveway was, how peaceful his garden was. If, somehow, the sounds of my screams escaped this basement, the only beings around to bear witness would be the butterflies, the jewel-bodied hummingbirds, perhaps a single crow in the distance.

Wilkens turns around, a curved pair of shears dangling from his fingers, the blades open and hanging like legs from a hammock. The dim basement light throws a weak shadow across my face as Wilkens looms over me, smiling hopefully with shears in hand. He manages to make it look like both a punishment and reward. "So, what's it going to be, Ella? Are you going to cooperate?"

That's when it hits me. Really hits me.

I'm going to die. I may actually die if I don't figure out a way out of this.

I can't run or fight my way free. The only way out? Wilkens would have to let me go. I have to make him believe he can let me out.

"You're right," I say, my voice raw from screaming. "I . . . I'm not well. I had a psychotic moment."

For the first time since I've woken up, Wilkens's face falters.

"Really?" He sounds unsure.

I scramble, chasing the thin thread of his uncertainty. "You said it yourself. I tried to hurt myself. I can't process how Sawyer betrayed— I mean, I've *barely* processed losing Hayley. You—you were just trying to help me. I know you were." Tears are spilling down my cheeks, stinging my bruised eye.

Please believe me.

Mr. Wilkens lowers the shears, face inscrutable as he considers me.

"I understand you were trying to help me." I lick my lips. I fight the bile rising in my throat at my next words. "I understand that—that you probably only wanted the best for Hayley. You didn't mean to hurt her. You never—"

I realize I've overplayed my hand when he drops the shears and presses his fingers into his eyes.

Stupid, stupid, stupid. Like he'd ever believe I'd think what he did to Hayley was okay.

"God*dammit,* Ella." His voice breaks.

I know then that there is nothing I can do.

Wilkens drops the shears to the carpet, sitting heavily in the chair before me.

"Shit, shit, *shit*. You think I wanted this? You think I wanted any of this? I like you, Ella. You're a good kid. Smart. And I loved—do you hear me?—I *loved* Hayley." He presses a fist to his heart, like if he doesn't hold it in, it'll burst out of him, bloody and beating on the floor between us. "I've been through so much already," he says. "Do you have any idea how *agonizing* it's been? And now? Now I have to do *this*? Are you going to make this easy? Or is it going to be hard and messy?"

It takes me a moment to realize he's crying. A high, thready whine in his throat as he rocks back and forth in his chair crying.

Maybe it's the fact that I finally understand that I have no way out of this. Maybe I've finally begun to see the scope of this whole thing, who S really is, what happened to Sawyer.

Maybe it's the fact that *I'm* the one who's going to die, and he's crying harder than I am.

Whatever the reason, all my grief, all my fear, all my sorrow calcifies. Presses into a sharp, shiny diamond of fury.

"You pathetic sack of shit," I spit. "You hurt my best friend. She loved you; she trusted you, and you seduced her and then made her bleed. You—you ran us off the road! You *killed* her. You made me put Sawyer in jail!" It's half accusation, half realization. My head pounds, a howling, heavy pain. "It was all you, the whole time. That diary was you, you're S, you're the one, *you're the one who should be in prison*—"

"What do you know?" He shoots to his feet, paces like a tiger. "What was your childhood, hm? Bedtime stories and both parents at your school concerts? You couldn't possibly understand. I was five, and when it went quiet in my parents' bedroom, when the crying and the crashing stopped, I was wondering if he'd killed her. I was wondering if my mother was dead and I was next. You know what that's like? What that does to someone?"

Wilkens clasps his hands in front of him. "I loved her. Everything

I did was for her. To protect her. I saw Hayley's future the first time I saw her. An overdose at nineteen. Alcohol poisoning at twenty. She was beautiful—and destined to self-destruct. She understood what happens when your dads are faceless and violent, and your moms are Phoebes. Everything I did was to protect her."

"How can you possibly think all this?" I rasp. "That anything you did was okay? You *killed* her!"

He drops his chin, the fight going out of him. "I don't care if you believe me or not. But this is the truth. I'm not a monster, Ella. I was just trying to talk. She wouldn't pick up my calls. I was terrified I'd never see her again. Which . . . I know. Ironic." He lifts a fist to his mouth. "She forced my hand, Ella. I had no choice but to follow you, to chase . . . I just wanted to talk, Ella. Just wanted you to pull over and talk. When your car broke through the barrier, I nearly died. A part of me *did* die. I pulled over straightaway. I looked down over the drop-off, called out. But the car was so far down the embankment. I was about to climb down when a car started to come around the bend. I had to leave; they'd get the wrong idea. God, I nearly drove off an embankment myself when I found out that Hayley . . . Hayley was gone."

"You're right, Sam," I spit. "You're not a monster, because monsters . . . well, they can't really help it, can they? Rabid dogs, raccoons. There's no conscious thought. To call you a monster is to excuse you. You're the reason Hayley is dead. You killed her. And you nearly killed me. Both that night and every night for six months." I take a ragged breath. "I never put down that boulder of guilt. It nearly dragged me down into the depths too."

"Ella," Wilkens says, pinching the bridge of his nose.

But I'm not done. "You get off on thinking you're so smart. That you're so wise." I lift my chin at him, sneer. "You didn't teach me *shit*. But Hayley did. She taught me that I could be loved at my most human, my ugliest, my bloodiest. She taught me to be brave, *and* she taught me it's okay if I'm not quite brave yet. She protected me while trying to teach me to protect myself." I swallow hard. "I'm just a slow learner."

I know this can't end any other way, but at least I can have a few moments of peace. *I didn't kill Hayley.* The tears that fall feel cleansing, carrying a poison from my body.

"Ella, delaying's only going to make this all worse. I'm going to ask you one more time. Your choice. Are you going to make this easy? Or hard and messy?"

I force myself to lock eyes with Wilkens, to make my face stone. To make him look at me when he ends my life. And that's when I see it. A figure. Tall and slim, dressed all in black, masked and hooded. It creeps down the stairs, Sam's signed bat raised above its head.

The hooded figure is one step above Wilkens. It lifts the bat high, the *To Sam* glinting in the dull basement light.

"Hard and messy," I say.

The bat cracks down into Wilkens's skull, the sound as explosive as a bullet. He grunts, falling forward, but manages to stay on his swaying feet. He presses a hand to his head and groans when it comes back bright ruby red. The hooded figure raises the bat once more, bringing it down like a hammer.

Wilkens falls, soundless, crumpling to the ground.

The figure drops the bat, pulling back the hood to reveal short hair wrapped in a bun, one side shaved. Next comes a pale face, thinner than I remember but with the same dusting of freckles across high cheekbones, the same sparkling emerald eyes.

"Hey, Ella."

For a second, I wonder if I've already died. If Wilkens did kill me after all.

Because standing in front of me . . .

It's Hayley.

chapter 34
hayley

I don't condone violence, I really don't.

But I'm making Sam a special case, just this once. And God*damn* does it feel good to ring his skull like a bell, to feel the crack of the impact traveling up the wood to vibrate through my fingers, the ones he broke, the ones that will always be a little crooked.

He hates blood, would never touch me when I was on my period, so I loved hearing him squeal after seeing the red on his palm. But it was a huge risk coming back here at all. Sawyer knew there was no other option but urged me to be quick.

"It's all for nothing if anyone but Ella knows," he said.

So here we are, Sam out cold on the floor.

And then it's Ella and me, me and Ella, alone in Andrew Samuel Wilkens's basement.

I'm nervous, suddenly. Even after all I've been through, after all I've had to do, I'm nervous.

Because she's the last person in the world I want to ever hate me, and she's the first person in the world to have every reason *to* hate me. I know what I put her through. What I had to let her believe.

I'd hate me too. Even after knowing all I know, the reasons why I did it.

I'm struck with the urge to free her without revealing myself. I could cut her free, press the folded letter into her hands, and sprint away before she could act. The coward's way. I know I'd never do that, would never do that again to Ella, but as I meet her eyes, feel the shame bubbling in my throat like a boiling cauldron . . . it's tempting.

Even stronger is the urge to take her back to North Carolina with me, to figure out all our next steps together, like we always planned. The yearning for it all nearly bowls me over.

But there's no way I'm not out of time.

Ella starts to sway in her chair, like she may faint, so I drop the bat to the ground and rush to her side, put my hands on her shoulders to steady her.

"I know," I say fervently. "I know. I . . ."

Five minutes. I might have five minutes, tops, before my life is over.

"Shit," I spit, squeezing my eyes shut.

The letter will have to do.

I open my eyes, and Ella's face is a landscape of conflicting emotion, the hurt and confusion and love coming off her in thick, choking waves.

"The police will be here in five minutes," I explain. "I called them from your phone upstairs. So say you managed to sneak away and call them before he caught you and dragged you down here. I told them you thought he had a gun." I jerk my head at the lethal-looking pruning shears. "That'll be good enough, don't worry."

I pull my Swiss Army knife from my back pocket, heavy as a stone, reach behind her to saw at the zip ties around her wrists. "Okay, Ella.

This was in your back jean pocket. It took you a while, hours even, but you managed to free your wrists. You waited till he had to take a leak to do your ankles."

The zip ties come apart with a snap. Ella's arms dangle behind her as soon as they're released. She doesn't move a finger. I punch away the guilt that threatens to take over and switch to sawing at the plastic ties at her ankles.

Her eyes have never left me, and I don't think I've seen her blink once. The plastic ties snap, and her ankles fall apart, limp like her arms. I give the knife a cursory wipe and slide the blade back into place before taking Ella's hand and gently placing it in her palm.

"This is your knife. It was in your back pocket. You managed to free yourself." I close her fingers over the cold metal. Her hands are freezing. She's still not blinking.

I turn around, chewing my lip as I stare at Sam lying facedown, the bat beside him. *The bat.* I leap to my feet, snatch it, and wipe the handle with my sleeves, careful not to grab it with my bare skin.

"He brought this down. Wasn't sure if he was going to beat you with it or not, wanted to have the option to threaten you. When he came back from the bathroom, you surprised him when his back was turned." The Swiss Army knife is still clutched in her palm, so I lay the bat across her lap.

When she catches it with her other hand, I release a breath I didn't know I was holding.

"Ella . . . I wanted to—"

Sam groans and twitches. I almost snatch the bat from Ella's lap, give him another thwack, but in the distance comes my warning bell. The sound of sirens, growing steadily louder.

I fall to my knees before Ella, shove my hand in my pocket, and pull out the folded letter.

"I say it all in the letter, Ella. It's not enough, not near enough." I stuff it deep inside her sock, under her arch so it won't fall out. "But it's all we have."

I cup her cheek, her uninjured side, and hold her eyes, still so wide and opaque.

"Okay, Ella." I touch my forehead to hers. "You freed yourself. You hit him with the bat. I was never here. I need you to say it."

The sirens are louder, closer. Ella still says nothing. My heart beats violently in my throat.

"Ella. You freed yourself. You hit him with the bat. I was never here." Silence. "Oh, Ella, I know. I *know*. But I need to hear you say—"

"You were never here."

Tears spring to my eyes as I pull back to take in Ella, her beautiful face, the defiant set of her jaw surprising and new.

"You're not a baby bird anymore, are you?" I whisper. "You're an eagle. A phoenix. My Ella with eyes and hair of fire." I lean in and press my chapped lips to her cheek, soft and cold as fresh cream. "I love you forever, Ella. No matter what you decide."

And then I'm gone.

chapter 35
hayley's letter

My dearest Ella.

Shit. How do I start this? Do you know how many times I've begun this letter to you? Last night, I knocked my water over all the papers on the table and tried to pretend it was an accident, and not an act of shame, an act of cowardice.

But no more excuses, Ella. I love you, and you deserve to know everything.

I wanted to tell you about Sam. It's no consolation, I'm sure, but know that it was you I wanted to tell most of all. Especially in the beginning, that era of magic, when he was pulling flowers from behind my ear and I went to bed and woke up smiling, always smiling.

As you can imagine, he wanted it to stay secret. He'd tell me I was wise beyond my years, that we were basically the same age, but we had to be so careful just the same. He'd certainly be fired, jailed even ("The ham-fisted laws hold no space for nuance," he would complain), and until I was eighteen, we had to sneak around in silence.

I'll admit it to you, Ella. I couldn't believe he'd chosen me. Even now I'm ashamed to write those words. Which is why I'm writing them. It's hard to light a candle in these corners of my soul I've spent years hiding. But I'm learning that I can be embarrassed while knowing I have no reason to be embarrassed. And that is how I feel when I think of how grateful I was simply to have Sam choose me.

You see, after seeing Phoebe give her love out so willingly, to anyone who showed her the least bit of attention (to anyone except me, *may I add), and seeing what it cost her, over and over again, I* swore *it would never happen to me. I would never choose a man over myself. Now I understand nothing is quite so simple.*

After all, don't we all just want to be loved? Want to be seen and still chosen? Who wouldn't split their fingernails scrabbling for that?

That being said, it's no excuse. What has happened between me and Phoebe is beyond repair. Ella, I decided a long time ago that I wasn't going to let Phoebe know I was alive. For now, at least. For forever, maybe (I don't know how I'll feel when I'm fifty if she's still alive). It seems harsh, and maybe it is. But the damage is done, and I truly believe we're better off apart.

We can't choose who birthed us, who raised us, but we can *choose our family. Maybe Phoebe loved me in the only way she could, but I deserve better. I deserve to be protected, to be cherished, to feel* safe. *Instead, I was an inconvenience to her. A burden, a thing that stood between her and her chance at love.*

The way she didn't protect me with Sean was a breaking point, the way she chose him even when I told her that he made me uncomfortable, that he looked at me in my towel, and that I was sure he was stealing, from us or someone else, because I know there's no way he could afford the gifts he gave her or half the things he bought. When I asked him about a gold chain he got Phoebe, he got this dangerous, furious look in his eyes. "You accusing me of stealing, Hayley?" he said a deadly quiet voice that made me too scared to go any further.

None of it mattered. Only when he cheated on Phoebe with a younger woman, when her mighty ego was cut to the quick, did she throw him out.

I used to wrap my contempt for Phoebe around me like armor. I swore I'd never be like her, breaking her body and her heart over and over, just for any hope that someone might keep her for longer than a day. I vowed to myself I would never be so dumb. So weak. I would dole out my love like favors, by appointment to the queen. And men would feel lucky *to love me. But this was all fear disguised as armor, a recipe for shame.*

Everyone was safe before Sam.

I liked Sawyer. But I specifically chose him because of just that. I would only ever like him dearly. Of course he was hot and fun and good. He never pushed for more and was, I think, in mutual like with me. And the truth is we worked best as a trio. Things were always better when you were there, Ella. Even Sawyer said so. It was perfect.

And then along came Sam.

What can I tell you about those early days, Ella? He had this gift for convincing me I was so very lucky to be loved by him. He was a magician, pulling rabbits out of hats, a house of mirrors.

He distracted me with passion I'd never known. I never saw his hands moving closer to the lever, that trapdoor he called love.

He told me to stay with Sawyer, that it would make it safer, draw less attention. It felt cruel, but I took comfort in the fact that by the time Sam and I were enmeshed, Sawyer's and my relationship had reached a pleasant tepidness.

It's not always easy to spot the red flags—I know this now. A jealous comment here. A disparaging comment about his ex-girlfriend there. He'd pass them off as compliments. "You're so much more beautiful than my last girlfriend, so much cooler and more reasonable. She'd never let me do this." I wasn't immune.

Tell me more, *I'd think as I wondered how I could be even cooler, even more reasonable.* Tell me how you love me the most. Please. Love me the most.

I'm not going to go into detail here. I'm still working through the shame of it, processing it, and honestly, Ella, this isn't what this letter is about. It's about filling you in on what actually happened and why I had to do what I did. But you do at least need to know that I started feeling scared all the time. And then ashamed of being scared. And then ashamed for feeling ashamed of being scared.

Here's the thing about Sam. His jealousy knew no bounds. At first it was just random guys. But then he started to get really, really *jealous of you. He was no longer just jealous of anyone I could possibly cheat on him with. He was jealous of anyone I would spend time with that wasn't him. And, of course, who would that be but you?*

As time went on, he kept pushing the boundaries of just how far he would go to make sure he knew where I was at all times, who I was with, what I was doing.

Then I got pregnant. My worst nightmare. That's when I became truly trapped. It would have been difficult to get an abortion with *a supportive partner. But with Sam? It was not outside the realm of possibility that his rage would be deadly: Rage that I wouldn't want his child. Rage if I* did *have his child. My only option was for me to hide it from him. Or I tried to, anyway. Because,* God, *I was terrified. Obviously, I wouldn't be able to hide it forever, but hopefully I'd have enough time to figure out* what the hell I was going to do.

Instead, I was able to hide it for exactly four hours. And that's when I figured out he had AirTagged my car to keep track of me at all times. He'd snuck into the pharmacy, gone through the trash.

I had been right. The pregnancy pushed him over some kind of edge. He managed to be both possessive of and threatened by the potential baby. He loathed the fact that I wasn't over the moon about it. I didn't even tell him the extent of it, how I'd sobbed in my car after I found out, how I'd started Googling Planned Parenthoods within driving distance.

That's when I started finding AirTags everywhere and realized just how trapped I was.

Then, one day, Sawyer caught me between classes while I was huddled in an alcove during a breakdown. I'd been acting so strangely; he'd known something was up. I'd been avoiding him, putting off any discussion that would lead to anything real. But he looked at me with such concern, such lack of judgment, and I was so hopeless, I grabbed his hand and pulled him into an empty classroom and locked the door.

I told him everything. As much of a facade as our relationship had become, I was still worried about his reaction, expected him to be hurt or mad. I would have understood.

He took it as well as anyone ever could.

You know Sawyer. He's a good guy. And he's human. He asked for time to process everything and agreed to keep up appearances in the meantime. And sure enough, after a few days, he came to me, admitting that while he had been hurt initially and upset, ultimately what he felt for me was . . . understanding. He confided in me that he, his mom, and his brother had stayed in a domestic violence shelter a few hours away from here when he was younger.

He knew I was a victim, and he wanted to help in any way he could.

We started to make plans. But it was hard. Nearly impossible.

As each week passed, Sam managed to demand more of my time, get more controlling. The only time Sawyer and I were able to speak were stolen moments at the water fountain or an empty classroom when we were supposed to be in class.

It was exhausting, and I began to feel hopeless.

But then Sam took pity on me. He could tell I was floundering, adrift. He "let" me have a slumber party with you. We were at your house, and I had barely spoken. I felt like a husk. A carapace filled only with shame and despair.

Naturally, you noticed. Oh, Ella, I wanted to tell you. You gently asked, in different ways, over and over, what you could do to help. But it wasn't safe. It wasn't just me in the crosshairs anymore.

That night, Scott was having a party.

Sawyer told me you don't remember much from the party. He also told me . . . Oh, Ella, I cannot express how much it hurts me that you blame yourself. Maybe . . . I don't know, maybe if you know everything, you'll absolve yourself. Realize that you have only ever been the best friend any human being could hope to have.

So, Scott's party.

Of course, Sam would have never let me go to it. And, normally, you would have balked at the idea. But I couldn't bear the idea of sitting there all night in silence with you, unable to break open and let everything out. I couldn't bear the hurt look on your face when I refused to open up. You were so desperate to do something for me that when I suggested we go, you leapt off the couch to change.

I searched my purse thoroughly, pressed along the inseams, just in case Sam had been industrious enough to stitch an AirTag within the lining. I knew there was an AirTag somewhere on my car. I'd found all the old hiding spots, and he'd gotten creative (read: learned how to dismantle and then re-mantle sections of it), so I'd given up trying to pry them out.

What I hadn't counted on was him AirTagging your *car.*

Right before we walked into the party, my phone rang. These little "check-ins" were pretty standard at this point. I shooed you away, told you to go inside, scope out the place.

He seemed a little weird on that first phone call. On edge. I chalked it up to this being our first night apart in weeks. But then the texts started. Asking where I was again. "Just making sure," he kept saying. It was a little unusual to do this after a phone call, but it was still nothing compared to other things he'd done before.

I found you, drinking a beer (Ella, it was a Natty Light—a nun would have to drink three of those to get as drunk as she'd get after one kombucha), and you told me Sawyer wasn't there, you'd searched the whole party.

My phone kept buzzing. With each text Sam sent me, my paranoia began to get worse. He always seemed to be one step ahead of me. Nothing felt out of the question anymore. Had he hired a private investigator to follow me?

I began to look at every person's face in that sweaty, crowded house, half certain that they were agents for Sam. And you noticed, Ella. You knew something was wrong. And you had clocked that I wasn't drinking.

While I had no *idea what the future held, I wasn't gonna drink while pregnant. I snuck to the kitchen, grabbed four empty cups, filling three with shots of vodka and, making sure no one saw me, the last one with water from the sink.*

"Who wants shots?" I yelled, holding up the three vodka cups above a churning dance floor. There were cheers and yells, and three hands shot out from the crowd to grab the cups. I took a confirmatory sniff before shooting the water, making a face afterward, like God, that's strong.

I did that two more times, just for good measure, and after the third one, I caught your eye across the room, looking concerned, beer still in your hand. I wanted to tell you not to worry, that it was the most hydrated I'd been all day.

My phone kept buzzing and buzzing. When he got like this, it was impossible to respond. How do you respond to fifty texts sent in a matter of minutes? You wait, batch send a reply. They were usually around the same theme anyway and one reply would cover dozens at a time.

But then I heard a different notification. He was FaceTiming.

I was horrified. If he was willing to risk FaceTiming me, where you or your family might have seen his face . . . I knew I was in trouble. Even if I didn't pick up right there, he'd know something was wrong if I didn't call him back within five minutes.

You tried to peer at my screen. "Who is that?"

"Sawyer," I blurted. "Wait here. I gotta call him back."

"Why not just do it—"

But I was already gone. I found Scott, who was already trashed, and asked him to point me to an empty room I could borrow. God, I cringe now at how his eyes lit up. It didn't register then, of course, what he thought I meant. He gave me directions to his parents' room on the second floor.

My dress was red and low-cut, so I grabbed a T-shirt from the closet and started the FaceTime.

"What are you wearing?" Sam's hair was all standing up, like he'd been pulling at it, and his eyes were already wild.

"I had to borrow a shirt from Ella's mom," I lied smoothly. "I spilled ketchup all over my pajama shirt. It's in the wash."

"Is that her parents' bedroom? Why are you in there?"

"We're all watching a movie downstairs. The whole family. I'm so sorry, that's why I haven't had a chance to reply to your texts, but I came up here so we could have privacy. They've paused it for me, actually. I feel bad to make them wait. Did you need anything, baby?"

Sam looked at me like he wanted to reach through the screen and yank my earlobe to bring me closer, a preferred move of his.

"So you're at Ella's right now?"

I broke into a cold sweat. "Of course, Sam. Where else would I be?"

He nodded. "Where else would you be?" He said it slowly, like a threat.

"Nowhere, Sam. I'm at Ella's." I hoped the reception was bad enough that he couldn't see all the color leave my face.

There was a knock on the door.

I panicked. "That's Ella's dad, crap, I gotta go, I think he needs to change—" I clicked the end button before the pounding continued.

Immediately, I doubled over, dry heaving. I'd never hung up on Sam, not even accidentally. Oh God, he was going to kill me. And he knew *I wasn't at your house. How?* How?

The door opened, and Scott strolled in. Well, more like swayed and stumbled in.

"Sorry it took me so long," he said. "I have to tell you . . . I'd always hoped you felt the same. I was too nervous to tell you how I felt—"

"Wait, what?" Ella, I had no idea what he was talking about. And besides that, his timing couldn't possibly have been worse. "Scott, sorry, I have an emergency, I gotta go."

"No—Hayley!" He sounded so sad, so desperate. I almost felt bad. "Hayley—I'm pouring my heart out to you. I've never done that. I'm, like . . . telling you that—I'm, like, in love with you or whatever."

"Scott, you're not in love with me. You'll be super hungover and forget all about this tomorrow." I was gentle. Scott's an ass, but I didn't delight in crushing him. He's got problems; we all do.

I bolted out of the room because we had to get the hell out of there. *And Scott followed, yelling. "Hayley, stop, wait—please? I just . . . when we're fighting or sparring or* talking *. . . it's the most fun I have, like, ever.* Please *don't turn me down.* Please? *I don't know how— Wait!"*

But I was already back in the living room. Scott tried grabbing my wrist, begging me. And then, my God, Ella, he was crying. *I pray he remembers none of that. I think he would go into witness protection if he realized he cried in front of another human being.*

After I peeled Scott off me, I found you frowning at a bowl of pretzels at the snack table.

"We need to go." I grabbed your shoulders. "Now."

"What are you wearing?" You blinked at me, concern cutting slices between your brows.

"Shit, I forgot." I ripped off the T-shirt, which said, WINE NOT? *and urged us to the door.*

"Hayley," you tried saying. "Hayley, what's going on?"

"No time."

Before I got in your car, I froze on the curb, something occurring to me. He knew where I was. I'd made sure to clear my phone of any tracking app, any location sharing. My purse was clear. My dress, my bra, my clothes were clear.

But your car . . .

"What are you doing?" Your concerned frown deepened when I dropped to my knees, looking at your tires, slipping my fingers into the space between the spokes, beneath your car's undercarriage.

"Can you pop the trunk?" I called from underneath the car. Ella, you looked so worried, but you did it anyway, only for me to scramble to my feet and shut it again after I came up empty-handed. He'd put it somewhere on there; I just knew *he had.*

But we were out of time.

We got in the car, but you didn't start it.

"Ella, please, *let's go." I figured if we got to your house, we'd be safe. Sam couldn't risk raising suspicions with parents of a student. He'd leave us alone. I figured maybe he'd cool off, and it wouldn't be so bad the next day.*

You swallowed, looking nervous. "I had a beer." You turned to me. "Hayley, you seem so scared and—and not okay. Want me to call my parents?"

"No, no parents. Ella, you had a single beer, like, over an hour ago." My phone buzzed. "Go, go now!"

Your face pinched, the way it does when your mom yells at you in front of me, and you turned on the car and got us out of there.

I thought we'd make it. We weren't that far away.

Then a car appeared behind us, out of the inky-black night. We were being followed. Don't panic yet, *I thought.* Other people in the world drive cars.

But most other people don't flash their brights.

I needed a safety net. I pulled out my phone and texted Sawyer my current location. Fern was working a double at WH, so he'd had to stay home with Callan. But I knew in an emergency, he could take Callan to the neighbor's.

And it was definitely an emergency.

Might need help. Be ready. E's driving, S is chasing us.

I looked back over my shoulder, and yes, this car was definitely speeding up. The headlights loomed larger and larger. Oh God.

The car was going to hit us.

I screamed, twisting in my seat to try and get a better look. I'd never seen you look so scared. I wanted to comfort you, but my mind was gone from terror.

"Drive faster!" I shrieked, unbuckling my seat belt. I needed to see. Needed to know for sure. I twisted in my seat to get a better look.

"What are you doing?" you yelled, even as you blessedly slammed your foot on the gas.

I caught a flash of the Ford symbol on the hood, saw that it was a car the color of jaundice and infection. And then I knew for certain.

"Oh God," I wailed. "He's trying to kill me!"

But it wasn't just me in the car, was it? It wasn't just me anymore.

I turned to you, my best friend. An impossibility.

"He's gonna kill us," I said just as the road began to take a slight left and Sam crashed into the bumper, sending us careening right.

It all happened so quickly.

There was the screeching howl of metal and machine as we broke through the metal guardrail and rolled down the slope. Your side took the brunt of it, and you cracked your head against the window before the airbags inflated, knocking you out.

I couldn't believe we were alive. I checked your pulse and started to cry when I felt you breathing. Three feet more to the right, and we would have been in the river below.

My window had exploded. So had nearly all of the windshield, and I had a few nasty cuts on my face from the spray of glass. Tentatively, I stepped out of the car, shaking so hard I had to kneel, terrified I would tumble over the edge to a watery grave.

He had finally done it. Tried to kill me. Us.

I pulled out my phone and started dialing 911. But immediately, I thought of Sam's uncle Rick, who worked on the force. He didn't know about us, but Rick was a family man. When it came down to it, who would he choose? His beloved nephew or a teenager from a broken family?

And even so, could I prove what he'd done? There'd been no witnesses. And unless Sam was in jail for good, for forever, I would never be safe.

"Holy shit! Ella! Hayley!"

I saw Sawyer's car at the top of the embankment, parked so crookedly the nose was peeking over the side. He slid down the hill, knocking pebbles and rocks down as he made his way to us as quickly as he could.

"No," *he cried when he saw you, still, your eyes closed.*

"Not dead," I said, beginning to cry. I was still in shock. "Sawyer, Sawyer, if anything happened to her—" I broke off on a sob.

"Took some basic CPR courses after Mom . . . well, you know." He climbed into the front seat, gently brushed your hair from your face, assessed you, serious and grave as a surgeon. Sawyer called to me over his shoulder. "Her pulse is strong. That's good, I'm pretty sure. But I'll feel better when she's in an ambulance."

I cried harder, tears of relief. He leaned out of the car, keeping a hand on you, never taking his fingers off your pulse. "He's not going to stop, Sawyer. Not until I'm dead."

"Thank God you're okay. I mean, are you—"

"Fine. I haven't called the police yet because of Rick."

Twisting in the seat, Sawyer examined the seat belt retractor. He shot me a look.

"You weren't wearing your seat belt?"

I shrugged. His eyes got stormy for a second, then they cleared. "Actually . . . this works."

He looked at the windshield, out toward the river, and then at me. He pointed down, where the water roared below, the rapids more violent than usual. I peered over the side, then looked back at the car, assessing the angle, the impact.

"To be clear . . . are you suggesting what I think you're suggesting?" I breathed, still processing it.

Sawyer's eyes narrowed, his mouth a tight line. "You said it yourself. He won't stop until you're dead."

I stared at you and made a decision. "I can't. I can't do it. Ella's gonna think she killed me. She'll blame herself. I won't put her through that."

Sawyer nodded. "Okay. But what will Sam put her through?"

I stared at you again. You had a cut above your right eyebrow that was bleeding, a rivulet of red staining your lavender shirt. Your lip was split. You would most certainly have two black eyes.

"No." *I bowed to the ground, pressing my face into the dirt, rocks and sticks digging into my skin and wounds. "Oh God, I can't believe I'm going to do this to her." I rocked back and forth, weeping.*

Sawyer gave me thirty seconds before he cleared his throat. "We're already pushing it, time-wise."

"I know, I just . . . will I be able to reach out in a few weeks? We'll get her a burner phone, and . . ."

Sawyer shook his head no. "She's only safe if you're out of the picture."

"Ella can keep a secret."

He sent me a sharp look. "There's a chance she'll see Wilkens every day senior year. Don't send her into the shark tank covered in blood." After a beat, he softened. "One day, though, Hay. Maybe one day."

It would have to be enough for now.

Because the seat belt retractor had been bent on impact, it was obvious I hadn't had one on. It made the most sense that I would have flown through the windshield into the river.

Sawyer asked me to hold your wrist while he used a rock to punch a larger hole in the windshield. When a giant chunk of glass fell into the car, he grabbed it too quickly, slicing a gash into his palm.

"My blood can't be in here," he growled, throwing the glass into the river. "But yours has to be. On the windshield. Hair too, if you can."

I had plenty of cuts and wounds to choose from. I pulled out bloody strings of my hair, laying them carefully across the jagged edges of glass.

"Good enough?" I asked.

"It'll have to be."

I kept my phone, my dress thankfully having pockets, but everything else stayed in the car.

Including, to my agony, you.

I made Sawyer promise to watch over you, to keep you safe from Sam. Then we decided it would be best to dial 911 from your phone. It wasn't hard to sound disoriented and injured, to pose as you to the operator. In just a few words, I managed to say you'd crashed, were injured, and didn't know where your friend was before nestling the phone into your hand.

Sawyer and I stayed as long as we could. Honestly, we pushed it.

"Sirens, Hayley. We cannot *get caught."*

"Ella, Ella, Ella, forgive me," I said in a ruined voice, leaning over to kiss you goodbye on your cheek.

Sawyer drove me to a shelter, and that was the night that Hayley Miller died, and Hazel was born.

Just in case, I won't include my last name or what state I'm in here in this letter.

I will tell you that Hazel has a good life. For the first time in a long time, a safe *life. I met a lot of wonderful people at the shelter. And one of those wonderful people drove me four hours each way to finally get my abortion.*

Ella, I have never felt such relief. The only thing that stressed me about the procedure was the IV. I'm embarrassed to admit this, but I'm terrified *of needles. But other than that? The relief was so strong it was almost spiritual. I'd been so nauseous every waking moment. But worse was that when I pictured my future, I just saw a black hole.*

After the procedure, for the first time in a long time, I saw Germany in my future. Paris. A bachelor's in psychology. A small apartment with a girl named Ella and a cat? (I know, I know, I'm getting ahead of myself.) The point is . . . I had a future I could imagine wanting to live.

When I said this all in group, I was worried some of my new friends would judge me. That they'd say it was wrong to feel the way I did. Selfish. But you know what? Not one of them judged me. Not a one. A couple people spoke up, said they related.

That's one of the most comforting lessons I've learned here: Anytime I get up the guts to admit to a thought or feeling that I've been stuffing down into a barrel of shame, one that feels absolutely unforgivable, at least one other person says, "Same, girl." It's usually way more than just one, a full chorus of "Same, sister, same."

I keep thinking about everything I never told you, everything we never said, wondering if it all could have turned out differently if only I'd confided in you. Maybe everything would have been exactly the same, but if we'd just talked, maybe I would have at least felt less alone.

On a completely different note . . . well, Sawyer and I talk. Text, phone calls. We debated how big a risk it would be, keeping in contact. But we figured if we used an encrypted app, and we were very careful, we'd be safe.

And the truth is . . . I needed it. I left behind everyone and everything I'd ever known. Suddenly and violently. I was relieved to be safe, of course. But I was also deep in a well of grief. I missed you. I missed our friends, the comfort of anything familiar.

I can't tell you how many times I've asked him if we could bring you into the loop. A couple times he almost relented. But in the end, we decided it was too much, too dangerous. At least while you were still at North Davis.

So I asked him to tell me all about you. Something he loved to *do. I don't want to say his words for him, so I won't go into that. But* I do *want to tell you that . . . you two together? Like,* duh. *You guys work. You guys fit. I was never happier than when we three would hang out. Now my two closest friends are together and . . . what I'm trying to say, Ella, is* don't you dare feel guilty about it. *Okay? Okay.*

I'm not going to send this letter until it feels safe enough. Not sure when that will be, but if you're reading this, it's probably safe enough for Sawyer to give you my new cell number.

That is, if you want to maintain contact with me.

I love you, and of course I want you in my life until you need that incredible, *museum-worthy denture mug. Which, I'm hoping it made it out of the kiln . . . ? Though you certainly have had far harder things to deal with these past few months than checking the back of Ms. Langley's shelves. If you want, I can always make you a new one. A local potter volunteers and teaches classes at the shelter, so I've actually gotten pretty good.*

All that to say— Well. You know how I feel.

I don't want to presume to know what you're feeling, and whatever you do feel, you absolutely deserve to feel. Which is probably a lot. I won't ask for your forgiveness, because it's hard to feel like I deserve it after everything I put you through.

But I hope, at least, after reading this, you can understand why I did what I did.

And that never, not for one iota of a millisecond, did I ever, ever, ever *stop loving you more than anything else on the whole damn planet.*

Love,
(For the narcs) Hazel
(But for you, always and always, my Ella Bird) Hayley

chapter 36
ella

This hospital room is a little nicer than the one I stayed in all those months ago. There's a lamp on the side table, glowing soft and warm, and the view out the window is of trees and, in the distance, mountains. It's a shame, really, as I'm only going to be here for a *very* cautionary twenty-four hours.

"Are you sure that's *all* she needs?" Mom's standing at the foot of my bed, smoothing the white sheets with her hands, over and over. Dad, standing next to her, subtly takes her hand, pats it kindly.

"Her CAT scans were perfectly normal. Other than her bruising, we didn't detect any other physical issues. Honestly, in any other case, she would have been discharged a while ago. Since it's her second head-related injury in less than half a year, we wanted to be sure." Dr. Shepherd shoots me a reassuring smile.

I like her. She's been patient with all of my parents' questions, and earlier, when she caught a local news reporter trying to slink into my room, she yelled at him to "Get the hell out of here before I give you an enema!"

My mother sniffs. "Slight bruising. He should go to jail for life. That terrible, terrible man."

"I don't think you'll get much argument from any of us, Mrs. Graham." The doctor scribbles some notes on my chart.

"And if he doesn't, when he gets out, I will kill him mys—"

"Oookay, sweetheart, there are too many reporters around for you to be saying things like that." Dad cranes his neck to peek out the hospital door before giving Mom a look like, *I'll help you hide the body*.

"Ella, hit that button if you need absolutely anything. I'll be your attending until you get discharged tomorrow." Her smile softens. "You're a very brave girl, Ella. I hope you know that."

As she exits the room, Dad dabs at his eyes with a tissue and Mom squeezes my foot so hard it almost hurts. I lean back in the bed, my eyes following the clouds, but I'm not really seeing anything.

"Ella, you okay? You are so quiet. What's wrong? Do you have a headache?" My mom flutters around my feet like an anxious bird.

Jess is sitting in a chair by the bed, playing her Nintendo Switch. "Gotta say, Ella. Super impressed at you bashing in the asshole's head."

"I didn't exactly bash his head—"

"Damn right, bashed him good," Mom snarls, her eyes full of murder.

Dad and I exchange looks.

I throw Mom a bone. "You know, I wouldn't mind a snack."

"I have dried mango, tamarind candy, pastillas, polvoron . . . Oh, wait, no polvoron, it's all crumbled at the bottom of my bag . . ." She's digging through her purse like a raccoon, her bangs sticking up in the front. I feel a swell of affection so immense, it's like I swallowed a hot air balloon.

"The tamarind candy," I say, "please." It's not salted (which is my favorite) and I know Lola sent it to us three years ago, but I unwrap the sweet gratefully, taking a nibble.

Dad puts a large hand on my shin, giving it a gentle squeeze. Mom comes to the head of my bed, frowning at my pillow.

"That looks uncomfortable. Let me fix it."

"I'm okay, Mom."

"I can just—"

"Mom," I sigh, sinking back into the cushions. "I'm good." I'm so tired. My brain shut down hours ago.

Mom nods, still hovering at my elbow, her hands nervous, antsy things, looking for something to do. She looks down, sniffs wetly, and I realize that she's beginning to cry. Which would make this the second time in my life that I've seen my mom cry. There's a sniff to my right, and I realize that Dad's starting to cry too. Which would make this the second time this hour that he's cried.

"Ella," my mother says. "I'm sorry. Your father and I both are. We should have been there for you. You've been dealing with so much . . . so much all alone. I hate that you couldn't talk to us, tell us everything that's been going on. We had no idea how to handle everything that happened with Hayley and the accident . . . didn't know how to be there for you. But we should have tried harder. Better. We should have let you know that no matter what you've done, no matter who you are, no matter *what*—" Her voice hitches. "That you would always be our perfect Ella to us. Just as you are."

I swallow hard. "Even if I never rejoin the swim team?"

Both Mom and Dad nod.

"Even if I never go to college?"

Mom and Dad look at each other. "Well, let's not go too far . . ."

I smile, relieved, actually, that their expectations are still there, that I haven't changed them so irrevocably.

Mom tucks my hair behind my ear. "We love you more than anything. Nothing could ever change that."

"Nothing ever!" Dad sobs, scooping me up from the bed for a bear hug.

"Wait." Jess lifts her eyes from the Switch to look hopefully at Mom and Dad. "Does this mean I can finally get my eyebrow pierced?"

With a slow turn of her head, Mom levels Jess with a stare. "Never."

"Aw, come on, Smella gets all that *no matter what* stuff, so why doesn't that apply to—"

"Jesslyn Marie Trinidad Graham," Mom snarls. I swear the lights dim briefly as she speaks.

"Joke *lang*, Ma!" The unflappable Jess looks briefly terrified. When Mom's not looking, I see Dad touch his eyebrow and give Jess a secret thumbs-up.

Right now, all I can manage is a smile. Don't get me wrong, all of this is filling the fractures of my soul with sunlight. But I'm still processing, still absorbing.

I mean, up until four hours ago, I had thought Hayley was dead. And four hours before that, I had thought Mr. Wilkens was the only person in my life I could trust.

I'm gonna need a minute.

"Knock, knock," calls a voice from the door. Seema strides in, carrying a bag of Doritos, a Bugs Bunny plushie with a single, upsettingly large front tooth, and a Paw Patrol balloon. She tugs the string of the balloon. "Yeah, I know. Hey, but it was either this or a happy retirement balloon, which just felt wrong."

"Chase was always my favorite," Jess says, staring at the Mylar swaying in the air-conditioning.

"A girl after my own heart," Seema says.

"Seema," my mom says. "It's good to see you. Are you feeling better?"

"Much," Seema says. "I'm really sorry for the way I left."

Mom flaps her hands. "Oh, I'm just glad that . . . I'm just glad."

"Me too," Dad says, his eyes on the muted football game on the TV in the corner.

Jess eyes Seema and me in that shrewd, elusive way of hers before she gets up and stretches. "Ma. Dad. Let's go get some Chinese food. Unless"—she looks at me—"you want something else?"

"Chinese sounds amazing." I sigh. "Thanks, Jess."

I tell Mom and Dad I love them, and Jess herds them out of the room. Seema toes off her shoes, pulls a chair closer to me, and props her feet up on the bed, knocking her feet into mine.

"What if I'd had a broken toe?" I say, arching a brow at her.

"I knew you didn't. Your chart's hanging outside the door. I needed *something* to read while I was waiting for your family to finish apologizing to you." She tosses the bag of Cool Ranch Doritos on the bed, along with the Bugs Bunny plushie.

"Seriously, Seema?" She grins. I open the Doritos and shove a couple in my mouth. "I can't believe you remember my favorite flavor."

"How could I forget? You fell asleep on the couch with your hand in a bag of them once. Smudged the dust all over our brand-new, snow-white couch that cost two thousand, three hundred and twenty-eight dollars and twenty-two cents. With tax. How do I know how much it cost? Because my parents reminded me over and over and I was almost never allowed to invite friends over again."

I turn my head slowly to her. "I . . . am really sorry about that."

Seema reaches over, grabs a handful of chips. "Don't be." She shoves them all in her mouth, every single one. "The smudges were mostly mine. I just blamed all of them on you."

I throw a Dorito at her, which she ducks expertly.

After tossing the chip into the waste bin, she faces me, suddenly serious. "I'm . . . really sorry for sort of losing my shit last night.

Everything you said just . . . well, it hit on what my therapist likes to call 'Big Ouchies.' Most of what I said . . . I didn't mean. I mean, you were going through a lot more than I realized. I mean, Wilkens? Seriously?" She shakes her head. "I had no idea. I am so sorry."

I sag back into the bed. "I'm sorry too . . . Truth is, you were right. I haven't been a good friend."

Seema shrugs. "To be fair, you were going through some serious piles of shit. Like. A school faculty member almost *murdered* you this morning. I mean, *damn*."

"Sure, but . . . I have no idea what you've been going through. And that's . . . that's not okay, Seema." I play with the soft gray ears of the Bugs plushie. "I'll do better."

She gives me a wide, lopsided grin. "You better."

I hold Bugs Bunny up, wiggle him a little. "Can I ask . . ."

"What, you can't tell?" Seema reaches over and shows me the bottom of his foot. There's a Six Flags Over Georgia logo on the fuzzy white heel.

I throw my head back and laugh. "Don't tell me . . ."

"Yeah, yeah, I did. When I saw the news, I did the unthinkable. The impossible. I braved Atlanta traffic, drove all the way to Six Flags, *bought a ticket*, waited in line to get in the damn park, went *shopping*, like to more than one gift shop, bought this plushie, got a corn dog, *got a funnel cake*, got back in the car, *stopped to get a balloon*—"

I hold up a hand. "Seema. I will treasure this Bugs forever. That's honestly one of the coolest things anyone's ever done for me." I frown. "And the weirdest."

"Yeah, well. I felt bad about last night. If I'd spent the night, we could have nipped this whole thing in the bud. That asshole would have broken into your room and I would have karate-chopped the crap out of him."

"You know karate?"

"Nope. I just get *super pissed* if someone wakes me up before noon." Seema picks at crumbs on her shirt. "Seriously, though, Ella. How're you holding up?"

"How am I holding up?" I echo, leaning back and staring at the ceiling. "Let's see . . . I became terrified of my boyfriend because I was convinced that he was an abusive killer."

"Yup."

"Someone broke into my bedroom, and I falsely sent said boyfriend to jail."

"Yup."

"The person who *actually* broke into my room was the school psychologist, who then almost killed me with pruning shears."

Seema pauses her loud, messy chewing and turns her head slowly to me. "Ella. That's messed up."

"Yup."

We laugh, try and catch chips in our mouths, and speculate on why they made Bugs Bunny's tooth nearly as long as my thumb. I need this. A few minutes of normalcy.

I don't know how I feel about Hayley's letter yet.

About Hayley.

I mean, the truth is, what I feel is everything. *Everything.*

When I saw her face, my heart exploded, my brain exploded.

I love her, of course. I always will. But she's right. I'm not her baby bird anymore. Whatever happens next, it'll be different.

I watch Seema yawn and grab an unused pillow off my bed. And I think, *You know what? Different is good.* I understand that Hayley did what she did because she had no other option. She did it to save her life, and she did it to save mine.

I'll need some time to recover, to process, but I have no doubt that whatever relationship Hayley and I grow into will be richer and deeper for everything we've been through. Healthier, even.

Baby birds are bound to their nest. They are at the mercy of everyone around them. They cannot feed themselves; they cannot protect themselves. I am more than that now. So much more.

My family returns, and Seema stays for dinner. Jess shows Seema her Pokémon team on her Switch. Mom tells me that if I *really* want to, we can watch the extended editions of *Lord of the Rings* when we get home. Dad pretends to faint from horror, doing it so well that he almost actually falls out of the chair. I realize that this might be the happiest I've felt since before Hayley made her Great Escape. And I think if I can feel this good on the same day that a school staff member tried to kill me, then I'm probably pretty lucky.

After the meal, I nod off twice midconversation, so everyone leaves to let me sleep. I nestle back in the bed, and as I drift off to sleep, I think of Hayley.

chapter 37
sawyer

When a cop comes to get me, and it's not Officer Rick, I take it as a hopeful sign. When that same cop hands me my phone and wallet, I know Hayley did it. The officer won't even look me in the eye when he tells me I'm free to go. I open my mouth, about to say, *Not even a sorry, Officer?*

But haven't I learned my lesson? Well . . . I'm trying. So I keep my mouth shut.

I'm waiting in front of the station for my mom to come get me, squinting in the late-afternoon sun, when a cop car pulls up and someone very familiar is pulled out of the back seat.

"This is bullshit! I didn't steal anything—my boss is just a paranoid asshole!" A handcuffed Sean Adams is pleading with a red-faced cop who's dragging him out of the car.

"A paranoid asshole with state-of-the-art security cameras. Hope you enjoyed your expensive toys while you could. You're gonna be staying with us for a while." The cop gives him another yank.

We make eye contact as Sean passes me, and I give him a little wave. He swears loudly before the front doors of the station shut behind them both.

My mom pulls up a few minutes later.

"You might be the happiest person I've ever picked up from prison. Do I want to ask?" Mom eyes me when I get in the car.

I shake my head, failing to bite back my manic smile. "Let's just say that, for once, justice is served. And it is really satisfying."

"So you did hear. I was wondering if you had."

Sean vanishes from my mind. "Heard what?"

Mom frowns, pulling out of the parking lot. "Just type 'North Davis High student news' into your phone."

When I do, Wilkens's mug shot is on every page. I hold my breath as a I scan the articles, skip through the news videos.

Ella's okay. In the hospital. But alive. Very, *very* much alive. I sag back against my chair.

And nothing about Hayley. Wait. That's not true. There is a mention in one news segment.

> *New evidence is pointing to the possibility that Andrew Wilkens was also involved in a hit-and-run incident this past May that may have caused a car crash resulting in serious injuries for seventeen-year-old Ella Graham and the death of another North Davis High student, seventeen-year-old Hayley Miller . . .*

I'm tempted to shoot Hayley a message through our encrypted app right now. But we agreed: no unnecessary risks. I'll wait until I'm alone.

We pull into the driveway, but Mom stops me before we get into the house. She scrutinizes my face, her hands on her hips. I shove my hands in my pockets and hang my head. Whatever's coming, I deserve it. She squints an eye and pokes my cheek.

"What—um, what—"

"I'm trying to see how many tattoos you got in the clink. No teardrops, this is good. You get any 'Mom' tattoos?"

I let out a whoosh of air. *"Mom."*

"Ah, there he is. My whiny little Saw-Saw. Come on, I bet you're hungry. Callan's over at a friend's house for a while, and I called out of work, so I can actually make you something."

I follow her into the kitchen, grab the wood glue from the shelf, and crawl under the crooked kitchen table. There's the clinking of pots and pans, the sound of the fridge door opening and closing. I examine the table leg, and, yeah, wood glue's not gonna do too much more. But I just sit there for a minute.

"So . . . you're not mad?"

The metal clanging pauses. "Sawyer, I saw the news. All I want to do is shake you and have you tell me everything and cry over the fact that you three had to deal with that man. I'm just . . . giving you space. You talk when you're ready. In the meantime, how do scrambled eggs sound?"

I crawl out from under the table and stand. "Got anything else?"

"Oh, certainly, sir. Of course, sir. We have omelets as well."

"Right. And lemme guess. If I don't like that, I have the option of hard-boiled eggs?"

Mom clucks at me, fanning a hand in my face. "Don't sound so disappointed. We also have soft-boiled."

I tell her scrambled sounds perfect, and she sings to herself as she moves around the kitchen. I lean against the wall, staring at mug shots of Wilkens.

When Hayley first told me, I felt as helpless as a child, overwhelmed with conflicting emotion.

"Can I have a minute?" I'd asked when she first told me about her and Sam. "Some time to just . . . think about this? Is that okay?"

"Take your time," Hayley had said sadly.

So I let myself feel the rapid rushes of jealousy and hurt and anger and worry, processing them as fast as I could. After I'd taken a few days, I met back up with Hayley, and we talked at length.

"I'm sorry," she'd told me. "I'm so sorry I've been lying to you. For not breaking up with you."

I was leaning back against the whiteboard, arms crossed, my mind on overdrive.

"Wilkens told you not to break up with me?"

She nodded.

"He told you to keep it all a secret?"

Another nod.

"And now you're pregnant . . . and he hits you?"

She bit her lip, clearly trying not to cry, but tears started to flow anyway. I pushed off the wall and reached for her hand.

"May I?"

Off her nod, I gently took her hand, turned it over. Delicately, I peeled back her sleeve, swore violently when I saw the purple-yellow thumbprints, a healing bruise the size of grape.

I exhaled through my nose, a sharp rush of air.

"Mom, Callan, and I spent a few months in a domestic violence shelter when I was a kid. Callan was just a baby, but it was a decent place. It's a few hours from here. I can take you."

"He'd find me," she whispered. "He'll always find me."

I stared at the window, thinking. "I know how this sounds, but . . . Phoebe?"

"Doesn't know. You're the only one who does now. She wouldn't be much help anyhow."

"Not even Ella knows?" The realization surprised me.

But she told me, "He's pathologically jealous. Lately, especially about Ella. So I've been avoiding her. I'm scared that Sam might . . . It feels ridiculous to say, to even imagine. But he makes these comments."

"It's not ridiculous." The muscle in my jaw ticked. "I know you wouldn't love this, but . . . the police? I'll go with you."

"His uncle's a sheriff here. They're close. Sam has made it clear that Rick has always protected him—"

"Hayley. Being with you is illegal. The moment Wilkens first touched you was illegal, and so was everything that followed," I said, not unkindly.

"I suppose." She shrugged.

I took a step back, giving her space before asking, "Hayley . . . can I give you a hug?"

It felt like the first real hug we'd ever shared.

"Thank you," she whispered. "I always knew you were a good guy, but . . ."

"Come on," I said, pulling back. "Of course, Hayley."

"I want you to know . . . In a way, I did love you." She grimaced. "That came out bad. What I mean to say is—"

"You don't have to explain. Ditto. You're one of my closest friends."

"Maybe you need more friends," she said.

I breathed a laugh, a soft exhale through my nose. "Yeah, maybe." I got serious. "Listen. For now, we still say we're dating. Nothing suspicious. Everything stays the same publicly."

"Thanks," she said, clearly relieved.

"Maybe you're not sure yet," I said carefully, "but do you know what you're going to do about . . ." I dropped my eyes to her stomach.

"I'm not sure yet."

"None of this is your fault, Hayley. I can support you now, help you figure this out."

"Okay," she said. "Yeah. We'll figure something out."

And we had.

Truthfully, I'd known something was up with her. A few signs that felt familiar in a bad way. But I hadn't wanted to push it. Didn't know what to ask. But when she told me, it was worse than I'd thought. Way worse. Those bruises . . . and her and Ella's safety at stake?

Leaving Ella in the car the night of the accident was *agony*. We had only been driving a few seconds when I saw the ambulance stop at the mouth of the bridge in my rearview mirror. I'd been terrified we'd get stopped, and wondered what would happen if we were. Would we be arrested? We'd tampered with a crime scene and fled. The only thing I knew for certain was it would land Hayley right in the palm of Wilkens's hand.

I thought it could only get better after I'd gotten Hayley settled at the DV shelter we'd found. I had thought wrong.

The real agony began when school started, and I had to see Ella suffer.

Hayley and I would turn it around and around, whether we could tell Ella the truth, whether she was safer knowing versus not knowing. And then when I started to fall for Ella? God, what a mess.

"So . . . you gave her a ride home. What's wrong with that?" Hayley asked me.

"I almost kissed her, Hay. I wanted to. Bad."

"And?"

"You don't see a problem with that? If we started dating, I'd have to lie to her every day about the biggest thing in her life. How long d'you think I can keep that up for?"

And then that day I saw her in the hall with Wilkens, standing next to Scott. It was like a reminder of the main mission: Keep Ella safe. I'd gotten too close to her. The closer she was to me, the closer she was to learning about Hayley, and I'd seen how close Wilkens was sniffing around. With his forked tongue, he'd have it out of her.

I knew I had to stay away from her, keep an eye at a distance.

Which is why I immediately hooked up with her afterward.

When Hayley told me she was going to give her the letter, I figured that was it for Ella and me. I mean, hell, not that things had been going well between us. Regardless of Wilkens steering her suspicions onto me, I had acted poorly.

I keep getting flashbacks of her eyes at the corn maze, when I grabbed her arm. Between that and the night when Callan ran from me, I haven't been able to look myself in the mirror. A dread as heavy as a brick has been riding around in my gut day and night.

Mom appears at my side.

"Eggs are done. Wow." She points to my phone, where Wilkens's mug shot is still on my screen. "You're still looking at that?"

My shoulders shake. "Mom," I say. "I don't . . . I don't want to be like him. Like Dad."

Mom lifts her chin, nodding slow as a monk, and puts a hand on my shoulder.

"So don't be." She says it softly. "I'm not saying it's easy, Sawyer. It's not. But I *am* saying it's a choice. You're not a werewolf, Saw." She gestures to the photo of Wilkens. "He's not a werewolf. He can't blame moonbeams, some*thing* that transforms him into a completely different creature. He wants us to believe that he only wakes up in the aftermath, that he's as horrified as us, that he had *no* part in the torn clothes scattered around him and the blood on his hands. He might even believe it."

Mom brushes a lock of hair from my forehead, reaches over to pick at the collar of my shirt.

"Your father blamed alcohol. Blamed anger. But you think I've never been as drunk as him? That I've never been that angry? When he worked as a mechanic, his boss was a nasty old codger. Your dad had left an oily rag on the counter by accident, there for the customers to see. In front of the entire crew, a few customers even, his boss ripped into him, told him what a failure he was, how irreconcilably dumb he was, how incompetent. What'd he do? Not a damn thing.

Silently packed his locker and left. How angry do you think he was, Sawyer? Did it seize him like the full moon? Did he black out and then come to, his boss beaten to a bloody mess in front of him? Look at his ruined knuckles with horror, like his fury and violence was something that had happened *to* him?"

She cups my cheek, her palm cool and smooth as a stone from a river.

"No, Sawyer, of course not. He kept his mouth shut. Drove home in silence. And then that night, you cried when he said you couldn't have more steak fries at dinner. Your chubby little hands opened and closed as you whined for more . . . and when you didn't stop, he grabbed a fistful of steak fries and smashed them into your face, grinding them into a pulp against your cheek. They were still hot from the oven, and you were screaming, and I was screaming, and I finally got you away from him . . ." Her voice shatters into a million pieces.

"I don't remember," I say, rubbing her back. "Why don't I remember that?"

"Oh, Saw." Mom clasps my hand, squeezing. "You were only two."

I give her a minute. Take one for myself.

"How?" I finally ask, my voice low, jagged around the edges.

"First, you take accountability. What you did the other night was *not* okay. Slamming the table, throwing that toy."

"You're right. I haven't stopped being sorry." I drop my head. "I fought with Ella the other night. I knew—had a feeling, rather, that Mr. Wilkens was bad news. She was talking to him a lot, and I was worried for her safety. I was so scared, so frustrated, so overwhelmed. I . . . destroyed a bale of hay in front of her. Kicked the crap out of it. Raised my voice at Ella. I immediately felt awful. God. I felt . . . I feel so guilty, Mom."

Mom nods. "Good. You should. That wasn't okay either."

"I won't do it again. Either of those things. Or things like them.

No matter how upset I am." I gesture to my chest. "I think I bottle a lot up. I don't know. None of it's an excuse, I just want to make sure that I don't—that I *never* do it again."

Mom hums. "Okay. I'm glad to hear you're gonna work on it. I'll support you and hold you accountable to that."

"Thanks." I close every browser with Wilkens's face on it.

"You're welcome, Saw. Eggs?"

"Please. I think . . . I'd like to see Ella for myself. I'm not going to stop worrying about her until I just—*see* her. You know?"

Mom scoops eggs onto her own plate. "All right," she says tentatively. "She may not want to talk to you."

"I accept that."

"Ever again."

"That would . . . hurt. But I'd accept that too."

Mom eyes me. "All right. Good."

By the time I get to the hospital, the sun's starting to set. Ella's asleep in her bed. I debate about leaving, having seen her safe.

But I'm greedy. I want to hear her voice. See her eyes.

I sit down, deciding that I'll only stay a few minutes. If she doesn't wake up by then, I'll go. Try another day. But as soon as I sit down, I realize I haven't slept in over twenty-four hours, and it flattens me like a tractor.

I don't even notice I've fallen asleep until Ella's voice rouses me. I open my eyes to her trying to hand me a pillow. And she's okay. Ella's okay.

She says my name. And she sounds *happy*.

And like a damn sentimental fool, my eyes fill with tears.

chapter 38
ella

Sorry," Sawyer says, wiping at his eyes. He looks embarrassed, color rising on the high points of his cheeks, and despite all the shit that has happened between us, the fact that I now know he knew Hayley was alive all along and never told me, just the sight of his face has my stomach flipping.

"Sorry for what?" I ask.

Sawyer barks a laugh. "Where do I start? Do you want the full list or an abridged version?" He shakes his head. "But before all that . . . are you okay? I mean, that's a dumb question. You're in a hospital bed and Wilkens tried to kill you and your best friend came back from the dead and—"

"Sawyer," I say, "I'm okay. And as for Hayley . . . It's gonna take some time to process, of course. My emotions are complicated, but ultimately?" My eyes fill with tears. "My greatest wish in the world came true. Hayley's alive. She's *alive*, Sawyer."

His smile is soft and crooked. I want to trace his mouth with my fingers.

"I'm sorry I didn't tell you, Ella. I kept wanting to. We both did, honestly. We'd flip-flop. She'd beg me to tell you, and then I'd beg her to tell you . . . ultimately, we were both just so, so worried about what Wilkens would possibly do to you, or her, if he found out she was still alive. Hayley knew him better than any of us. I had to trust her. And in the end, she turned out to be right." He sucks at his teeth. "Tell me. Was watching him get clobbered on the head as satisfying as I'm picturing it?"

"Better," I say. "When the police picked him up off the floor, he peed himself."

"That," he says solemnly, "is disgusting. And fantastic."

My fingers twitch. They desperately want to press against Sawyer's knuckles, follow the whorls of his skin. But I keep my hands tucked tight against me.

Because we have to address some big things first. And with how Sawyer's dark brown eyes are so heavy with remorse, we seem to be on the same page. I clear my throat.

"That night at the corn maze . . . you really frightened me."

"I know." Sawyer swallows hard, squeezing his eyes shut. "God, Ella, I'm so sorry. You'll never know how sorry. That was . . . That was not okay."

"No," I say. "It wasn't."

He nods. "I talked to my mom about it. I'll make the same promise to you as I did to her. I'll never do anything like that again." Sawyer's brow is furrowed. Earnest. "I have work to do. Lots of work. Mom mentioned therapy, gave me books to read . . . but even if I'm not where I need to be, there are lines I will never cross again."

"Like yelling and breaking things?" I raise a brow.

Sawyer winces. "Exactly. At the very least. Doesn't matter how I feel."

I duck my head to meet Sawyer's swimming eyes. "I'm glad to hear you say all this. Obviously, saying it is not the same as *doing* it."

"Of course," Sawyer whispers.

"But," I say after a pause, "I'm willing to give you a chance to prove it." A glimmer of hope sparks in Sawyer's gaze. "It's okay to be angry, Sawyer. It's *not* okay to yell at me or punch, throw, or kick things. You do anything like that again, that's it for us. Understand?"

"Of course," Sawyer repeats fervently. "It's more than I deserve. I'll earn it—I'm so sorry. Just so, so sorry—"

He cuts off, confused when I laugh. I shake my head. "I'm not laughing at you. It's just . . . that's almost an Ella amount of sorrys you're tallying up tonight."

Sawyer breathes a laugh, his shoulders relaxing. "This is different. My sorrys are warranted." He tilts his head, regarding me. "But you know? I haven't heard any unnecessary sorrys from you in a while. In fact, I get the feeling that you finally realize you never had anything to be sorry about."

"Ah." I squeeze one eye shut at him. "Yes and no. Yes, in general, I'm done being the walking apology. And no because I *do* want to say sorry for sending you to jail."

Sawyer laughs good-naturedly, and he lets me take his hand. When we touch, he falls into a serious silence, looking down at our threaded fingers.

"You didn't send me to jail, Ella," he says quietly. "Wilkens sent me to jail. You were his victim."

I take a deep breath and nod. For a minute, we just sit in silence, together in the soft dark. The light filtering through the cracked door shifts, and that scar on his brow, that delicious slice of silver, glimmers.

Suddenly, I want so very badly to kiss him.

"Ella," Sawyer bursts out, "I've always . . . *Listen*. Before Hayley and I . . . before I ever spoke to either of you . . . I always saw you. I'd be playing hacky sack in the courtyard and I'd have to tell myself, *Okay, you're not allowed to look at the girl with the long dark hair for five kicks.* But I'd only ever make it to three. Or two. I never made it to my full five."

I blink, surprised. "Why didn't you say something?"

He shrugs. "I didn't know you, but I knew *of* you. Straight As, high achiever, functional family . . ." He sighs, a sound that breaks my heart. "What would you want with me?"

I raise an eyebrow and trace figure eights on the inside of his wrist. "A lot of things."

"Ah. That . . . that is distracting, wow. I'm trying to—to tell you something, here. When Hayley invited me to sit with you guys, I was pretty stoked to get to know you. But I knew it was never gonna happen. And then Hayley and I happened. And, you know, it worked. We'd been through the same trenches together. The history with our dads, all that. And when we got together . . . I put a block up, a mental barrier. Thou shalt not covet thy girlfriend's best friend, et cetera, et cetera."

"Uh-huh . . . why are you telling me this?" I drag my fingernails up the insides of his arms, and he shivers with pleasure.

"I didn't want you thinking I did Hayley dirty. And I wanted you to know that . . . well, I've always . . . to me, you're just . . ." He looks at me like I could ruin him with a single word. "You're incredible. And I want you."

Even though Sawyer and I have talked about his behavior, that we've both agreed on the parameters of his second chance . . . I wonder if I should wait. Give it time. Let the dust settle on all these revelations, these withheld truths. But if I'm being honest, I'm sick of waiting. Of shoulds. Of shrinking back in the shadows while other people pick at the banquet table first.

And after everything today, I want to go after what I want.

I decide that I deserve that.

To unapologetically and fullheartedly step toward what I want.

"I want you too," I say, and I kiss him.

He tastes like orange juice and chocolate. Kissing him feels like breathing, like finding something better than breathing.

"Ella." He breaks away from me, panting. "You're in the hospital. You need to take it easy." I smile against his lips. "And you're making it really . . . *difficult.*"

I nuzzle against his neck. "Funny. I thought you were gonna say I was making it really—"

"Well, yes." He shifts uncomfortably. "That too."

Sawyer's crooked grin squeezes my heart. "You're right," I say. "We have all the time in the world ahead of us."

His eyes light up. "Yeah?" he says.

"Yeah," I say. "But first—" I cradle his chin and dip his head toward me. Finally, *finally*, I press my lips against the scar on his eyebrow. "You have no idea how long I've wanted to do that," I murmur against his skin. I pull back to find his cheeks pink as he blinks furiously.

"Wow. I— Uh, sorry. I don't know why that short-circuited my brain so much. Words are hard to— Sorry."

"You know," I say wryly, "I'm beginning to wonder if that's your favorite word. *Sorry.*"

He shakes his head, laughing and leaning forward to kiss my forehead.

We spend the rest of the night murmuring to each other about anything and everything, finally able to be fully raw and open with each other for the first time. We fall asleep together, and when I wake up, he's still asleep in the chair next to my bed, his head at my feet, his hand in mine.

The sun is pink and gold as it comes over the horizon. Two hawks soar in the distance, silhouettes in the sky, rising and rising above the clouds, out of sight.

chapter 39
ella

I spent the first few months of the year infamous. Now I'm getting a taste for famous. It's okay, but it feels a little bit like stolen valor since Hayley was the one who *actually* swung the bat.

She tells me that it was, undoubtedly, a team effort, and the fact that I had to spend the whole morning with Sam was way harder than any old bat swing. Sawyer agrees, and I'd be lying if I said that a part of me doesn't love the excessively deferential way the sophomore boys part for me in the halls, or the fact that I can say hi to Beth, Rachael, and Nia without the weight of discomfort.

Sam's arrest is the talk of the town. Not just at school, but even in the grocery line, on social media, at the drive-thru. It would get old a lot faster if I didn't think about how much I know that entitled asshole must hate this.

While I was in the hospital, I got an expensive bouquet of flowers with the note *It's cool you didn't die. It's cooler that you almost killed the school psychologist. I'm a huge dick, I know. I was probably too much of a dick to you. —Scott (P.S. First step is awareness)*

When I read it, I thought about Hayley's letter, the vast amount of emotion that Scott keeps buried.

Our new school psychologist is incredible. Ms. Powell holds a master's not only in psychology but also in social work, and one of her first points of order was to hold a very well-attended seminar about domestic violence. I see a lot more students in and out of her office than I ever did with Wilkens.

Sawyer meets with Ms. Powell once a week. She gives him homework, and he's never missed an assignment from her. When I point out that he almost never did homework in class, he points out that no lesson has ever felt as important as the ones Ms. Powell is teaching him. I can't disagree.

And just last week, when he thought no one was looking, I saw Scott slink in there. Maybe there's hope for him yet?

Currently, I'm at the zoo with my whole family, plus Sawyer, Callan, and their mom. When I invited Seema, she told me that my mom had already invited her, and *duh*, of course she was gonna be there.

Callan is on Sawyer's shoulders, and he has decided that he wants to be a gorilla when he grows up.

"What does he mean 'when he grows up'?" Sawyer mutters in my ear.

"Fern," my mother asks Sawyer's mom, "how do you like working at an elementary school?"

"You know? I . . . love it." Sawyer's mom smiles so hard she presses a hand to her cheek. "I really love it. The pay is phenomenal, and I get to work with kids, and I get to eat lunch with Callan every day. It's my dream."

"How'd you find it?" Dad asks.

"It took some searching. One of the places I interviewed with liked me but wasn't able to hire me. But the receptionist there had a friend who's a teacher at Callan's school, so I was recommended for an admin role. I turned out to be a great fit."

"All right, Ratatouille, I'm done. Yep, Alfredo is taking a break." Sawyer peels Callan from his back, who is shouting, "Anyone can cook! Anyone can cook!"

Seema and Jess dash up to me.

"You gotta come see this: This monkey was staring Jess in the face, screaming, and he's got the most hugest, most raging . . . Hello, crowd of parents, how are we doing today?" Seema flashes them her widest, toothiest smile.

"Same as ten minutes ago," Sawyer's mom says, eyes twinkling.

"What's the monkey got?" My dad seems genuinely interested.

"A banana," says Jess.

"Huh. Well, I could have guessed that." Dad looks longingly at a food cart. "I'll be right back."

Sawyer appears to my right, Callan-less but with very messy hair. "Wanna get ice creams for everyone?"

We take everyone's order, and Callan is very disappointed when he is not allowed to have three of everything. But when I lean over and tell him there might be crayons in the gift shop, he perks right up.

"If he eats them, *you* will be brushing them out of his teeth," Sawyer says.

While we're standing in line, both of our pockets ring at the same exact time. We pull out our phones.

H

OMG. SAY HI TO MY NEW ROOMMATE.

I squeal when we get the picture she sends of a little black kitten with four white paws.

H

I'm naming her Smella

Jk jk jk.

"Are you kidding me? You told her that nickname?" I grumble.

Sawyer suddenly finds a very interesting crack in the concrete.

H

Name is pending, but you two will have to meet her sometime soon.

"Is that a thing?" I whisper eagerly. "You think we can visit her? See her in person?"

"Anything's possible." Sawyer swoops in for a quick kiss.

We manage not to drop any ice creams, and Callan doesn't ruin anyone's shirt but his own, and this is heralded as a great triumph.

When we're all standing around the giraffes, watching their long purple tongues curl around the branches, I turn away from the animals, gaze at my family and friends, this giant group of people I love.

It wasn't that long ago that I thought I was alone, that the world was this spike-filled maze that was impossible to navigate.

As isolating as it was, it also felt safer that way. Without anyone to hurt me—and more importantly, without anyone for me to hurt. But I see now this was just a lie birthed from shame. A lie people like Mr. Wilkens exploit. People who want to convince you that you're as alone as they are.

Especially when you never were.

I will never replace Hayley, and luckily I don't have to. Distance has nothing on our love, and though I miss her, for now it's enough to have a picture of her new kitten in my pocket. To feel Sawyer's hand in mine. To have Seema's arm around my shoulder. To see Mom's smile when Jess and Callan ask Dad and Fern if they can have money to feed the giraffe.

I was too lost, misled, and scared before to see them, but they were always there. Even in the dark, they were only ever a hand's reach away.

I may not know what will happen or where I'll end up, but with the love of my family and friends, I'm no longer scared of the future. Far from it.

In fact, as a very dear friend of mine would definitely say: "All right, let's see what you got."

author's note

If you or a loved one are in an unsafe situation at home, here are some resources available for you to seek confidential support.

National Domestic Violence Hotline
Call: 1-800-799-SAFE(7233)
TTY: 1-800-787-3224
Text: "START" to 88788
TheHotline.org

Love Is Respect
National Dating Abuse Helpline
Call: 1-866-331-9474
TTY: 1-800-787-3224
Text: "LOVEIS" to 22522
LoveIsRespect.org

Rape, Abuse & Incest National Network
National Sexual Assault Hotline
Call: 1-800-656-HOPE(4673)
RAINN.org

National Resource Center on Domestic Violence
Call: 1-800-537-2238
NRCDV.org

National Coalition Against Domestic Violence
Full list of resources: NCADV.org/Resources

acknowledgments

I have an unbelievable amount of people to thank from the bottom of my heart. And to start off, I'd like to thank *you* for reading this book. Thank you, thank you, thank you. You've given me so much by taking a chance on this work. Whether you loved it or hated it, I'm still happy you took the time to read it.

Make no mistake, no book is made by a single author alone, and without the brilliance and efforts of so many people, this work would be nothing more than a scattered, messy pile of too many words and too many fart jokes (still on the fence as to whether there's such a thing).

My first, wholehearted thank-you goes to my editor, Lanie! I'm absolutely the luckiest to write with you. Thank you for making my writing shine and showing me the ropes, and only ever being the kindest, most encouraging creative collaborator. What would I do without you? (Probably have ten extremely unnecessary chapters of *Lord of the Rings* references alone.) Thank you also to Romy Golan and to everyone at Rights People for being my champions overseas.

I owe a huge hug and big thank-you to Eliza, who connected Lanie and me in the first place. The truth is, I'd never have written this book if you hadn't put us in touch, and I'm constantly grateful for you.

I have so much gratitude for all the folks over at Penguin Random

House for putting their faith in me. I'm humbled and honored by everyone who worked to make this book what it is—if this book speaks to you, it is truly only because of all the hard work and creative vision of Jen Klonsky, Simone Roberts-Payne, and their team. I'm still pinching myself every day that you took a chance on me. Thank you to Natalie Vielkind for ushering this through production, Kelley Brady for the gorgeous cover, and a big thank-you to the brilliant Janet Rosenberg, whose copyediting skills elevated the manuscript and made me look like I know how to properly use punctuation.

I also could not have done this without the support of my loved ones! Thank you to Bex Carlo, who has taught me *so* much and been a loving, brilliant support since the beginning of my writing journey. My happy place will always be a frosty kombucha with you at *our* table.

All my love and gratitude to Allison, Amaris, and Joanna, my GFFs. Thank you for wishing on that dandelion that I would finish my draft in time. I have no doubt that this is the sole reason why I made my deadline, because that is the power of GFF love, full stop! I love you three forever and ever and can't wait until we're all living together again! (I assure you, I'm still saving up for that compound, y'all.)

Oh, what would I have done without Michael and Will? Shriveled into a pile, that's what. Without the loving support, encouragement, and endless wisdom and brilliance of both Michael and Will, I wouldn't be where I am. Thank you for indulging me with late-night Zooms where I was pulling my hair out, even when it was past all of our bedtimes. Thank you, Michael, for sticking with me throughout the years (especially *those* years), always making me laugh no matter the hour and circumstance, and *especially* for enduring my infodumps about Lalo. Please don't expect those to end anytime soon.

Huge shout-out to my St. Pete crew! Even if we're all scattered across the continent now, my love for y'all crosses all the state lines. Thank you for always supporting my ambiguous spacework. A heartfelt thanks to Kevin, who kept me sane over the summer by playing lots of *RDR2* poker with me and talking me off ledges. And thank you to John, who will definitely read this because he's definitely read everything I've ever written. And especially a very heartfelt thank-you to those of you who've supported me since my fanfics: You will always, always have a piece of my heart (especially you, Si!).

To Jess and Kyle, who are family. I love you both so much. Thank you for loving me relentlessly and thinking I was enough when *I* certainly didn't during my aimless-crying-on-y'all's-couch twenties. And, Jess, thank you for being my Hayley. It wasn't always easy to grow up where we did (but then again, is growing up ever easy?), but at least I had you . . . and chips.

Thank you to my brilliant, beautiful mother. I hope to one day be half as brave, strong, and sharply witty as you. I owe more than I can ever say to you, Mom. Thank you for all your sacrifices so that I can live this life I never thought possible, and for your patience with my painful journey of trying to learn Tagalog. Mahal kita.

Dad has literally been telling me I could be a writer since I was spelling *please* as *qlease*. I never believed him, but he's always believed in me. Thank you, Dad, for being the best father any human could ask for. You're the dad I wish Hayley and Sawyer could have had. I don't know what I did in a past life to deserve you, but I'm grateful beyond measure. Love you beyond the moon and back.

Thanks to Peetz, who I love a stupid, immeasurable amount. He's always been my bastion of mirth and laughter when I'm at my worst. I'd follow you to the ends of the earth to headbutt you at three a.m., bro. Thank you for showing me important things, like YouTube videos of the soothing sound of fourteen pitched-down crying babies.

If I've ever written a cool, funny character, it is only because I have

Vic, the Coolest Person I Have Ever Known, as inspiration. If I try to explain *just* how much I love Vic and what they mean to me, I'll literally melt into a pile of cheese, so I'll just say thank you for always supporting me nonjudgmentally, especially during my many (*many*) questionable crushes on cartoon characters.

Even though she shan't be bothered to read this, I have to thank my little heart outside my body, Pabu. During nearly the entirety of me writing the book, she was curled in my arms as I typed, where she merrily purred and farted in my face. She only walked across my keyboard a few times and never deleted anything a lifesaving Command-Z couldn't fix. I love her an unhealthy, unreasonable amount, and I can't imagine writing without her.

And finally, I must thank the love of not just this life, but all my lives following (I'm counting on having actual eternities with you), the Babs. No words exist to encompass the entirety of my feelings, but you prefer when things are short, anyway.

So, Babs?

Thanks.